Doom Patrol

OTHER FIVE STAR WESTERN TITLES BY L. P. HOLMES:

River Range (2006)
Roaring Acres (2007)
Riders of the Coyote Moon (2010)
Singing Wires (2011)
Desert Steel (2011)
Orphans of Gunswift Graze (2012)
Once in the Saddle (2013)

DOOM PATROL

A WESTERN DUO

L. P. HOLMES

FIVE STAR
A part of Gale, Cengage Learning

GALE
CENGAGE Learning®

Detroit • New York • San Francisco • New Haven, Conn • Waterville, Maine • London

GALE
CENGAGE Learning°

LIBRARY OF CONGRESS CATALOGING-IN-PUBLICATION DATA

Holmes, L. P. (Llewellyn Perry), 1895–1988.
　　Doom patrol : a western duo / by L. P. Holmes. — First Edition.
　　　pages cm
　　"A FIVE STAR WESTERN."
　　ISBN 978-1-4328-2703-8 (hardcover) — ISBN 1-4328-2703-0 (hardcover)
　　I. Title.
　　PS3515.O4448D66 2013
　　813'.54—dc23　　　　　　　　　　　　　　　　　　　2013008293

First Edition. First Printing: August 2013
Published in conjunction with Golden West Literary Agency
Find us on Facebook– https://www.facebook.com/FiveStarCengage
Visit our website– http://www.gale.cengage.com/fivestar/
Contact Five Star™ Publishing at FiveStar@cengage.com

Printed in Mexico
1 2 3 4 5 6 7 15 14 13

ADDITIONAL COPYRIGHT INFORMATION

FOREWORD
BY JON TUSKA

L(lewellyn) P(erry) Holmes was the author of nearly six hundred Western stories for magazines and dozens of Western novels. He was born in a snowed-in log cabin in the heart of the Rockies in Breckenridge, Colorado, on January 4, 1895. According to Holmes, almost from birth he had an urge to write. The youngest of five brothers and one sister, Holmes moved with his family when very young to Jamestown, California (which he always called Jimtown), and later moved to a ranch outside Napa where his father and his brothers built the ranch house in which he grew up and in which, later in life, he would again live. Holmes was an avid reader. He loved Rudyard Kipling (and could recite many of his poems from memory), James Oliver Curwood, Robert Service, and Stewart Edward White. He also loved pulp magazine stories. "My first readings of the pulps go back to when I was a ten-year-old kid on a far-out, lonely cattle ranch, days when, in our ranch house at least, there was no telephone, no electricity, no radio, and most certainly no TV," he once recalled. "In short, no means of entertainment of any sort—except *reading*. Once a week, Mother would get all her bartering products together and one of my older brothers would hook up the team to the spring wagon and drive her to town. There, at the old Rochdale Union grocery, Mother would barter her ranch products for such kitchen necessities as flour, sugar, and salt, spices, coffee and tea. While this was going on, my brother would hit the nearest news and

7

magazine source and buy up some of the latest magazines—all pulps. Of these, two titles were musts: *Blue Book* and *Adventure.* Others were *All-Story, Complete Story, Everybody's*— these I recall offhand. And they would be read by all members of the family, from cover to cover."

In Napa he met and fell in love with Lydia Marie Hillman who was born in 1898. It was a romance he would live again and again hundreds of times in his fiction. After graduating from high school, Holmes went directly to work driving a gasoline truck for Standard Oil. He and Lydia were married in 1920 and were living in Stockton when their only child, a son, Perry, was born.

Deciding that now was the time to write, Holmes bought himself an old Underwood typewriter, and once home at night after a full day of driving the truck, he punched out stories, using two fingers. Sometimes Lydia would find him asleep, his head on the keyboard. Holmes must surely have read O. Henry's "The Caballero's Way" (1903)—the story that was later to inspire the Cisco Kid character in movies, radio, and television— because his first published story owes more than a little to its plot. "The Passing of the Ghost" appeared in *Action Stories* (9/25). He was paid 1/2¢ a word and received a check for $40. "Yeah—forty bucks," he said later. "Don't laugh. In those great far-off days, a pair of young parents with a three-year-old son could buy a lot of groceries on forty bucks." That first story opens with a daring daylight hold-up by a bandit known as the Ghost because he vanishes so completely after each robbery. Clay Fisher is the deputy sheriff of Pima County. He notices that the Ghost was wearing a gray neckerchief spotted with blue. Checking with the local storekeeper, Fisher learns that such a neckerchief was sold to Anita Valencia, a Mexican girl who lives in a desolate cabin with her aged father. Fisher scouts the place at night and sees the Ghost moving in the darkness near a shed. A phantom form rushes from behind the shed just as the deputy tells the Ghost to raise his hands. The Ghost fires at the phantom and the deputy fires at the Ghost. The phantom was Anita. She is killed instantly. Before the Ghost expires, he asks Fisher if Anita will be all right and the deputy tells him she will recover.

Holmes was learning his craft in the late 1920s and virtually all his stories during this period depend entirely on plot. In "White Blood" in *Western Story Magazine* (2/20/26) two gunfighters interrupt their gunfight when a small boy runs into the street between them, chasing his puppy. They befriend the boy and, when he is kidnapped by the border bandit, Brick Sloan, they ride to his rescue below the border although, in the process, one of them has to sacrifice his life so the other can take the boy to safety. When the sounds of distant shooting come to them, the boy asks the remaining gunfighter what it is and he tells him: " 'It's the last stand of a very brave man, laddy. . . . And the vindication of a wolf . . . a noble, old wolf.' " In old age Holmes could say with justifiable pride: "You name a Western pulp and I was in it at one time or another."

One of his chief markets in the 1930s was *Five Novels,* edited by John Burr for Clayton House, and after the magazine was sold to Dell Publications in 1933, edited by Florence A. McChesney. Being primarily concerned with plot, Holmes tended to work and rework the same plot elements with slight variations. "The Six-Gun Trek" in *Five Novels* (12/33) concerns Marion Henderson's attempt to get her Loop and Cross cattle outfit to a new range on the Chinquapin Plateau. Her way is blocked by Clint Kramer who intends to throw up a barb-wire fence across Medicine Valley to keep trail herds from passing through it to the plateau region. With the help of Terry Brooks, a young rancher in the district, and his crew, Marion is able to accomplish her goal. Holmes had made a study of Ernest Haycox and, as the years passed, his debt to him would become greater and greater. Even this early the Haycox destiny theme, so commonplace in Holmes's later novels, is present when Terry asks Marion if she believes in it. " 'I don't know,' she said. 'I'll answer you better a month from now.' " Terry responds: " 'If destiny's workin', I hope it makes up its mind before then.' " Holmes still dealt with this theme in a light-hearted way and it had, for him, none of the fatalistic inevitability it had for Haycox until much later. In "No More Fences" in *Five Novels* (3/39) Holmes was still reworking his range hog plot. Jim Allerdice is a small rancher who has been grazing his herd on a summer range and must now bring the herd down for the winter. He is frustrated in this by Skull Gunther who has fenced Twilight Pass, the only way back to Jim's home range. The plot is complicated by the fact that Gunther has living with him his niece and nephew as a means to seize their inheritance. Denny, the boy, bolts first and Nancy, the heroine, is sequestered in town by Jim who hires Denny to ride for him. In a tribute to the villain by the same name in Haycox's *Free Grass* (Doubleday, Doran, 1929), Gunther's right-hand gunman in this story is also named San Saba.

Once Holmes's career as a magazine writer became sufficiently successful, he moved his family back to Napa to a house on three acres of ground about three and a half miles outside of town. He did his writing in a room called the Den, typing his first draft on yellow bond. Lydia, who had gone to secretarial school as well as college, would type Holmes's finished manuscript, with corrections and word changes inserted by Lew in pencil, on white bond, and this was the copy Holmes would submit to his agent. A carbon copy on yellow paper was retained. Not all of his stories were accepted. Those that were not he placed in manila folders in a closet in the Den. His son Perry, when he was in his early teens, would read those stories in the folders and many years later could remember the way they had moved him. Later, when Perry was away from home, Lew destroyed all those stories, thinking they were of little use to anyone. His writing day would begin after breakfast and he would work all morning. His afternoons were spent often in town, visiting with a regular group of friends and, occasionally, calling on the blind Western author, Charles H. Snow, who Holmes always called Judge Snow (because he was Napa's Justice of the Peace from 1920 to 1924) and who frequently served as the model in later novels for the local judges in Holmes's imaginary Western communities. It was the closeness Holmes maintained with this regular group of friends in town and the pleasure he took in going hunting or fishing in the area where he lived that ultimately became the inspiration for the ambient communities conjured by his imagination in his fiction. Holmes became such a crack marksman with a shotgun that even at the age of eighty-nine he hit ninety-nine out of a possible one hundred at the Napa Rifle and Pistol Club, a feat written up in *Sports Illustrated* (10/1/84). He also had a fine baritone voice and would frequently sing at local musical productions accompanied by his wife on the piano and was involved both in barbershop quartet singing and appeared with Lydia in many amateur theatrical productions. Once a year in September he would go hunting and camping with one of his brothers to the Modoc country in the northeastern tip of California. "I like room to flap my wings," he wrote on an insert to one of his novels. "When crowds move in, I move out. Skyscrapers are too high for me, but mountains never are. I live now where the shadow of one strikes every morning. I'm a lucky and a happy man."

His first hardcover novel was *Roaring Range* (Greenberg, 1935), the first of five he would publish between 1935 and 1941. The pacing he learned from the pulps is evident in these book-length narratives, but also some of the less attractive elements: characters inadequately drawn, sometimes just named in order to be killed, and a vague sketchiness even about the heroes. He did, however, as he would in novels that came later, develop his plots in these early stories through using the Haycox device of multiple points of view. Notwithstanding, in *Bloody Saddles* (Greenberg, 1937) one is struck by the dearth of female characters other than the heroine, a circumstance not true even in the pulp novels he was writing for *Five Novels*. Buck Comstock is the hero and the plot, as so often in Holmes, depends on the reliable range hog device: Leek Jaeger and Frank Cutts, owners of the J Bar C, frame Buck because they want to take over all three of the fertile valleys in this ranching district. *Bloody Saddles* was an expansion of Holmes's earlier short novel, "Outcast's Doom Patrol" in *Big-Book Western* (3-4/37). All stories seem to have their proper length—which may be why expansions, such as this was, are less than successful. The short novel actually has more dramatic and focused storytelling and, therefore, is far more appealing. And so it is the magazine version, retitled "Doom Patrol", that is included in this duo. Contemporary reviewers who do not remember the era of fiction magazines tend to call this kind of first book publication a *reprint,* but it is scarcely that, since this story as it stands never appeared in book form prior to its inclusion here.

Holmes was a frequent contributor to *Thrilling Ranch Stories* from the Standard Magazines group and the principal editor there, Leo Margulies, preferred extended fight scenes as much as F.E. Blackwell, the editor at Street & Smith's *Western Story Magazine,* preferred pursuit plots. Holmes always obliged Margulies. His fight sequences are always developed with unusual intensity and vividness as well as in most of the later novels.

When, at the advent of the Second World War, Perry Holmes joined the U.S. Navy and was sent to the Pacific theater, Lew stopped writing novels and took a temporary job, working at a Napa River shipyard, the Basalt Rock & Shipbuilding Company. This cut into the time he could devote to his writing although he did continue to contribute to the magazine market. Indeed, unless his pulp fiction is read from this period, the transformation that occurs in his post-war novels would come as something of a shock compared with the novels predating the war years. Another, even more important development, which began occurring in Holmes's magazine fiction, was the two-fold emphasis he now placed on secondary characters and the creation, at least in embryonic form, of a sense of a vital community as a background for his stories. Already in "Thirsty Acres" in *Ranch Romances* (First September Number: September 2, 1938) strong characterizations and a ranching community stricken by drought are effectively evoked. There are two conflicts in the plot, so related that as one is resolved the other comes to the fore. Sheriff Bill Waller is an older man, his character so deftly presented that when he is murdered his loss to the story—as to the community—has a definite impact. I included this short novel in the collection, *Stories of the Golden West: Book Six* (Five Star, 2005). In the Haycox mode, Holmes was adding interiors to his heroes and heroines in pre-war short magazine novels such as this. During the war, the stress on interiors extended to secondary characters as well. In "Blood on Her Spurs" in *Lariat Story Magazine* (9/44), he tried to introduce purely emotional scenes into an action narrative, and it is notable that Holmes was again working and reworking his materials, striving always to improve the quality and depth of his stories. Among the unusual ingredients in this short novel are Marva Roblin who runs her small cattle ranch during the day and works as a faro look-out at night at the Sugar Pine saloon. The protagonist is Jim Tunstall. Marva, a *femme fatale*, takes a quirt to one of her men when he fails in his attempt to murder Jim at the hotel.

Dakota Blue, an old-timer, becomes Jim's ally in saving the Morrison ranch from rustlers. As Holmes aged, his characters in the second half of life were given increasingly prominent rôles in his stories, as would also be the case with D.B. Newton and Lauran Paine. In "The Longhorn Trail" in *Ranch Romances* (First January Number: January 12, 1945) trail boss Jim Ladd is gun-whipped off his horse by Nick Bodie who with his gang then steals the Walking Diamond herd that is on its way to market. Jim survives the dangers of the roaring Little Devil River and is found and cared for by an old pothooks, Happy Jack, another of Holmes's very engaging old-timers. Both of these short novels will be collected in a forthcoming L. P. Holmes Western trio.

Holmes's later novels, while strictly traditional in structure and always with a ranch romance conclusion, remain among the most polished examples of their kind, all of them produced during Holmes's Golden Age, which extended from 1947 to 1970. Outstanding examples of such books would be *Somewhere They Die* (Little, Brown, 1955) and *The Plunderers* (Dodd, Mead, 1957). In fact, Holmes received a Spur Award from the Western Writers of America for *Somewhere They Die* and Dick Powell, prior to his sudden death, hoped to develop the property into a film to star John Wayne.

During most of these years Holmes was a client of the August Lenniger Literary Agency and, consistent with Lenniger's policy, every time Holmes switched publishers, he was given a different name. In the pulps, if two Holmes stories appeared in the same issue, he adopted the pseudonym Perry Westwood for one of them. This is also the name under which *Six-Gun Code* (Fawcett, 1953) was published, another range hog book and one which Holmes himself later revised and published under his own name as *Payoff at Pawnee* (Popular Library, 1981). These titles also belong among his best work.

It must also be admitted that some aspects of Holmes's Western fiction, even during his Golden Age, were already hackneyed in terms of the development of the traditional Western until that time, such as relying on Haycox's prototypical plot with the theme of the two heroines (one of whom the hero must choose), the "destiny" theme that became as oppressive at times as in Haycox's fiction from the 1930s and in which the confrontation between the hero and villain occurs because it has been fated to happen, and the terrific fistfights that Holmes continued to narrate with a vitality equal to anything in Haycox and even in Luke Short. "Delta Deputy", a four-part serial in *Ranch Romances* (Second May Number: 5/22/53-First July Number: 7/3/53), is notable in this regard not only for its unusual setting—the rangeland between two rivers—but also because for the first time in a Holmes story the hero is bested in a fistfight, revealing a vulnerability that Frank Bonham and Peter Dawson were also exploring in their Western stories as they moved increasingly away from the Haycox model. However, equally basic to Holmes's Western fiction during this period are his own very individual themes: the loyalty that unites one man to another, the pride one must take in his work and a job well done, and the innate generosity of most of the people who live in Holmes's Western communities. There are generally progressions in these novels, changes through which a number of characters must pass, and the need of some people (even, albeit not especially, female characters) to have to learn the hard way. In "Orphans of Gunswift Graze" in *Action Stories* (Summer, 1948), appearing in its first book edition as *Orphans of Gunswift Graze* (Five Star, 2012), nothing, absolutely nothing, is the same at the end as it was at the beginning, not merely because the evil element has been destroyed but because the various characters have changed and matured. Also, although Holmes's Western communities are often imaginary, there is an increasing awareness of the physical land. Holmes's heroes are never alone but bound to others by imperishable ties of friendship and to the places in which they live. What is more, whether Holmes created these communities himself or set his story in an actual geographic location, his stories make them so desirable and populated with such interesting and well-developed secondary characters that often a reader would indeed like to live there.

Throughout his career Holmes undertook to expand only a few of his pulp novels into subsequent book-length novels. This is unfortunate because much of his finest work is still to be found only in pulp magazines, in particular the stories he wrote for Florence A. McChesney at *Five Novels,* for Fanny Ellsworth at *Ranch Romances,* for John Burr at *Five Novels* and later, during the 1940s, when Burr was its editor, for *Western Story,* for Malcolm Reiss at *Action Stories* and *Lariat Story Magazine,* and for Leo Margulies at *Thrilling Ranch Stories* and *Masked Rider Western.* At his best, Holmes's style, his striking images, and his craftsmanship leave a lasting impression. Through his magazine stories and foreign language versions of his novels, Holmes received regular correspondence from readers all over the world who enjoyed his fiction for its many virtues, not the least of which was his ability to conjure poetic landscapes and create idyllic moods. "They rode in lengthening silence," he wrote of Dave Howison and Sue Kleyburg in *Showdown on the Jubilee* (Avalon Books, 1970), "their horses breasting an ever-deepening tide of twilight shadow that filled all of the basin's far reaches. Against the rioting crimson of a sunset sky the Cold River Rim was a purple-black barrier. East, the Sentinels were turning a smoky blue, and high up on old Chancellor, touched by a final flame of sunlight, an aspen thicket burned brightest gold." The imaginary West in Haycox's early fiction, or most of Luke Short's, is filled with danger. Holmes's imaginary West by contrast is a place readers long to return to, time and again, which perhaps explains in part his success during a career that spanned more than sixty years. As the bartender puts it in that same novel: " 'I got to admit I liked things the way they used to be. Everybody friends.' " That is the way it was for L. P. Holmes and in the life he lived in the Napa Valley, even after Lydia died in 1974. In his finest fiction he invariably shares this inner sense of well being with his readers and so it is unlikely they will ever forget him.

CONTENTS

★ ★ ★ ★ ★

WOLF BRAND

★ ★ ★ ★ ★

I

It was quiet before the storm and none sensed it more truly than did Vike Gunnison. It was like watching the clouds gather about the hoary crest of Battle Peak, knowing that suddenly the unnatural quiet would be torn apart by the blasting of thunder and the white sword of lightning. Only here, along River Junction's single street, the piled-up forces of hovering explosion were human rather than cosmic. Ironically enough, the day itself was fair and soft, the tag end of a late spring, and the lazy breeze lifting in from the river ruffled the cottonwoods, scattering bits of white fluff from the trees until the air seemed full of the drifting, cottony snow.

The settlers from Middle Valley had held their meeting and Reese Bagshaw, the lawyer they had hired to go East in their interests, had given them the bad news. So now the settlers were prowling up and down the street in twos and threes, small groups of grim, harried men with desperation and growing truculence in their eyes and manner.

Two of them who Gunnison knew rather well approached and made as if to pass him, unseeing. But Gunnison stepped in front of them. "I'm sorry, boys," he said, "sorry that the news Bagshaw brought was bad."

Joe Spicer, a gaunt, raw-boned, middle-aged man, accepted as one of their leaders by the settlers, gave Gunnison a hard, almost unfriendly stare. "I wonder," he growled. "I wonder if you really are, Gunnison."

Under the tan, Gunnison's lean face darkened slightly. "Many things have been said about me, Joe," he stated quietly. "But even my enemies have never called me mealy-mouthed. Just because I'm a cattleman is no sign I can't have sympathy and understanding for a group of people who have been given a dirty deal."

Spicer hesitated, then said awkwardly: "I take it back, Vike. You've been decent to us settler folk right from the start. But I understand that Marsten is aiming to organize the cattlemen to stand behind Collingwood and his railroad."

"Henry Marsten doesn't represent the feeling of all the cattlemen, Joe . . . not by a jug full," Gunnison said. "Marsten acts like he does, simply because he is Marsten. You've got to consider that."

"I know," said Spicer wearily. "But right now all I can consider is the fact that Collingwood has got those two hardboiled marshals of his, Niles and Haggerty, circulating around with a pocketful of eviction notices. Once they try and serve them, there will be trouble, Vike. We settlers have tried to abide by the very letter of our agreement with the railroad and by the law. But when that law denies us simple justice, then we can only fall back on the oldest law of all, and the first one in the book, the law of self-preservation. There may be some that Collingwood and his cussed railroad can bluff out. But there are plenty more of us who are going to fight, come what may."

"Right!" rasped Spicer's companion, a stocky, powerfully built settler named Ellison. "The law! Look at it, in Buell Hess and his sheriff's star. A man supposed to see that justice is done for all people in these parts. Where is he now? Why, tagging along at Collingwood's heels, like a bootlicking cur on a leash. Collingwood has bought him, body and soul. So much for the law. Justice . . . hell!"

There was little Vike Gunnison could say. These men were

fundamentally right in their contentions. "If," drawled Gunnison finally, "I might offer my advice, it would be this. Hang on
. . . and try and hold on. Make your resistance passive. Put the
weight of initiative squarely on Collingwood. Make him do the
moving. Don't give him the slightest chance to charge you folks
with violence. You've got to view this as a long-term fight.
Somewhere along the line a break may come. If it does, and
your skirts are clean, it will be all to the good."

"Sound advice," admitted Joe Spicer, "but hard to follow
when the pressure is on you like it is on us right now. But we'll
do our best. I think it would be a good idea, Tim, to round up
as many of the boys as possible and get them out of town."

"I hate to give Collingwood the satisfaction of feeling he's
run us out of town," growled Tim Ellison. "But I reckon you're
talking sense, Joe. Let's get about it."

The two settlers hurried off, and Gunnison headed for the
Midnight, common center of gossip and news in the town. On
his way he had to pass the hotel and standing on the hotel
verandah was a group of four. Henry Marsten, his daughter
Katherine, Abel Collingwood, and Buell Hess, the sheriff.
Marsten called: "Oh, Gunnison! Like a word with you."

Gunnison hesitated, shrugged, and climbed the steps. He
nodded curtly to the men and tipped his hat to Katherine
Marsten. "Hello, Kate," he said. Then he faced Henry Marsten.
"Well?"

Henry Marsten owned the Dollar outfit, over on South Fork,
biggest and richest cattle outfit along the river. He was a big
man, gone somewhat to flesh. In his manner was a slight swagger, arrogant with the too-conscious pride of a man who had
definitely succeeded in life—hard-headed, self-opinionated, and
none too tolerant of the same privileges for others. He flushed
slightly at Vike Gunnison's cool tone.

"It's like this, Gunnison. Looks like Mister Collingwood has just about got those settlers on the run. It is my thought that, if the cattle interests line up solidly behind the railroad, the settlers will realize how completely their game is up and clear out of Middle Valley with less chance of troublemaking. I just wanted to know how you stood about the idea."

Gunnison's laugh was as curt as his manner. "I'd rather turn horse thief than back the dirty deal Collingwood and his railroad are trying to put over on those settler folks."

"Strong words, Gunnison, strong words," said Abel Collingwood sharply.

Gunnison turned and looked Collingwood up and down with a slow, long scrutiny. And he thought that sight of this man always would, as it had from the first, arouse a hostility within him, deep and strong. "Words of truth, Collingwood," he said.

Collingwood's black eyes met Gunnison's gray ones in a long, measuring stare. He shrugged his heavy shoulders irritably. "Your sentiments are hardly practical, Gunnison. My company made a business arrangement with the settlers. If they can't hold up their end, that's their fault."

"You and your railroad made a deal with them, yes," agreed Gunnison. "But now you're out to double-cross them. Collingwood, you may have some people fooled, but not all. You and your railroad brought the settlers into this country. The proposition listened good. Your railroad was out to get a subsidy title to all that Middle Valley land. And the settlers were encouraged to come in and settle there with the understanding that they would be allowed to buy their lands from the railroad for a dollar an acre, when and if the subsidy grant went through. Otherwise, they could prove up on their sections according to regular homestead law. Either way would leave them sitting pretty, working toward ownership of a chunk of good land, with a railroad right at their doorsteps to serve them. It listened good and would be good, if you and your crowd would shoot square. But it is plain now that you don't intend to. You got your subsidy grant all right, like you knew you would from the first. And now you are threatening to run the settlers out unless they pay your railroad fifteen dollars an acre. If a man can't pay that much, which means all of them, you kick him out and pay him not a red cent for all the work and improvement he's put into his land. Now you may call that a business arrangement, but I say it ain't half a step removed from highway robbery."

Dark blood beat up in Collingwood's face. "You'd have a case, if you had the facts, Gunnison," he said harshly. "But you're mistaken in the vital point. My company quoted no set price to the settlers. The agreement was that the price per acre would be as low as was compatible with grading and construction costs. And. . . ."

Vike Gunnison shrugged and laughed curtly. "That's a lie, Collingwood, and you know it."

Abel Collingwood was as tall as Gunnison, who stood an even six feet. He was heavier through the shoulders. He was a man used to authority, masterful, driving, alert, a man who usually prided himself on the mastery of his mind over his emotions. But the lie had been thrown in his teeth and Kate Marsten was there to hear it, which was all the spur necessary to Collingwood's already simmering anger. He took a swift step forward and drove a slashing right fist at Vike Gunnison's face. Back along the years when he had been climbing to his present post of authority, Abel Collingwood had known the rough-and-tumble life of the construction crew and grading camps. That he had climbed was tribute of a sort to his physical and mental prowess. Also, there was an instinctive ruthlessness that made the neck of a prostrate opponent a legitimate footstool, providing it advanced the personal ambitions and welfare of Abel Collingwood. So the railroad superintendent had no reason to doubt his ability to take care of himself in physical combat. He overlooked one thing. The physical does not always remain as sharp and responsive as the mental. Life had been easier in the past year or two and long hours in an office chair had dulled the fine edge of his physical condition. He realized this a trifle desperately as the supple, wiry, saddle-toughened figure of Vike Gunnison swayed lithely out of the way of the blow.

Then a clap of thunder crashed against Collingwood's jaw and he was flat on his back on the rough and dusty boards of the hotel porch. Vike Gunnison was standing over him, slightly crouched, swaying a bit from side to side, gray eyes full of white lightning.

Collingwood shook his head dazedly as he got to his feet. But before another of those thunder blasts could come his way, Henry Marsten and Buell Hess were pressing Vike Gunnison back.

"Enough of that sort of thing, Gunnison," growled Marsten. "You had no call to do that."

There was a rasping, sardonic note in Gunnison's laugh. "Who threw the first punch, Marsten?"

"He did. But you flung the lie in his face, first."

"And I stick to both. The lie and the punch. And he can have some more of the same if he wants it. Hess, you poor, slick coyote, take your paws off me. Quick!"

Sheriff Buell Hess was long and gangling with a narrow, horsey face. A strange furtiveness had come out in the man of late. It was gall and wormwood to have to obey Gunnison's scornful command, but there was a deadliness about Vike Gunnison just now that Hess feared more than he did scorn. He backed away, mumbling something. And Gunnison might have torn loose from Henry Marsten for another shot at Collingwood, had not Kate Marsten taken a hand. She stepped between the two men, facing Gunnison.

"No, Vike!" she said sharply. "As a favor to me. No! Please go now!"

A strikingly handsome girl, Kate Marsten, with her wealth of ash-blonde hair, her classically perfect features, and her full, strong figure. Slowly the cold, bleak fire died out of Gunnison's eyes and he nodded.

"All right, Kate," he said.

He turned and dropped swiftly down the steps in a clash of spurs. There he found waiting for him the two Vestal boys, Luke and Coony. Small, wiry men, the Vestal brothers, with a hint of Indian blood in their thin, dark faces, they seized upon Gunnison joyfully.

"Finest sight I ever laid an eye on," chortled Luke, the elder. "Mister Abel Collingwood, flat on his back from a lovely smack, right in the teeth. Vike, you old horse thief, I'm buying you a drink for that."

"I'll make it a pair," vowed Coony. "If Luke and me can't get any pay from Collingwood for that corner of our range he ran his railroad across, then we sure enjoy seeing somebody take it out of his hide."

Gunnison had himself in hand again, with the cold, explosive fury that had convulsed him retreating into the background. He even managed a grin at the Vestal brothers. "You two seem to be doing all right. How come Hess lets you pack your guns in town? I've got in the habit of leaving mine home."

Luke Vestal spat through his teeth. "An hour back he told us to go over to his office and leave 'em there. We told him to go braid his tail. We told him that long as those two railroad marshals, Niles and Haggerty, were packing shoulder guns, we'd keep packing ours. He backed down, then."

Buckboards and other conveyances were rolling out of River Junction. Evidently Joe Spicer and Tim Ellison had persuaded most of their fellow settlers to get back to Middle Valley. Gunnison and the Vestal boys waited for several rigs to pass, then went on across to the Midnight. Just before they reached the swinging doors of the saloon, Gunnison saw Al and Cherry Derian ride up to the hitch rail of Miles Letterman's store. Cherry's white Stetson hung by the chin thong to her saddle horn and her tousled dark curls glinted in the sunlight. She caught Gunnison's glance and threw up a slim arm to wave at him, a quick, impulsive gesture so characteristic of her.

Inside, the Midnight was pretty well crowded, several riders and cattlemen being present, along with half a dozen of the younger and more truculent settlers from Middle Valley who Joe Spicer had been unable to persuade to leave town. These young hot-bloods were in a little group by themselves at the far end of the bar.

Andy Killian, who owned the Elkhorn, and Ed Lutz, who owned the Wagon Wheel outfit, a pair of grizzled, leathery, hard-bitten cattlemen of the old school, were having a beer together and made room for Gunnison and the Vestal boys. They wanted to buy, but Luke Vestal would have none of it, explaining that it was his treat and telling them of the punch that had laid Abel Collingwood low. At which the two old-timers snorted their delight, and made Luke detail the whole thing, after which Andy and Ed pounded gnarled fists on the bar and called loudly for service.

"Served Collingwood right," vowed Andy Killian. "Me, I got no use for a slick crook like him."

Gunnison took a small beer, warmed more than he cared to admit by the approval and support of these staunch friends. As they put their glasses down, two more men came into the Midnight—Niles and Haggerty, Collingwood's railroad marshals. Haggerty was short and thick and red-faced. Niles was taller, thinner, with a beaked, ferret-like countenance. Both wore store clothes, both moved at a swagger. They went straight over to the group of young settlers and Haggerty pulled a sheaf of folded papers from his coat pocket. He thumbed through them, then said harshly: "Which one of you birds is Jorgenson . . . Knute Jorgenson?"

A big, strapping young settler with a round, placid face, sea-blue eyes, and a shock of bleached yellow hair nodded and said: "I am Knute Jorgenson. Why?"

Haggerty shoved a paper at him. "Here's why. You're officially served with an eviction notice."

"Eviction notice? What is that?"

Haggerty barked a harsh laugh. "An eviction notice, you big, dumb sod-buster, is an order for you to get off of railroad property. If you'll bother to read that paper, providing you ain't too dumb to read, you'll notice the dates written into it. Those dates mean you got just one week to move out in, one week from today. Either that, or you pay the railroad fifteen dollars an acre for that section you're on, fifteen dollars an acre, cash on the barrel top."

Haggerty riffled through his papers again. "Farman," he barked. "Chris Farman. Which one of you is . . . ?"

"Wait a minute." It was Jorgenson, and he had a hand on Haggerty's arm. "I don't want this paper. I'm not leaving my land and I'm not paying fifteen dollars an acre. I will pay one dollar an acre, which was the agreement the railroad made with me in the first place. No, I don't want this paper."

Haggerty snarled at him: "So you don't want the paper, eh? Now, ain't that just too bad! Get this, you big, dumb ox. You got the paper and it means just what it says. You pay, or you get off that land. And if you try and make a fight of it, you'll get thrown off. And me, Buck Haggerty, will do the throwing. Understand?"

Jorgenson's sea-blue eyes took on a chilly glint. With slow, deliberate moves he tore the eviction notice in shreds. "Here is what I think of you and your paper," he said. "And if you try and run me off my land, you'll get just what the paper got." Then he threw the shreds of paper in Haggerty's face.

The marshal spat a curse and slashed a quick, swinging blow at Jorgenson's moon face. It was a heavy punch and might have floored a smaller man. All it did to Jorgenson was to rock his head back and leave his lips split and bleeding. Jorgenson swung his great ham-like hand, palm open and flat, in a ponderous slap. It caught Haggerty across the side of the face with a spat like a splitting board, and it knocked the marshal spinning into a card table, which skidded and upset. Haggerty, raging, whirled back. As he came, his right hand was up under his coat, clawing hard at his left armpit.

Vike Gunnison, who, along with the Vestal boys, Andy Killian, Ed Lutz, and others, had been watching and listening to the whole thing, leaped forward, yelling at Jorgenson: "Look out! He's going for a shoulder gun! Haggerty, don't try it! Don't try . . . !"

Gunnison had just a stride too much to cover. Haggerty lashed a snub-nosed gun into the clear, stabbed it level, and the report of it shook the room with thunder. A shivering jerk ran all through Knute Jorgenson's big figure. A vast and stunned surprise showed fleetingly in his wide, blue eyes. Then his jaw dropped, his yellow head lolled to one side, and he crumpled down, shot through the heart. And Haggerty, carried completely away by his fury, drove another slug into the group of settlers. One of them, his right leg shot from under him, staggered and fell.

"You damned crazy wolf," gritted Vike Gunnison. He smashed Haggerty on the jaw with a driving fist.

Haggerty hit the floor, rolling completely over. But the fellow's rage seemed to make him impervious to ordinary shock. He came up on one knee, cursing thickly, and he threw the next shot at Gunnison, who felt the burn of the slug across his ribs. Gunnison gathered himself for a headlong leap at Haggerty, hoping desperately to beat the fellow to the next punch. But as he did so a second gun roared behind him. Haggerty shook under the impact of the slug, then dropped forward on his face.

A fourth time a gun shook the room with hammering report and Niles, the other marshal, walked blindly into the bar, bounced back, and went down, in a sprawl. As he fell, a gun skidded from his limp fingers.

Gunnison turned, a little dazedly. There stood Luke and Coony Vestal. Both had guns out and both guns were smoking. "Niles," said Luke Vestal jerkily, "was aiming to get you by a sneak, Vike. Now you see why Coony and me were packing our guns. You better go home and strap on yours. From here on out you're liable to need 'em."

The room was dead still for a long moment. From the first shot to the last only a few ticking seconds had elapsed. Yet gaunt and red-handed tragedy now filled the room with suffocating tension, where cool peace had reigned before. It had happened fast. No man could have guessed the start, and it was all over before any man could have stopped it. Now three dead men, and a wounded one lay on the Midnight floor and Vike Gunnison could feel warm stickiness seeping down his ribs.

He said tonelessly: "Thanks, Luke, Coony. You saved my skin that time. I won't forget. But now you'd better leather your guns and slope. Hess will be here on the run. Slide out and make for your bronc's. Don't waste any time, but don't act like you're in too big a hurry. By the time Hess finds out what happened, you can be clear of town. I'll make this up to you, someday."

"We didn't aim to start no gun play," said Luke. "It was one of those things."

"Lucky for me you had guns," said Gunnison. "You're wasting time, Luke."

"Right," grated Coony. "Come on, Luke."

They holstered their guns and slid out the door.

Vike Gunnison looked around. "Meet with your approval, gentlemen?"

"Suits me," twanged Andy Killian. "Niles and Haggerty came looking for it. And shot down two unarmed men. And came close to getting a third . . . you, Vike."

"Plenty close." Gunnison nodded. "I owe Luke and Coony plenty for that."

Only one of the settlers spoke. He was staring at the still forms of Niles and Haggerty. "The dirty dogs," he growled bitterly.

There were shouts from the street, and the pound of running feet. The swinging doors slammed wide and Buell Hess charged in, followed by Abel Collingwood and Henry Marsten.

Hess howled: "What's going on in here? Who was shooting?" He broke off suddenly as he saw the men on the floor, the balance of his words running off in a whistling, diminishing gasp.

Abel Collingwood dropped on a knee beside Haggerty, turned the limp figure over. He looked at Haggerty, then at Niles. "Dead," he snarled. "Both of them. Shot to death."

"They had it coming," said Andy Killian softly.

Collingwood surged to his feet, face working with fury. "Who did this?" he yelled. "Who murdered my men?"

"They weren't murdered," growled a settler in answer. "But they were murderers. They shot down Knute Jorgenson and Bob Wayne, who had no guns. Shot them down over nothing."

Vike Gunnison had edged over to the door. He glanced out. Luke and Coony Vestal were just untying their broncos. Another fifteen or twenty seconds and they would be clear.

Now the bartender spoke. "The Vestals did the shooting, Mister Collingwood. Luke got Haggerty and Coony got Niles."

"Ah-h," spat Andy Killian in flaying contempt, "you damned squealer." Then Andy moved over to the door beside Vike Gunnison.

Nobody heard Andy. Collingwood was snarling at Buell Hess. "The Vestals came out of here just before we came in. Get after them, Hess, quick!"

Buell Hess charged for the door, but found Vike Gunnison and Andy Killian blocking his way. Gunnison shoved a stiff arm against Hess's chest. "They saved my life," he growled. "They get their chance for a getaway if I have to smash you down, Hess. Back up."

Hess hesitated. That was all Gunnison. For Luke and Coony Vestal were in the saddle and spurring for it. They galloped into the alley alongside the hotel that led to the open country beyond. When Gunnison finally stepped aside and let Hess go, Luke and Coony were safely away.

Hess charged outside, heard the fading clatter of hoofs, then came back in, cursing and livid with rage. "Damn you, Gunnison!" he yelled. "I got a good mind to. . . ."

"Change it," snapped Andy Killian. "I'm backing Vike's hand, too."

Collingwood raged at Hess. "Get after those killers! What are you coming back in here for, you fumbling fool? Get after them!"

"They're gone," said Hess sullenly. "I'll go after them as soon as I get a posse together." He glared at Gunnison. "And you, smart guy, you're going to be one of that posse."

"Not this day, or any other," retorted Gunnison coldly. "I wouldn't ride in a posse of yours, Hess. I'd sooner be dead."

"That goes for me, too," chimed in Andy Killian. "Don't waste your breath trying to tell me I got to. Because I won't."

"Likewise here," said Ed Lutz.

Hess was choking with anger, unable to find words. So Collingwood spoke, gone cold and quiet now. "Go collect your posse elsewhere, Hess. And don't come back without those Vestals, in their saddles or across them."

Hess stamped out. Vike Gunnison moved over to the settlers, still numbed and made indecisive by the tragedy that had taken the life of one of them and crippled another. "You better get that wounded man over to the doctor," he said quietly. "You'll also want to take care of Jorgenson, too, I expect."

Collingwood said: "Not so fast there, Gunnison. Stay put, everybody. I still got some questions I want answered."

Gunnison turned on him. "Listen close, Collingwood. I don't know who sold you the idea that you're running things in this town and valley. It's an unhealthy idea, for you're not. Get rid of it. All right, boys. Move your men out."

Again came that clash of personalities. Again frosty gray eyes won in combat over boiling black ones. Collingwood said nothing more while the settlers went out, carrying the dead Jorgenson with them.

Collingwood turned to the bartender. "We'll put Niles and Haggerty in your back room, Stude. I'll have them taken care of, later. Lend a hand."

Throughout it all, Henry Marsten had not said a word. Now he moved over to Andy Killian and said: "Those Vestal boys always have been bad medicine. It don't surprise me none that they've gone clear past the edge."

Killian looked at Marsten closely. He said bluntly: "That's got a funny sound, Henry. Like you was trying to drop your loop on something whilst straddling a fence. Get clean on one side or the other. I got no use for a fence-straddler. I know where I stand. I'm for Luke and Coony Vestal."

Ed Lutz touched Andy Killian on the arm. "Vike got a little lead scratching himself in that ruckus, Andy. Maybe you didn't notice it, but I did. Let's get him over to the doc."

They left Henry Marsten standing there, uncertain, red of

face, a trifle choleric. They steered Vike Gunnison to the door. "I saw you flinch, Vike," said Ed Lutz. "Haggerty nicked you, didn't he?"

"Across the ribs," admitted Gunnison.

"You for the doc," said Ed.

II

It was nearly an hour later when Vike Gunnison left Dr. Stuart's office and headed for Letterman's store. The pony that Cherry Derian had ridden into town was still tied there. As Gunnison entered the block of shade thrown by the store overhang, Cherry herself came out of the place. Her face was sober and grave.

"Vike! They told me you'd been hit."

Gunnison shrugged. "Just a little scratch across the ribs. Where's Al?"

"Buell Hess took him as a posse man. Vike, I saw them carrying out those . . . those. . . ." Her voice went tight, seemed to choke a little. "Tell me all that happened . . . and why."

Gunnison did so, acting as matter-of-fact as he could. When he finished, Cherry stared straight ahead into the afternoon sunshine. "I . . . I thought we'd outlived our shooting days in this valley," she said finally.

"So did I. I haven't packed a gun in the past two years. A little mistake," Gunnison added dryly, "that came near costing me my skin today. I'm not making that mistake again."

Again Cherry was silent for a time. Over south and west, where the railroad right of way was pushing steadily out along South Fork toward Hunger Gap, a freight engine spilled the mellow blast of its whistle. Until six months ago, the vast peace of the valley had never been shattered by such an alien sound.

"I hate it!" flared Cherry Derian in sudden fierceness. "I hate the railroad and all connected with it. For it has done things to our beautiful valley, Vike. And it was a happy valley before."

Gunnison nodded silently, as he looked down at her. He thought that here was an outburst typical of this range-bred girl, for Cherry Derian was never one who would approach life cautiously. She knew but one gait, which was headlong. In the saddle she rode high and light. When afoot she had a forward-leaning, tiptoe sort of manner that suggested a bird about to take flight. In the slim grace of her was a deathless, exuberant vitality and courage. Her blue-black hair, worn short and always looking as if it had just come through a tussle with a high wind, entirely became her. Against the dusky richness of her skin her mouth was startlingly soft and red, a mouth that could hold for hours at a time a faint and elfin half smile. She could be a vixen with her dark eyes, filling them at will with a slumberous languor, or crinkling them with teasing mischief. Or make them wide and sober, as now. As headlong as she was in lesser things, so she was in the virtue of defiant honesty.

"Yes," she said again. "I hate it. I suppose it might be called progress, but if the price of progress has to be this sort of thing, then I want none of it."

"I've heard that progress always demands a price," said Gunnison. "But the price paid today was entirely an unnecessary one."

Cherry said: "Do you think Buell Hess will catch up with the Vestal boys?"

A ghost of a smile touched Gunnison's lips. "Not if Luke and Coony use their heads, he won't. Those boys were born and raised in the Monument Mountains and know every foot of them. How come Al went along with the posse?"

Cherry made an impatient gesture. "You know how Al is, Vike. Cautious, conservative, strong on what he calls law and order. The good citizen who must not shirk his duty. Oh, he's my brother and, of course, I adore him. But there are times when I could cheerfully pull his ears. This is one of them."

"You sound," drawled Gunnison, "as though you hoped the Vestals get clean away from the sheriff and posse."

"I do," Cherry declared. "I hope they make a complete fool of Buell Hess."

Gunnison managed a chuckle. "The way you rawhide the majesty of the law. *Tch, tch.*"

Cherry tossed her curly head. "I don't care. I can't be a hypocrite."

"That posse may be gone for a day or two. You aiming to wait for Al?"

"I am not. I'm going home."

"Then I'll squire you as far as the forks of the trail. Wait till I get my bronc'."

Riding out of town, they had to pass the hotel. Henry Marsten and Abel Collingwood were there on the hotel porch again, as was Kate Marsten. As Gunnison and Cherry went jogging by, Kate moved to the edge of the porch and called: "Oh, Vike! Could I speak to you a moment?"

Gunnison hesitated and Cherry said softly: "Go ahead, my friend. The queen calls. Don't mind me. I'll be riding slow. You can catch up if you don't linger too long."

"I'll be along," said Gunnison briefly.

He did not bother to dismount, but slouched in his saddle as well as his bandaged ribs would permit, as he looked down at Kate Marsten.

"Could you stay in town for the evening, Vike?" she asked. "Dad is figuring on holding a meeting of as many of the cattlemen as he can round up. He wants you there."

Gunnison built a wary cigarette. "Meeting . . . for what?"

She hesitated just a moment. "To decide on some sort of policy that will see that such a thing as happened today does not occur again. Something of that sort."

Gunnison inhaled deeply and looked straight into the beauty that was Kate Marsten's face and eyes. He said slowly: "I'm afraid your father and me can't see eye to eye in this matter, Kate. I know what is in his mind and he can't convince me. So, it would only be a waste of time."

She gnawed a red underlie slightly. "You can be a very stubborn person, Vike Gunnison."

He spoke words that Cherry Derian had used but a few moments before: "I can't be a hypocrite, Kate. A man has to tie to his own convictions, or be one. Sorry. I'll be seeing you again."

He shook the reins and set off after the disappearing Cherry. Kate Marsten watched him go, a little flare of heat coloring her cheeks and the ripe curve of her lips tightened until it hinted of slight hardness.

As Gunnison caught up and dropped his bronco in stride again with her pony, Cherry Derian flashed an elfin glance at him from under long lashes. She murmured: "Of course, I can't be sure, but I'm wondering if the man's pulse is beating any faster. It should be, after an audience with the queen."

"You," answered Gunnison in kind, "are an unregenerate little devil. A regular hellcat."

"In the presence of such stunning competition, a poor soul like me must use some kind of weapons," stated Cherry calmly. "Even claws."

Gunnison grinned. "Meow!" he twanged.

Cherry stuck her tongue out at him, wrinkling her nose. "Why not?" she retorted. "Any woman is a cat when confronted by a vision of loveliness in her own sex that puts her completely in the shade."

Gunnison leaned over, stuck out a long arm, tucked a finger under her soft little chin, tipped her face up, and studied her at such critical length that Cherry grew slightly rigid, her cheeks flushing hotly, while a strange, blind breathlessness came into

40

her eyes. "When," said Gunnison slowly, "you get over being such a kid, and use a hairbrush occasionally, you'll be pretty attractive yourself, young 'un."

Cherry reined away, tossing her tousled head. "I was a wise old lady long ago, Mister Vike Gunnison. Much wiser than a certain fresh cowhand I might mention. And I do use a hairbrush, regularly. Is it my fault I was born under the curse of a cowlick?"

"Know just how you feel." Gunnison chuckled. "Got one myself."

As they rode along, the sun dropped from sight beyond Battle Peak and the smoky blue shadows of evening spilled everywhere. North, the smooth, tawny, folded flanks of the Sombrero Hills became a rampart of the palest, softest lavender. South lifted the Monument Mountains, blue-black in their dense cloak of pine timber, while high and far in the east where the bright copper of the sky had turned to a pale and cooling blue, a tiny puff of cloud hovered, like a fragment of rose-tinted cotton.

Cherry said softly: "Our beautiful valley."

III

It was after midnight when Sheriff Buell Hess and his posse got back to town, tired and dusty, hungry and thirsty—and without prisoners. Hess dismissed his posse members and headed for his office, where a light was burning. He entered to find Abel Collingwood there, sitting behind the desk.

"Well?" Collingwood rapped.

Hess shrugged. "They broke for the Monuments, like I knew they would. We picked up their trail and followed it as far as we could, but lost it in the timber when the darkness came on."

"You'll try again in the morning." It was an order, rather than a question.

Hess hesitated, then shrugged. "I'll keep my eyes open," he

41

said sullenly. "But I'm not going to ride myself to death pounding the Monuments from end to end. It wouldn't do a lick of good. The Vestals know those mountains like a book and the country is awful damn' big. A man who knows that country could hide an army in it. We'll have to play a waiting game for the Vestals."

"Waiting never curried any wolves," said Collingwood sharply. "Niles and Haggerty have to be avenged. I'll be satisfied with nothing less. The prestige of the railroad is at stake."

"Suppose we get one thing straight," Hess growled. "You know and I know that Niles and Haggerty asked for what they got. And. . . ."

"That is neither here nor there," cut in Collingwood. "Niles and Haggerty were railroad marshals, charged with serving eviction notices on those settlers and seeing that the notices were obeyed. If I allow their killing to go by without the killers being properly punished, what chance has any future marshal at the same job? Those settlers must be made to understand that the railroad means business. So, you bring in the Vestals."

Buell Hess threw his hat into a corner, dropped wearily into a chair. "Suppose I hand you one chunk of advice, Collingwood. I know this country and the men in it better than you do. Don't push them too hard, or too far. If you try and drive this thing to a showdown, your railroad will run into more misery than you can imagine. Oh, I don't mean necessarily from the settlers in Middle Valley alone. But there are a lot of cattlemen in this valley who don't care for you or your railroad. They're not all like Henry Marsten, Frank Todd, Judd Slocum, and Pinto Blodgett. You got that crowd seeing things your way, sure. But there's others who see it different and you can't laugh 'em off. Take Vike Gunnison, for instance. You push that jigger to a wide-open break and you'll think a chunk of white hell is loose in the valley. Then there is Andy Killian and Ed Lutz. No profit in stirring up men like them to a shooting frame of mind unless your hand is a lot stronger than it is now."

"You surprise me, Hess, showing such admiration for this Gunnison fellow," Collingwood sneered.

"I didn't say anything about admiring anybody," Hess argued stubbornly. "But I ain't fool enough to think that because I don't like a man he's something I can brush out of my way with a wave of the hand. I'm not over fond of a tiger, either, but that doesn't mean I'm going to stir that tiger up if I can help it, or figure it a sick pussy cat that I can scare off by yelling boo. I should think you'd have learned something about Gunnison today on the hotel porch. Well, what he gave you then is only a small sample of what he can hand out, should he get really started."

Collingwood instinctively fingered a swelling on the side of his jaw, while his face went turgid with anger. "I'm far from done with Gunnison," he snarled. "And I got no use for a coward, Hess."

Hess leaned forward, a glitter growing in his eyes. "Let's get something straight," he rasped. "You and me made a deal. I expect to live up to my part of the deal as far as possible. But there was nothing about that deal which said I had to take any damned sneers or dirty tongue-lashing from you. So, go slow on the name-calling. Understand?"

Abel Collingwood studied the gangling figure and the thin, horsey face of the sheriff and saw something there he had never noticed before. Here was a man neither very brave, nor all coward. One who would avoid trouble if he possibly could, but fight he would, if fight he must. Collingwood smoothed his tone and manner. "I take that back, Hess. Guess I'm on edge. But I want those Vestal brothers brought in. We'll have to figure some way."

Mollified somewhat, Hess growled: "Now we're getting down

43

to cases. If you're willing to take advice, I got a few ideas. I been thinking about them on the ride today."

"I'm listening," said Collingwood.

"All right. You'll be bringing in men to replace Niles and Haggerty. Let me pick those men."

Collingwood, who had gotten up to pace the room restlessly, swung around and looked sharply at Hess. "Go on," he said.

"You ought to realize by this time that force, and plenty of it, is the only thing that is going to move those settlers out of Middle Valley. They've dug in. They got cabins built. They've cleared a lot of acres of sagebrush and dug irrigation ditches. They put in a dam on Copper Creek, providing their own work and money to get that irrigation water. They've built fences, plowed ground, put in crops. They've made valuable property out of what was nothing but sagebrush flats. They know that. And they won't let go of it unless the fear of hell is thrown into them. A couple of railroad dicks serving eviction notices haven't got a chance. You've got to bring in a different breed of men. I know, Collingwood. Back along the years before I hit this country and began toting this star, I rode wide and far. I've seen a few things and learned a few lessons. I know what you got to do to handle a flock of sod-busters. And I know the kind of men you got to have to do that handling. Then, when the pressure is on, I'm not overlooking the strong probability of such men as Gunnison, Killian, Lutz, and maybe others siding with the settlers. Should they do so, your ordinary railroad dicks would be babes in the woods. It will cost you a little money, but if you let me get the kind of men I want, you'll at least get results, even if Gunnison and those others are fools enough to stick their noses in."

Collingwood took another turn up and down the room. "You speak of money," he rasped. "How much?"

"Maybe ten or fifteen thousand dollars. But . . . cheap at the price, considering."

"Get them," snapped Collingwood. "I'm beginning to get your drift. Any more ideas?"

"One. About Gunnison. Killian and Lutz will side him for keeps, providing he still looms as a strong man. But once he starts to slip, they're liable to think things over pretty serious before getting too far out along a limb. If there was some way we could sort of take the gloss off him. . . ."

Collingwood grinned, and there was a cruel, cat-like quality in that grin. "I'd been figuring on that myself," he admitted. "Gunnison cuts too wide a swathe with several people in these parts to suit me. I got a man out at Hunger Gap running my grading crew. Black Mike Brady. I've seen Black Mike break a man's arm like you would a matchstick. I've never known him to be whipped. Now, if some pay night, when the crew is here in town and Black Mike should sort of bump into Gunnison, and then take him apart . . . well, what do you think?"

Buell Hess grinned back. "It wouldn't hurt things a bit, and would probably help a lot. This Black Mike man of yours could go all the way and not hurt my feelings."

"I think he might," said Collingwood. "Meantime, you get busy about bringing in those men you spoke of."

Out at his Oxbow spread, Vike Gunnison had been taking things easy for the past ten days, giving his ribs a chance to heal. A little fever had come along, but he had whipped that with a couple of days in his bunk. Now he was up and around again, just about his old self. Cherry Derian had ridden over and spent a lazy afternoon with him. They sat on the ranch house porch, talking of light and more serious things.

Cherry had reported what her brother Al had told her about the failure of Buell Hess and his posse. Now and then, echoing faintly over the miles, had come the sounds of an engine whistle from railhead at Hunger Gap. At regular intervals the shuddering thud of dynamite explosions told of the construction crew activities as, with drill and powder, pick and shovel, the railroad gnawed its way along through the stubborn rock defiles of the gap. All along the valley, engine whistles also echoed as more rails, more ties, more powder and equipment were hauled in from the east.

Gunnison, seeing the shine of resentment in his visitor's eyes, laughed softly. "No use, young 'un. We got to live with that railroad from here on out. Got to make the best of it. Let's hope things quiet down."

"I know." Cherry sighed. "Things will never be the same, and that hurts in some funny, deep way. Well, I'd better be getting home. Al will call me a shameless little hussy when I get there for visiting a bachelor all afternoon."

"You tell Al to go soak his head." Gunnison grinned. "I was dying of loneliness. I love you for taking pity on me."

The dancing elves were in her eyes as she gave him a slanting glance. "Don't throw that word around so reckless, my friend. I might take you seriously. And that would be bad. Kate Marsten might hear of it."

"What's Kate Marsten got to do with it?" challenged Gunnison.

Cherry tripped lightly down the verandah steps, her little spurs tinkling. "I wonder, Vike. . . ."

Gunnison walked over to her pony with her, caught her by the elbows, and tossed her lightly into her saddle. Cherry, smoothing her divided skirt, said: "He's a fake. The man is a fraud. And here I thought he was all crippled up. Cherry Derian, you're a soft-headed ninny, taking pity on such a faker."

"You're a nice little lady with a heart of gold and goodness," corrected Gunnison. "I kiss your hand in gratitude."

He did so, before Cherry could pull back her hand. She

reined her pony away, dancing under the touch of the spur. Again that strangely lovely, blind, breathlessness was in her eyes. "Losh!" she cried. "The man's daft."

And then she would have ridden away, had not a rider come spurring up out of the town trail. It was Shad Guthrie, one of Gunnison's three riders. Shad was stocky, almost as broad as he was high, with a round face ordinarily mirroring a constant good-natured grin. But Shad's face was grim and serious now, his sunny eyes narrowed and bleak.

"Wait a minute, Cherry," said Gunnison, his bantering tone gone. "Shad's got news, and, if I know him, it isn't good."

Shad pulled to a halt and swung down. Gunnison said: "What's the damned railroad done now, cowboy? You got misery to unload. Let's have it."

Shad said slowly: "Misery is right. I hear that Middle Valley is an armed camp. Collingwood has brought in a crowd of tough ones, Vike. Riding men, bristling with hardware. Got a half-breed leading them, an *hombre* who goes by the name of Chino Chavez. They pulled a raid on the settlers last night, burned three cabins. Killed one man, crippled another. And caught in one of those burning cabins was a settler kid, maybe two years old. Its mother got it out just in time, but Doc Stuart has been working over the younker most of the day. He says it's a toss-up. He said something about third-degree burns."

Cherry gave a soft little cry of anguish. Gunnison's face pulled out of its lines of good humor and became as taut and hard as a carven mask. "Where was Buell Hess all this time?" he asked harshly.

"Supposed to be out looking for the Vestal boys. At least, that's what I heard in town."

"Go saddle yourself a fresh bronc' and cinch my hull on another," ordered Gunnison. "We're going to town, Shad."

Gunnison went into the ranch house, and from a wall peg

over his bunk lifted down and strapped about his hips a pair of gun belts and holstered guns. He settled the belts at just the right angle, slid first one gun, then the other out of the leather, spun the cylinders, opened the loading gates, and plugged the chambers in the cylinders full of fat, yellow, deadly cartridges. He donned his hat and a somewhat faded denim jumper, took a rifle in a scabbard out of a corner, and stalked out.

Cherry was still there, humped in her saddle, her eyes brooding. "You better scatter along home, young 'un," said Gunnison gently.

"No! I'm going to town, Vike. Doctor Stuart may need help with that poor child. I know enough about nursing to be of help."

Gunnison looked at her. "You're a thoroughbred, Cherry," he said quietly.

They rode fast, Cherry and Gunnison and Shad Guthrie, slamming along the trail down Oxbow Creek, to where it emptied into the North Fork of the Blue River, turned east along the river to where they could ford at the usual shallows. From there they pounded straight on into town.

In front of Dr. Stuart's place was a rickety buckboard with a gaunt, tired-looking team of ponies. A settler was humped despairingly on Dr. Stuart's steps.

Cherry said: "Please, Vike, don't do anything to add to my worries." Then she spurred over to the buckboard, swung down, and ran into Dr. Stuart's house.

There was another buckboard, tied in front of the hotel and on the dash a stamp iron had burned a Dollar brand. It was Henry Marsten's buckboard and Gunnison headed that way. "Drift around a bit, Shad," he ordered. "See if you can pick up any new developments. I'm going to run down Marsten."

Spurs clashing, Gunnison crossed the hotel porch and went in, and saw Henry Marsten immediately. The Dollar owner was at the hotel bar, talking to Pinto Blodgett and Frank Todd. All three of the cattlemen seemed in very good humor, but their laughter cut short as they saw Gunnison prowling toward them.

Pinto Blodgett, an untidy-looking sort with a blotchy face, pointed at Gunnison's guns. "Better not let Hess catch you wearing those hog-legs, Gunnison. He won't like it."

"He'll have to get used to them," Gunnison shot back. "Because they stay there until this valley is clean of snakes again. Marsten, what do you think of your friend Collingwood, now?"

Marsten flushed. "What do you mean?"

Gunnison waved an impatient hand. "You know damned well what I mean. Don't try and be so cursed heavy and wise and pompous. There's cold turkey in the air. Let's get down to cases. You know of that raid on the Middle Valley settlers, of course. How does it set with you?"

Marsten drew a deep breath. "As long as you ask me, I'll tell you. It suits me fine. I'm not a hoe-man lover. I never have been. Cattle country for cattlemen, I say. I'm all for anything that will run those sod-busters out of this country."

"Even if it means burning babies to death in their own cribs?" shot back Gunnison harshly.

Marsten hesitated. "That was unfortunate, I admit. But it was the settler's own fault. They've been warned, served with eviction notices. And the way I get the story, they started the shooting in the first place."

"Besides," put in Pinto Blodgett, "the kid wasn't burned to death. Just singed a little." He laughed, hoarsely, as though he had cracked a joke.

Gunnison's face thinned to a terrible bleakness and white cavities quivered at the corners of his nostrils. "Blodgett," he crackled, "you're a dirty, slobbering hog!"

The room went very still. Pinto Blodgett swung fully to face

Gunnison. Thunderous fury burned in his slightly blood-shot eyes. "I ain't got a gun," he said thickly.

Gunnison jerked one of his, slid it along the bar. "There's one . . . as good as the one I got left. Bust yourself, if you don't like what I called you."

Blodgett half reached for the gun, hesitated, let his hand fall at his side. Then Henry Marsten, a look of real alarm on his face, slid the gun back to Gunnison and stepped between him and Blodgett.

"You can't be serious, Gunnison," he protested. "Great Lord, man! Do you realize what you're going . . . or trying to do? You'd start war running all through the range? You've gone loco."

Gunnison laughed harshly as he re-holstered his gun. "Listen, Marsten. I always knew you were a pompous big mouth. But I never figured you a complete jackass. I was wrong. You are. Here you stand, backing the hand of the most ruthless, crooked, greedy polecat ever to hit the Blue River. Yeah, I mean Abel Collingwood. You know that he's bought up the man who is supposed to represent the law in this valley. You know that Collingwood brought those settlers in here in the first place. They didn't just find their way in here. The railroad and Collingwood put the bait out to bring them here. They knew that the subsidy land, once it was cleared and had irrigation water on it, would be a gold mine. So they brought those poor devil settlers in to do the dirty work. Now they're aiming to rob them of their hard work and sacrifice. That is what your friend Collingwood has done and is doing, Marsten. On top of that he turns two bloodhounds loose, Niles and Haggerty. They start shooting and get rocked off by a pair of good boys, the Vestals. And Collingwood, and you, declare them murderers and fugitives. Now Collingwood brings in a gang of gun-throwing wild ones to shoot and burn and loot. And you still call him friend, and put your OK on what he does. Speaking of fools, Marsten, you're the biggest one unhung. And mark my words, when Collingwood gets through using you, he'll drop you like you were a five-striped skunk."

Just as Gunnison finished his verbal blast, Judd Slocum came in. A grizzled, raw-boned, leathery-faced old-timer with deep, sun-puckered eyes under shaggy brows. Slocum owned the Sugar Loaf spread over under the slopes of Battle Peak. With a glance he seemed to understand what was going on. He smiled grimly.

"Telling 'em off, eh Vike?" he rumbled. "Good! They got it coming if they're still backing Collingwood's hand. Marsten, I been looking for you. Wanted to tell you that I've changed my mind. After what happened last night, I'm all done. I want none of your fancy ideas. I might put up a fight to run hoe-men out of the country, but when it comes to burning babes as they sleep, I pass. Tell Collingwood and his crowd to keep away from me or I'll wring their necks."

With this, Judd Slocum turned and walked out. Gunnison laughed softly, though without mirth. "You see, Marsten? Think it over."

Gunnison started to leave then, but as he crossed from the bar room to the front door of the hotel, Kate Marsten barred his way. She looked worried, but stubborn. She walked with him out onto the porch.

"You've become difficult lately, Vike," she said. "Can it be that I've underestimated the wiles of Miss Cherry Derian?"

Gunnison looked at her gravely. "Cherry is over at Doc Stuart's, Kate, helping take care of a little settler kid that your friend Collingwood came close to burning to death, last night."

She seemed honestly startled. "Why . . . what do you mean?"

"Ask your father," was the terse reply. "He knows all about it. Now, I'm sorry. But I got some chores to do."

IV

Vike Gunnison caught up with Judd Slocum before the latter could get to Kettleman's store. He noticed that Slocum was carrying a gun. "Never expected to see you get out the old hardware again, Judd," he said.

Slocum grunted. "When a flock of wolves like Chino Chavez and his crowd begin riding my country, you bet I'm strapping on the old Peacemaker."

"This Chavez . . . who is he, Judd? You've heard of him before, maybe?"

"Kinda. He's a half-breed gun *hombre* that would do anything for a few dollars. And he's got a flock of the same kind riding under him. He's been in trouble in a half a dozen states. I don't know how Collingwood got hold of him, but he's here and raising hell. Things are going to be a lot worse in this valley before they get better. That's a prophecy you can paste in your hat."

"It looks, Judd, like there is going to be a wide split among the cattlemen of this valley. Which side are you going to be on?"

"Not Collingwood's, you can bet on that," rumbled Slocum. "Beyond that, I'm making no promises."

"I'm satisfied, Judd."

Slocum went into the store. Gunnison looked over toward Dr. Stuart's and saw Cherry Derian standing in the doorway. She waved to him and he stalked over that way. Cherry's face was very pale, but she looked relieved.

"The baby is going to live, Vike," she half whispered. "It is going to live. But oh, Vike, those poor little tortured arms and legs. . . ." Cherry's eyes filled with tears and her lips quivered and puckered like those of a hurt child. "I . . . I'm g-going to b-bawl, Vike," she wailed. "Loan me y-your shoulder."

She burrowed her tousled, dark head against him, her slim shoulders shaking. Gunnison slid an arm about her. "There, there, young 'un," he comforted. "I know just how you feel. It's no disgrace to cry when you're hurt. You'll feel better in a minute."

Apparently she did, for soon her shoulders quit that convulsive shaking and she pulled away, dabbing at her eyes. "I'm n-not as b-big a b-baby as I seem," she whimpered. "T-thanks for the s-shoulder." Then her head came up in the old valiant, gallant way and she managed a smile at him through the welling tears.

"You bet," approved Gunnison. "Chin up."

She wrinkled her nose at him and went back into the house, and Vike went on the prowl for Shad Guthrie. He found him just coming out of the Midnight.

"Well?" asked Gunnison.

"Nothing new," reported Shad. "Chavez and his crowd aren't in town just now. I hear they got a camp out along South Fork somewhere."

"They'll probably show up in town after dark," said Gunnison. "We'll stick around. I want a look at that half-breed."

Kate Marsten was vastly disturbed. For one thing, she had stood watching Vike Gunnison after he left her on the hotel porch, had seen him catch up and talk with Judd Slocum, and then go over and on to Dr. Stuart's place where he met Cherry Derian. It was too far for her to see what was on Cherry's face or to hear any words, but not too far to see Cherry bury her head against Gunnison's shoulder, nor to see his arm go about her slim, dark-haired figure. Kate Marsten had gnawed a lovely lip over that, then gone in to see her father and ask him what Gunnison had meant when he had spoken about a burned settler child. Her father had proven evasive and ill-tempered, and finally Kate had told him she was taking the buckboard and going home, to which he offered no objection. Now, as she whirled along, the spirited team reeling off the miles at a sparkling trot, she was frowning and wondering and thinking about a lot of things.

Kate Marsten had been spoiled all her life. By the time she was born, the Dollar Ranch was already strongly entrenched. By the time she was old enough to understand the meaning and advantages of worldly wealth, she was surrounded with it. The death of her mother while Kate was still very small had left Kate the sole object for Henry Marsten's affections. The beauty that had been endowed upon her by Nature was an added treasure. All men, it seemed, admired her until she had come to view these attentions as part of her special gifts from life. That she would be badly spoiled was inevitable, yet, fundamentally, Kate Marsten had a fine, clean strength about her, too, and a level head, when she wanted to use it. She was using it now, thinking about Vike Gunnison. If she had known any special preference among men who had sought her company, it had been for Gunnison. The lean, brown, clean-cut virility of the man, the cool, dauntless strength and courage so plainly a part of him, an agile mind, an easy, drawling humor—these things put him apart from others, somehow. Even so, Kate Marsten had taken his attentions slightly for granted and now she was wondering whether she wasn't being faced with a penalty for that casual manner.

Of course, in the past few months, there had been another admirer, Abel Collingwood, a handsome man, a doer, a man who built things, made things go, a man apparently destined to move high up in his profession. Kate was not entirely unsusceptible to these things. She admired the idea of a man being masterful, a man of authority. There was sharp contrast between Abel Collingwood and Vike Gunnison. Gunnison was the spirit of the range country, lean and rangy and free in the saddle, with the fire of its sunshine and the grim strength of its storms in him. A figure, however, who would always be beyond the fringe of the busier world, slightly lonely, slightly visionary, a bit mysterious as he rode against the backdrop of the sunset shadows. While Collingwood was a part of the bustling world of inexorable progress, always pressing closer to the frontier, pushing that frontier farther and farther back to make way for modernity. True, there was one somewhat tarnished spot on the picture of Abel Collingwood. That was as she remembered him as he lay flat on his back on the hotel porch, driven 'here by one flashing potent smash by the fist of Vike Gunnison

Kate was still in her disturbing turmoil of thoug t when, without warning, the near pony of the buckboard tea n pulled up, hobbling and dead lame. Kate set the brake an climbed out of the rig. Examination showed that the horse h d picked up a severe stone bruise in the off front hoof. In fact, e jagged piece of rock had jammed into the tender frog an was still there.

Kate tried to remove it with her gloved fingers, bv it was too tightly set. She was back in the buckboard, search g the tool box on the dash for some implement to do the jo when she heard the patter of approaching hoofs. She looked p just as a rider swung to a stop beside the rig. He was a l le, cat-like man, very swarthy—ornately, almost flamboyan dressed in the best Spanish *caballero* fashion, black velvet users, skin-tight about the hips and thighs, flaring at the le bottoms and slashed with red silk, a short bolero jacket of the ame material, embroidered with scarlet thread. He wore huge black sombrero, heavy with a silver scroll band, two g is belted at his narrow hips, ivory-handled. His riding gear w equally fancy, hand-stamped and heavy with silver. His hors was coal-black, speedy-looking, spirited. There was a sinist handsomeness about the fellow, his features aquiline, a faint t ead of mustache on his upper lip. His eyes were bright, black, nreadable.

Kate's first impression was of a bold an admiring stare.

Then white teeth flashed in a quick smile and the heavy sombrero was doffed with an exaggerated sweep. *"Gracias, señorita,"* came the velvety, purring voice. "You are in trouble, no?"

Kate's first impulse was to ignore the fellow completely, to freeze him with a glance. Then she realized that this was a pretty lonely spot along the trail and that perhaps a little charm would be more effective than too much frigidity. So she smiled slightly and nodded. "Yes, I am. The near pony has picked up a rock in the off front hoof. I wonder if you would be so kind as to dig it out for me?"

"Why of a certainty, *señorita.*"

He was out of his saddle like a cat, was lifting and examining the offending hoof. He flicked out a knife, worked a moment, then dropped the hoof. Again the white-toothed smile, the sweeping bow. "It is done. And I, Chino Chavez, have been honored to serve one so beautiful."

There was no mistaking the fellow's open admiration. Kate felt the color creeping into her cheeks. She nodded. "Thank you so much," she said. She kicked off the brake, shook the reins, and the buckboard rolled on. Kate could feel those bright, black eyes following her.

As for Chino Chavez, he mounted slowly. *"Por Dios,"* he muttered. "Never have I seen such beauty. Hair like the kiss of morning sun on snow. Thees country . . . I am like it better all the time."

He watched until only a ribbon of amber dust marked the progress of the buckboard. Then he rode slowly south, toward the dense alder and willow thickets that there blanketed the banks of South Fork.

The railroad construction gang, their pockets heavy with wages, hit River Junction in a noisy, sweaty, thirsty avalanche. A switch engine brought them down from the railhead on a flat car and let them off opposite the town. They waded the shallows of South Fork carelessly and streamed into the street, heading mainly for the Midnight.

Swaggering along in the forefront was a man built like a gorilla. He had enormous, sloping shoulders and arms that hung long and heavily at his sides. He was bare-headed, his hair a matted, ragged black thatch. He had little, bleak eyes, deep-set under a slanting brow. His jaw was heavy and outthrust, his nose broad with thick nostrils and flat across the bridge as though broken at some past time. He was Black Mike Brady, boss of Abel Collingwood's jerry gang.

Shadows were deepening now. Yellow lights had begun to flare from windows and open doors all along River Junction's street. Standing back in the shadows, Vike Gunnison and Shad Guthrie watched the advent of the construction gang.

"Tough layout, Vike," said Shad. "Time they get a few shots of liquor under their belts, this street will be no place for a peace-loving man."

Gunnison shrugged. "I'm not interested in that crowd. I want a chance to face this Chino Chavez *hombre*. We're sticking around."

It was not long before a swelling bedlam of noise began to come from the Midnight. Shouts, curses, ribald songs were roared out as the liquor began to take hold of the railroad jerries. Two men bounced suddenly out of the saloon, stood toe to toe, swinging heavy fists. One of them went down. The victor swaggered back inside. The beaten one lay for a moment, got up, and also went in.

Miles Letterman came along the street, recognized Gunnison and Guthrie in the gloom. "They bring me business, that crowd," said the store owner. "Just the same, I'll be glad when the railhead gets beyond Hunger Gap. This town can do without that gang."

The night deepened and the regular citizens of River Junction sought their own firesides. They, like Miles Letterman, wanted nothing to do with that noisy, brawling crowd in the Midnight. Two riders came jogging in from the south. They tied in front of Letterman's store, then jingled toward the Midnight. As they entered, limned for a moment in the glare light of the door, Vike Gunnison stirred.

"I've never laid eyes on this Chavez hairpin, Shad," he murmured. "But one of those two sort of looked the part. Like a half-breed. Flossy Spanish get-up. Come on, I'm going to investigate."

Shad followed a trifle reluctantly. Shad was no coward, but he was cautious.

Gunnison stood for a moment, just inside the door of the Midnight, looking over the room. He saw his man immediately, where he stood with his companion, back to the far wall, watching and listening to the uproar with a sort of sardonic amusement. Gunnison pushed his way toward him.

Black Mike Brady was at the bar, drinking. Now the bartender leaned over, tapped Black Mike on the arm, and said, for Brady's ears alone: "Gunnison. The tall one with the blue jumper."

Black Mike swung around, took a look, nodded, finished his drink, and then began pushing through the crowd after Gunnison and Shad Guthrie.

Gunnison came into the clear, facing the swarthy rider in the velvet, flare-bottom trousers and the embroidered bolero jacket. "You're Chino Chavez?" he rapped flatly.

Chavez looked Gunnison up and down, his eyes narrowing warily. "And if I am?" he said thinly. "Then what, *señor*?"

"Get out of this neck of the woods . . . tonight! Take your

gang with you. Get far away. Or else you'll be open game, for a rope or a slug by the first cowhand who can get you over his sights."

Chavez said: "That is a broad and surprising order, *señor*. Your authority is . . . what?"

"These." Gunnison tapped the butts of his guns.

Bright, black, unreadable eyes stared back into Gunnison's flinty gaze, then glanced away. "I doubt your authority, *señor*," purred Chavez. "But I will talk of it with my men. Come, Tomás."

The two *vaqueros* headed for the door. Gunnison turned to follow them, only to find a gorilla of a man facing him—Black Mike Brady.

"Slow up, saddle-pounder," growled Black Mike in his rasping, guttural voice. "You're Gunnison . . . Vike Gunnison?"

"That's right," said Gunnison crisply. "What about it?"

"Just this. I don't like you. I don't like anything about you. And if you'll take off them popguns you're packin', I'll prove it to you. Or don't your nerve reach that far?"

A look of alarm came into Shad Guthrie's face. He caught Gunnison by the arm. "Go slow, Vike," he warned. "This has got all the earmarks of a raw set-up."

Gunnison was already unbuckling his guns and laughing, low and cold. "Why, of course, it's a set-up, Shad. Take these guns . . . and use 'em to see that they don't gang me. Now, Brady, step right up and collect, because you're going to receive payment both for yourself and your boss, Collingwood. Don't say I didn't warn you."

Black Mike Brady looked a trifle bewildered. He had expected this lean, rangy cowboy to do a lot of back-watering, like all others had done when faced with the threat of Black Mike's strength and brutal power, but the fool wasn't backing down a foot. He was even laughing, as though looking forward to something pleasant. Slow, sodden, brutal anger began to burn in Black Mike. He'd soon make this leather-pounder laugh out of the other side of his face. So Black Mike set himself and cut loose with a blow that would nearly have decapitated Vike Gunnison had his head remained where it was. But Gunnison's head did not stay put. It ducked smoothly out of the way. And then he let Black Mike have it with a blow that started clear from his toes, gathering momentum as it ripped up through his lean hips, up through a forward curving shoulder to find ultimate velocity in a leaden fist that ripped home with the smashing impact of a mule kick. Under that impact, Black Mike's nose was a complete wreckage and the bully foreman of the construction gang wavered backward, arms pawing aimlessly, little eyes dazed and numb with shock. A gasp of surprise ran over the room, then dead stillness.

V

Within the next five minutes Black Mike Brady found out that there was more than one kind of physical combat. It was one thing to grab some helpless and unfortunate devil, to twist and torture his limbs, to club him into senselessness, to wrestle him down and put the boots to him. It was something entirely different to be faced with a lithe, panther-fast fury that you couldn't get hold of, that you couldn't hit because it was constantly on the move, in and out, weaving and sliding and side-stepping each bull-like rush. It was something that hit you with fists that felt like chunks of lead on the end of whalebone.

Black Mike Brady was as strong as the ape he resembled, but it was a slow, clumsy strength that had to get set, that needed time. Against one of his own kind, Black Mike was a terror. Against Vike Gunnison he was just a mewling, gabbling, grunting, clumsy animal, muscle-bound and ponderous. Gunnison either side-stepped Black Mike's floundering rushes, or stopped them dead with thundering punches that shook Black Mike like a tempest. Once one of Black Mike's clawing hands caught Gunnison by the arm and Shad Guthrie groaned. But Gunnison writhed loose, though he left the entire left sleeve of his jumper in Black Mike's grasp. If he were caught and pulled into the grasp of those gorilla arms, it would be fatal, and none knew it better than did Gunnison himself. He speeded up the fury of his remorseless attack. It was like hitting something inhuman. Vike had hit his opponent as hard as he had ever hoped to hit any man, hit him a dozen such lethal blows. Yet, Black Mike was still on his feet, floundering, groping, clawing, swinging ponderous, lethal blows that met only air.

Gunnison slid in, lashed two ripping punches. He was going away when one of Black Mike's wild swings hit him high up on the left shoulder. The impact of the blow fairly flung Gunnison across the room, left his arm feeling dead and paralyzed. But Black Mike was too slow, too blinded by the punishment he had absorbed to follow up his advantage. Gunnison circled him, around and around, stabbing and slashing with his right, while waiting for his left to recover and become usable again.

It couldn't go on forever. Nothing living, not even Black Mike Brady, could continue to absorb such relentless, staggering punishment. Deep though the man's vitality lay, the continuous hammering reached it. His nerve reflex began to go. His rushes no longer had direction to them. His wild swings still had power, but they were slow and easily avoided. And with his left arm coming back to full strength again, Gunnison moved in to finish it, ripping at Black Mike's sagging jaw with both hands.

Slowly, like something mortally wounded, Black Mike began to crumple. His thick legs were spread wide, but his knees were trembling. Then, under a final blasting right hand that found the point of his chin squarely, Black Mike went down and lay there, inert.

Vike Gunnison backed away, breathing in hoarse gasps. The knuckles of both hands were raw. He was wringing wet with sweat. "He's a man," Gunnison mumbled thickly. "By heavens, he's a man! Too good a man to be doing Collingwood's dirty work for him. All right, Shad . . . we can travel now."

Shad was speechless. He had thought it a hopeless cause at first, and now it was victory. Shad wanted to yell, but couldn't.

No attempt was made to stop their leaving. These men of the construction gang had watched Black Mike Brady grind down more than one man to shattered helplessness. They had seen him strut and swagger. They had never seen him whipped, until now. They had never thought to see it. They could hardly believe their eyes. Yet there was Black Mike, still on the floor, still out. They were stunned, shocked to silence. And there was something like awe in their eyes as they watched the man, who had done the impossible, leave the place with clanking spurs.

While the fight had been going on, the door to the back room of the Midnight had been partially open. Now, as Gunnison and Shad disappeared out into the night, that door shut rather emphatically. Beyond it, Buell Hess faced Abel Collingwood. "Don't say I didn't warn you, Collingwood," Hess blurted. "I warned you that Gunnison would be hell on wheels, should you ever get him started. I tell you, that guy is a tiger."

Collingwood was in a black fury. He paced the confines of the small room, glowering and infuriated. "It's certain, now," he snarled. "Gunnison has to go. He's the focal point of all opposition to me . . . all the real opposition. The settlers can be handled, if left on their own. But Gunnison won't leave them on their own. He'll side them and bring others in to help him. I thought Brady was a man. He's not, he's just a big, dumb ox. I'll fire him."

Buell Hess looked at the railroad superintendent narrowly and something like a glimmer of contempt came into the sheriff's eyes. "I wouldn't," he said bluntly. "Brady did his best. No other man I ever saw could have stood up to and taken half what Brady took. I tell you, it's Gunnison. The man's a tiger."

"You said that before," spat Collingwood. "Shut up! I've got to think this out."

Buell Hess shrugged, relapsed to sullen silence. Then came a knock on the outer door of the little room, a door that opened at the rear of the saloon. Collingwood motioned to Hess, who turned the lock, cracking the door just a trifle.

"Chavez," came the soft announcement.

Hess let Chino Chavez in. Collingwood growled: "What are you doing here? You're supposed to be on your way to work on those settlers again."

The half-breed shrugged. "I thought there might be a change in plans . . . after that." He nodded toward the door separating them from the barroom.

Collingwood demanded: "What's that got to do with your orders? For that matter, I saw you crawl out there."

The half-breed's black eyes took on a crimson glint. "You are mistaken, *señor*. I did not crawl. A wise man bides his time. I am biding mine. But it is queer, is it not, *señor*, for one who skulks in back rooms to talk of other men crawling?"

A heavy flush suffused Collingwood's face. His lips trembled with some hot retort, but he managed to hold the words back. "Forget it," he snapped instead. "You've something on your mind?"

Chavez built a husk cigarette, lit it, and inhaled deeply. Blue smoke trickled from his nostrils, weaved up across his swarthy features. "It came to me, *señor*, that we are . . . how would you put it . . . wasting our punches? Yes, it would seem that is so. We would strike at the sheep while the lobo wolf sharpens his fangs."

"What you're driving at is that Gunnison is our first care. Is that it?" barked Collingwood.

Chavez shrugged again. "Does it not seem so to you, *señor*? After he is gone, the rest will be easy."

"And you think you might be able to do something about Gunnison?"

"I might, *señor* . . . ," murmured the half-breed.

"Meaning, of course, if there is enough money in it for you?" Collingwood asked.

"I do not work for my health, *señor*," purred Chavez. "No wise man does. But I work swiftly . . . and well."

"I'll think on it. I'll let you know. Lay low along the river. I'll get word to you."

Chavez nodded, moved toward the door. "Do not think too long, *señor*. He who strikes first, doubles his strength."

VI

The next morning Vike Gunnison was early in the saddle. He rode straight east, into the eye of the rising sun. In a little over an hour he was at the Long D spread, where he found Al Derian just in the act of catching and saddling. It struck Gunnison that Al Derian's manner was a trifle curt.

"I suppose Cherry is still in town, Al?" he drawled.

Al nodded. "Yeah, she is. I'm going after her now. Seems like she's doing everything but stay home and mind her own business."

Gunnison's hands, swollen and stiff from the effects of his battle with Black Mike Brady, tightened a trifle where they lay crossed on his saddle horn. "Cherry," he said softly, "can't help having a heart as big as all outdoors, Al. You should be very proud of that little sister of yours. She's a rather wonderful person."

Al grunted. "Oh, you could expect her to feel sorry for that settler kid. I guess any woman would be the same. But Doc Stuart is paid to do that sort of thing, and Cherry ain't."

"Some things in this life aren't a matter of pay, Al."

Gunnison never had been able to fully understand Al Derian. Never could brother and sister be wider apart in personalities than Al and Cherry Derian. Where Cherry was buoyant, impulsive, wholehearted, Al was inclined to be cautious, calculating, even a little dour, a good man, and sound, but a trifle self-centered and without a trace of the sparkle that emanated from his sister. They did not even look alike. Al had a round face, settled and florid, hair of a neutral, bleached shade of brown.

"I won't keep you long, Al," said Gunnison briefly. "But I'm out to sound out sentiment along the valley. Things are heading for a showdown in these parts. Collingwood has brought in this Chino Chavez and his crowd of wild ones, apparently to put the pressure on the Middle Valley settlers. That doesn't set well with me at all."

"You trying to build up a protective committee to wet-nurse those sod-busters?" Al asked, a trace of sarcasm in his voice.

"Not exactly. But this valley has long been free of any influence like Chavez and his gang. We had a good valley and a quiet, friendly one until that railroad moved in and brought a peck of trouble. If we cattlemen think we can sit back and let Collingwood do as he damned pleases along the river and still keep our coattails from being tramped on, we've got another guess coming. I don't like the idea of a flock of renegade gun bullies running loose in the valley, regardless of why or who for. Give that breed of cats an inch and they'll take a mile."

"And what would you suggest be done about it?" asked Al shortly.

"That we run 'em out," snapped Gunnison curtly. "If, in so doing, we do the settlers a favor, why that's all right, too. After all, those settlers have rights and they are getting a dirty deal from Collingwood. That's what I wanted to see you about, Al.

Where do you stand?"

Al Derian did not answer right away. He busied himself loop-
ing the latigo and setting up on it. And here, thought Vike Gunnison, was another characteristic of Al, always cautious about
committing himself, weighing all angles, calculating every move.
Even before Al spoke, Gunnison knew what the answer would
be.

"I can't get excited over what's going on between the sod-
busters and Collingwood. That's their dogfight, not mine," said
Al, almost sullenly. "I'm running a cattle ranch and have got my
own troubles. It'll keep me busy, looking after them without
worrying over something that doesn't concern me."

"I reckon it is all in the point of view." Gunnison nodded.
"Every man has a right to his own opinion. That's all I wanted
to know, Al. Say hello to Cherry for me."

Gunnison shook the reins and jogged off, still heading east.
Somehow he wasn't surprised at Al Derian's stand. He had
really half expected it.

Well to the east and way up against the flanks of the Sombrero
Hills, Gunnison rode into Andy Killian's Elkhorn and found
Andy on the porch, poring over some tally lists. Andy grinned
and settled back with a sigh of relief. "Every man has a cross to
pack," said Andy. "Mine is figures. I never have been exactly
certain what seven times seven comes to. Sa-ay, what's this I
heard about you more or less massacring Collingwood's pet
bully boy from his construction gang?"

"It was quite a ruckus," said Gunnison briefly. He held up
his sore and swollen hands. "Like hitting a brick wall. That's
minor stuff. What do you think about this Chino Chavez and
his gang on the loose, Andy?"

"Don't like it," said Andy bluntly. "Don't like it a bit. We
ought to do something about it."

"Ah," said Gunnison, settling deeper into his saddle, "that's the kind of talk I like to hear. Wonder how Ed Lutz feels?"

"Same way," grunted Andy. "We never have stood for no crowd of gun thugs running loose in this valley and I see no reason to start in now, even if, for the present, they appear to be throwing most of their punches at the Middle Valley settlers. That sort of thing can spread and I'm all for putting the fire out before it gets a good start. Ed was over last night and we were talking about it. He feels the same as I do."

"That makes three of us," murmured Gunnison. "And I think we can count on Judd Slocum. Henry Marsten, Pinto Blodgett, and Frank Todd are going to back Collingwood's hand. Al Derian . . . I just came from the Long D . . . figures to take no stand, one way or the other."

Andy snorted. "I can't savvy that guy. He wouldn't lay a ten-dollar bet on an antelope against a horned frog. Now if that little spitfire of a sister of his had the say. . . ."

Gunnison had intended on cutting south east to the Wagon Wheel from the Elkhorn. But now that Andy had told him that Ed Lutz felt the same as they did, he did not bother. Instead, on impulse, he headed almost due south, aiming to cross the river at Porter's Ford and see how things were with the settlers in Middle Valley.

Gunnison's thoughts were sober. In a long term view, things looked bad because it seemed an inevitable rupture between the cattle factions of the valley was in prospect. This might (and Gunnison hoped so) be no worse than just a stand, one way or the other. But tempers might flare, non-retractable words spoken or some incident setting off a blaze of guns. It was not a pleasant prospect, yet a man could not retreat from the call of his own conscience and sense of honor. It was a question of right and wrong, and Collingwood was wrong, as were those backing him. Silently Gunnison cursed the railroad. It had brought nothing but trouble.

A mile from Porter's Ford the trail crossed the point of a long ridge, running down from the Sombreros, and from this vantage point Gunnison had a good look down into Middle Valley. What he saw first of all brought him up high and alert in the saddle. Down there, on the far side of the river, two funnels of dust were traveling and lifting. The larger funnel was following the smaller one. Two racing dots were out in front of the smaller dust cloud. The best part of a dozen of the same kind of speeding dots were ahead of the larger cloud. The picture took meaning in Gunnison's mind. Two men, being chased by a larger group—mounted men, racing fast. Somehow he knew who it was. The Vestal boys, Luke and Coony, probably with Buell Hess and a posse after them.

Gunnison spurred down toward the ford. He saw that the fugitives would reach the river before he did and he was still a full quarter of a mile from the line of greenery that marked the river's course, when the two riders burst into view on his side and sped toward him, but not so fast now, for the one on the rear mount had a horse under him that was limping badly.

It was the Vestal boys all right, and Gunnison was out of his saddle even as they first saw and recognized him. It was Coony's horse that was limping. Luke and Coony seemed a trifle wary until Gunnison waved them up to him.

"You darn' fools!" Gunnison rasped. "Why didn't you stay back in the Monuments, where you belong? Want to stop a slug or get your necks stretched?"

"No." Luke grinned. "But we got tired and wanted a change of pasture. Thought we'd hit across for the Sombrero Hills for a change and we bumped right into Hess and a posse. It was fun for a while, but not now. Coony's bronco went lame, coming across the ford."

"I'm not blind," snapped Vike. "I see that. What do you think I'm getting off this horse for? All right, Coony, you and me are trading bronc's and saddles *now!* Get in this saddle of mine and ride. And quit scaring your friends to death."

Coony shook his head. "That'll leave you in bad with Hess. And I won't. . . ."

Gunnison reached up, yanked Coony out of the saddle, and threw him up on his horse. "You got no time to argue. They're almost at the river."

Coony said simply: "You're white as hell, Vike. We won't forget this."

"Git!" growled Gunnison again. "Or they'll be in shooting range. Drop into the ranch tonight and get a supply of grub. I'll be looking for you."

Luke and Coony lit out again and were out of sight across the point before the posse came out of the ford, horses and riders dripping wet. They came right on up to Gunnison, who had built and lit a cigarette. Buell Hess was in the lead and he drew to a plunging halt, staring at the horse that Gunnison held by the reins.

"That's the Grulla Coony Vestal was on," fumed Hess. "How come, Gunnison?"

Gunnison shrugged. "You guess."

"That bronco is lame," charged Hess. "You let him have your bronco."

"If I want to trade horses with a friend of mine, that's my business and his," drawled Gunnison. "Nothing for you to get high blood pressure about."

"You helped a fugitive from the law escape," said the badgered sheriff. "I can arrest you for that. I think that might be a good idea, I think. . . ."

"No, Hess," said Gunnison softly. "You'd better not try. You can't arrest me for anything. I don't recognize any authority behind your star any more. If you're just busting to enforce the law, why don't you go round up that half-breed, Chavez, and his crowd of wild ones? Why waste your time chasing Luke and Coony, or trying to bluff and bully me?"

"You're not telling me my business, Gunnison!" Hess yelled. "You're . . . !"

"And I don't want to," cut in Gunnison. "It's too dirty a business."

"Aw, what's the use?" growled one of the posse members. "We ain't got a chance to overtake the Vestals. I'm sick of this rat race. I'm going back to town."

"Same here," said another.

"And me," added a third.

Before his eyes, Buell Hess saw his posse melt away, heading back for the river. He yelled at them, but none paid him any attention. And soon just Vike and Hess were left. Gunnison laughed. "That's the worst of a posse, eh Hess? Never where you want 'em when you want 'em. All posses are like that. They get tired and thirsty easy."

Hess seemed ready to choke. He swallowed several times. Then he said, his voice hoarse and suppressed: "Listen, Gunnison . . . I'm telling you something. You're leading with your neck. So far you've been more or less top dog. There'll come an end to that. Don't say you weren't warned."

"I like to keep things even," Gunnison answered. "Now I'll tell you something. You're about through being sheriff in these parts. I'm not alone in figuring that you've plumb outlived your usefulness. Because you're not a sheriff any more. You're just a cheap sell-out, blinded by whatever money Collingwood has paid you when he bought you. You're worse. You're as bad as this Chino Chavez and his crowd, because you're permitting them to raid and burn and kill. Now don't say you weren't warned."

"You don't know what you're talking about," blurted Hess. "Your imagination is running away with you."

70

"You don't lie worth a damn, Hess," said Gunnison coldly.

Hess got a congested, choked-up look about him again, cursed viciously, swung his mount, and spurred for the river. Presently Gunnison followed, on foot, leading the limping pony that Coony Vestal had ridden.

At the river he worked over the horse a bit. The injury appeared to be a strained ligament and Gunnison gave it half an hour of water cure, letting the cool river water flow against the mare's leg as it stood in the shallows. When Gunnison, swinging carefully astride, rode out the far side of the river, the mare seemed to be making easier progress.

A couple of hundred yards beyond the river at this point ran the railroad right of way, while beyond the rails the settler lands of Middle Valley spread. Gunnison headed the Grulla along the tracks. He wanted to have a talk with Joe Spicer and some of the other settlers regarding the threat of Chino Chavez. Suddenly he looked up.

Coming along the railroad track at a weary, limping pace was a tall, rather young man, in an old suit of store clothes badly rumpled and dusty and showing every evidence of having been slept in out in the sage. Scuffed, dusty shoes, never meant for intensive walking covered his limping feet. The fellow could have stood a shave and probably a square meal, thought Gunnison, as their lines of progress met. But there was a cheerful, friendly grin on the young fellow's face as he nodded to Gunnison and said: "Your miles are long ones in this country, cowboy."

Gunnison grinned in return. "A lot of 'em behind you, eh?"

"Too many." The stranger sighed, sitting down on the end of a tie and waving first one foot, then the other, as though to cool them. "How much farther to this town of River Junction?"

"Around twelve miles."

The stranger groaned. "Damn that brakie who kicked me off that train last evening. Had I guessed how far I was from River

Junction then, I might have put up a heftier argument. But"—
and here he grinned again—"he was a big, stout feller."

Instinctively Gunnison liked this drifting stranger. "Looking
for work, maybe?"

"Maybe. Right now a square meal and a chance to rest my
barking dogs is more important."

"Might be able to do something about both," drawled Gunnison. "That cabin yonder . . . it belongs to a friend of mine.
Suppose we head that way and prospect this meal, first."

The stranger accepted with alacrity, and Gunnison dismounted and walked along beside him.

Joe Spicer was out behind the cabin, greasing a buckboard.
Gunnison noticed, as they came up, that the settler had a rifle
leaning against the tongue of the rig. Spicer even took a step
toward the gun, before he recognized Gunnison. Then he
waited, grim-faced.

"Hello, Joe," greeted Gunnison. "Here's a friend of mine
who has already walked a long way and faces the prospect of
having to complete the walk to town before he can get a much
needed meal. Maybe the missus could do something about that,
eh?"

"Sure." Spicer nodded, giving the stranger a swift, shrewd
scrutiny. "You, too, if you're hungry, Vike."

Gunnison shook his head. "Thanks, but I had a big breakfast
this morning."

The stranger said: "You're mighty decent, both of you. And
entitled to know the name of the man whose life you're about
to save. I'm Rex Desmond."

They shook hands all around. "I'm Vike Gunnison. This is
Joe Spicer."

Buxom Mrs. Spicer, the soul of hospitality, bustled around
getting a meal together for the stranger, who had a wash before
he sat at the table. Joe Spicer said: "Saw the Vestal boys go tear-

ing through with Buell Hess and a posse after them. And I could have sworn Coony Vestal was riding that bronco you just come in with, Vike."

"He was," said Gunnison. "Luke and Coony bumped into me on the far side of the river. I saw that Loony's bronc' was limping, so I made him take mine. Hess guessed what had happened and rawhided me some. While he was doing it, his posse quit on him and went back to town. Our estimable sheriff seemed rather upset."

"He's a rat," said Spicer harshly. "He isn't making the slightest effort to do anything about this Chino Chavez and his crowd of renegades that Collingwood has brought in to burn and murder and loot."

"I was coming to that particular *hombre,* Joe," said Gunnison. "That first raid won't be the last. What are you folks doing about the threat?"

"We got a guard out every night," said Spicer. "The next time Chavez hits us, he won't find us asleep and unprepared. We had a meeting after that first raid. And we've made up our minds. We're going to stick. Collingwood and his damned railroad made a deal with us folks. Now he's reneging on it. We won't stand for it. We stand ready to pay him a dollar an acre for our lands, which was the price agreed upon. But we wouldn't pay him the fifteen per acre he's demanding, even if we had it. And he can serve eviction notices until hell freezes. We stick. We don't get out."

"That's the spirit," applauded Gunnison. "Stay with it. You can look for help from a good half of the cattlemen in the valley. That includes Andy Killian, Ed Lutz, me, and probably Judd Slocum. Add Luke and Coony Vestal, if they can give any help while keeping away from Buell Hess."

"That's good news, Vike," said Spicer simply. "We can use your help."

While Gunnison and Joe Spicer were talking, the stranger, Rex Desmond, had been eating hungrily. Yet, a close observer would have noted that he was listening to every word passing between Gunnison and Spicer and that a cool, sharp gleam lay deep in his pleasant eyes.

The meal over, Desmond thanked Mrs. Spicer effusively. "Now that my stomach is full, I don't think my feet will hurt so much," he ended with a cheery grin. "Maybe, someday, I'll be able to repay you good folks in some way."

Joe Spicer wanted to hook up the buckboard and take Desmond to town, but the latter would not hear of it. "You've done enough, Mister Spicer. I'll make it all right now."

"I'm heading for town myself," said Gunnison. "We'll take turn and turn about in the saddle, Desmond."

So they headed out, up the valley. After a bit Rex Desmond said: "None of my business, of course. But I couldn't help overhearing what you and Spicer were talking about back there and I'm curious. What does this argument between the railroad and the settlers seem to be?"

Gunnison told him, sketching in the whole background of subsidy lands, the original agreement, and about how Collingwood and the railroad had gone back on their word and were trying to gouge the settlers out of their hard-won properties. "It's raw," ended Gunnison. "As raw a thing as I even bumped up against. Like any other cattleman, I'm a little wary of settlers, but this thing is too rough for me to stomach, especially the latest weapon Collingwood has brought in." And then Gunnison told of the raid staged by Chino Chavez and his band, of the burning and killing, and of the little settler child that came so close to being fatally caught in the flames.

By the time he had finished there was a strange, grim look to Rex Desmond's face and the cool gleam in his eye had deepened. But he said nothing more on the subject. From then on, until they reached River Junction, their talk was of less serious things.

Gunnison left the limping pony at the livery corral and he and Desmond went uptown, to the hotel. "If you're strapped for money," began Gunnison, "I can let you have a little, Desmond."

Desmond flashed him a strange look. "I've heard about the real men this Western country breeds," he murmured. "I believe it, now. Thanks, Gunnison, but I'm not entirely broke. I'll sleep in a decent bed tonight."

At that moment Kate Marsten came out of the hotel and she said: "Thank heaven. You've saved me a ride, Vike. I was about to head out for your ranch."

She looked at Rex Desmond a little curiously, and Gunnison introduced them. Then Desmond excused himself and went into the hotel.

"Must be something important, Kate," drawled Gunnison. "What you wanted to see me about, I mean. A long time since you considered to honor my ranch with a visit."

Kate colored slightly. "Mahomet must go to the mountain," she quoted coolly. "It is about us, Vike. We don't seem to be as good friends as we were at one time, and I'm worried. Am I entirely shameless, Vike?"

Gunnison looked at her gravely. Again her sheer beauty struck him like a flame. He felt a semblance of the old kindling. "No, you're not shameless, Kate. I think you want me to be honest. There is a change. It came with the railroad. I think that's the trouble."

She nodded. "We are both very stubborn persons, Vike. And I don't see any chance of either of us giving in. We . . . we used to have very joyous times together, before. I . . . I'm wondering if we couldn't find an answer somewhere, Vike."

She was looking at him with level honesty, yet far back in her

L. P. Holmes

lovely eyes he could see the old imperiousness, the old consciousness that she was Henry Marsten's daughter, and the demand that this fact be always understood and appreciated by everyone. He tried to be as gentle as he could.

"Maybe something will happen, Kate. We'll have to wait and see. Either you are wrong or I am. When the proof shows up, one way or the other, I think we'll know our answer. Until then"—he smiled gravely—"you are very, very beautiful."

She caught her breath. "I love those words, but I don't want you to speak them again, Vike. Not now. Because they may make of me either a coward or a fool. And I don't want to be either. Yes, we'll wait, and see what the future brings. Until then . . . good friends?"

"Why, of course," said Gunnison heartily. "We could never be enemies. Now I've got to wangle a bronc' with four sound legs."

He left her there, watching him with brooding eyes, as he swung across the street, lean and prowling, a man of the sun and the wind and the open range.

A man appeared at the door of the Midnight. Another showed at the corner of the hash house. A third slithered into view from the mouth of the alley by Letterman's store. Roughly a triangle, with Vike Gunnison in the middle.

Instinct chimed like a hard-struck bell in Gunnison's consciousness. He stopped, looked around, marked each of the three men—and understood. Those men were members of Chino Chavez's renegade gang. It stuck out all over them. Gunnison thought: *Here it is. I've walked into something, like an empty-headed sheep into a wolf den.*

VII

Vike Gunnison had never known the meaning of true fear. He did not know it now. A cold, icy, prickling sensation ran up his spine. But this wasn't fear, either, so much as the sharpening of nerve senses to a bleak and savage alertness, a blunt analysis of all factors. He took another long, slow look around. All three of the renegades had a pair of belt guns, but nothing else. That was something. It put the one at the alley mouth by Letterman's store far enough away to discount somewhat the fellow's effectiveness. But the one in front of the Midnight and the one by the hash house were both plenty close. They were the two he had to center on first.

There was no way of telling which of these two was the best man with a gun. That was a gamble he'd have to take. So he made his plans. He'd make the first shot count. Then there would only be two left, and one of them some distance away. . . .

At that moment a slim, running figure came out of Letterman's store, dark hair flying in the sunlight. Cherry Derian. "Vike!" she cried. "Vike! Look out! They're going to gang you!"

Gunnison heard the hard, sibilant curse of the one by the Midnight, so he crouched low, whirling, lean hands ripping at his guns. The renegade had made his draw, and Vike glimpsed a split second before he threw his own first shot, the sultry, lurid flare of flame that spouted from the menacing muzzle. His teeth were set for the impact of the slug. But there was no real impact, just a slight tug at the flare of his chaps, about hip high.

Gunnison saw a tiny puff of dust leap from the shirt front of the renegade, saw the fellow lurch. Then he was turned around, both guns rolling at the one by the hash house. What might have been a red-hot iron passed so close to his corded throat Gunnison could feel the skin tighten and sear. But he had the cursing, frantically shooting renegade under his flaming guns now, and he saw the fellow jerk and wobble as the lead took him. The renegade seemed to lose his balance, and he ran forward with shambling steps, straight at Gunnison, trying to regain it. Suddenly he plunged, landing on his face, and lay there. At the same moment something jerked Gunnison's right leg from under him and he went down in the dust himself.

He heard, as he rolled up on his elbow, a broken, despairing wail, with all a woman's heartbreak in it. Then the thunder of his chopping gun wiped out all other immediate sounds. He saw a burst of splinters fly from a corner of Letterman's store where his lead flew high, and he held lower and lower on the renegade by the alley. The fellow's nerve seemed to run out. He whirled and leaped for the shelter of the alley, just as Gunnison let go another shot. The fellow went down, but was up again, and he went into the alley at a lurching run, one leg dragging.

A small weeping and wailing avalanche hit Gunnison. It was Cherry. "Vike . . . you're hit!"

He brushed her aside and left her there, sobbing like a child, wringing her hands, while he sped, running clumsily because of a shot-off heel on his right foot, for the mouth of the alley. He swung into it, guns high and ready. But it was empty and he loped along it, bleak and purposeful. Before he got in the clear beyond the rear of the store, he heard the pound of racing hoofs. When he finally broke into the open, it was to glimpse his man, hunched in the saddle, one leg hanging loosely, the other spurring savagely and the frantic pony stretched out like a scared rabbit, already bursting away into the blanket of sage beyond town.

Gunnison started to throw a shot, then held it. Too far. Useless. He had winged the ambusher and there would be another day coming. So he went back along the alley, punching the empty shells from the reeking cylinders of his guns, plugging them with fresh loads from his belt. He had to walk on the toe of his right boot, to keep from jerking himself to pieces at each step.

The street was in an uproar, men appearing magically from

everywhere, shouting confused questions and answers. Cherry Derian was leaning against one of the posts that supported the overhang of the store, her curly head on her folded arms. Gunnison went over to her.

"Everything is all right, young 'un," he told her. "I don't know how I came out of it. Fool's luck, I guess . . . for I was a fool ever to walk into such a trap. But the best they could do was nick my chaps, singe my neck, and knock a heel off my boot. Everything's all right." He laid a hand on Cherry's small, hunched shoulder, but she shook it off, and ran into the store without looking at him.

Some of the crowd descended upon Gunnison and he answered their questions with grim terseness. Somebody said: "Two out of three is a damn' good average. You're either lucky, or awful good, Vike."

Miles Letterman was there and Gunnison said to him: "A stroke of business for you, Miles. I've got to have a new pair of boots. I'll string-halt myself trying to get around in these."

Vike Gunnison got away from town as quickly as he could. His face was a remote, still mask, betraying nothing of his real thoughts. He stayed only to see if there were any questions by anyone regarding the outcome of the gun battle. There was none. All were profanely eloquent in their praise and satisfaction over the outcome. So Gunnison got a sound pony at the livery barn and headed for home.

Now his thoughts ran free and grim purpose crystallized from them. Time for indecisiveness was long past. No longer could a man sit back and wait for developments. To do so was to invite destruction. The experience he had just emerged from proved that, and Gunnison knew what he was going to do. He was going to carry the fight to the enemy. They had asked for it. Now they would get it.

★　★　★　★　★

Henry Marsten was having a bad time of it. A daughter who he thought he thoroughly understood was proving unpleasantly intractable. "Anybody would think you were in love with Gunnison or some other such foolishness," Marsten complained, pacing up and down the living room of the big ranch house.

"And anyone would think you ready to condone dirty, raw-handed murder," retorted Kate hotly. "I saw it. You didn't. I . . . I don't know yet how Vike came out alive. It was three to one. They had him trapped in the middle of the street. A lesser man would have been done for, then and there. But Vike shot his way out of it. I don't know how he did it, but he did."

"As long as Gunnison came out with a whole skin, I see no reason for all this fuss," mumbled Marsten. "Good Lord. I had nothing to do with it. I admit I ain't over-fond of Gunnison and I certainly don't agree with him on this wet-nursing of those sod-busters in Middle Valley, but I wouldn't have a hand in planning to dry-gulch him or any other man."

"I'm not saying you had anything to do with it, Dad," Kate said. "But I know who did. Abel Collingwood. Once I thought he was pretty much of a man. I know better now. He's ruthless, crooked, treacherous, and he is never to put foot in this house again . . . never! I hope that's understood."

While Marsten was trying to think up an answer to this, there came a knock at the door, and at Marsten's grumpy summons it was Abel Collingwood himself who entered. There was a triumphant gleam in the railroad superintendent's eyes and his manner was jocular.

" 'Evening, folks," he said breezily. He would have said more, only he glimpsed the storminess in Kate Marsten's eyes. He said: "What's the matter? Something wrong?"

"Yes," said Kate curtly. Henry Marsten saw what was coming and tried to head it off with a warning glance. But Kate was not to be denied. "You are no longer a welcome visitor at this ranch, Abel Collingwood," she stated flatly.

Collingwood looked from daughter to father, and back again. "I'm afraid I don't understand."

"I'll make it clear for you," flamed Kate. "You know what happened in town today?"

Collingwood showed the slightest hesitation, then shrugged. "I understand that Gunnison killed two men in a gun brawl."

"Yes," declared Kate. "And I understand more. I know who set those three renegades after Vike. You did."

Collingwood's laugh was a trifle forced. "You're not serious?" he protested. "I think I can tell you why that took place. I had nothing to do with it. Gunnison brought it upon himself. I know that he faced Chino Chavez in the Midnight not long ago and threatened him. Evidently today's happening was Chavez's answer to that threat."

By the time he finished, dark color was surging in Collingwood's face, for Kate Marsten was staring hard at him with all the scorn and all the contempt that a beautiful woman can put into a single devastating glance. "Just one more lie," she said cuttingly. "And I'm tired of lies. I suppose you would deny having anything to do with Chavez and his crowd of renegades coming into this country in the first place. Yet it is strange that the things they do are all calculated to aid your interests. Such as raiding and killing and burning among the settlers in Middle Valley. And then the bare-faced attempt to kill Vike Gunnison, the one man in this valley who was smart enough to see through you from the very first and who is capable of organizing a really stiff resistance to you and your schemes. Oh, you fooled a lot of us with your smooth talk, your glib schemes. But many of us are getting our eyes open now. I am, for one. And there is nothing more to say except that you will please leave this house and ranch immediately . . . and never come back."

It was direct and final enough. Collingwood looked at Henry Marsten, as though for support, but the cattleman was staring out of a window into the night. So Collingwood, an ugly light in his eyes, shrugged, turned, and went out. And not until he was in his buckboard and rolling back toward River Junction did he make a sound, and then he cursed, long and savagely, and voiced thick-toned threats.

In the kitchen of Vike Gunnison's Oxbow ranch house, four men sat at the table. Gunnison himself, Shad Guthrie, the Vestal brothers, Luke and Coony. The last two were eating voraciously, but listening while Gunnison spoke.

"The time for dilly-dallying is past," he said. "Once and for all it is going to be settled as to just who is running this valley. Either it is the decent, self-respecting people, or Collingwood, his crooked sheriff, and his gang of cut-throats under Chino Chavez. Tomorrow morning we organize and move. Andy Killian and Ed Lutz will ride with us. The settlers in Middle Valley will ride with us. We're going to force Collingwood's hand."

"Count Coony and me in," mumbled Luke Vestal, chewing busily. "We're tired of dodging and running from that clunk-headed Buell Hess and his posses. We want to make a stand."

"I've got work for you," Gunnison said. "I want you to do some scouting and locate where Chavez and his crowd are hanging out. I heard they were in camp somewhere along South Fork. Maybe they are still there, maybe they have moved somewhere else. But find 'em and report to me. It will put a double risk on you, of course, but if you don't pull any more fool stunts such as riding right through the middle of the valley in broad daylight, you should get by all right."

Coony grinned. "Buell Hess was fit to be tied when he found out you'd given me a sound bronco to get away on, eh, Vike?"

"He seemed a little put out," Gunnison agreed. "Now, when

you finish eating, you two boys get some rest, then line out to locate that renegade crowd."

"We don't need no rest," said Luke Vestal, stretching his arms. "Since we been on the dodge, we've put in most of our time laying around. What Coony and me want is action."

VIII

Vike Gunnison waited around the ranch until noon of the next day. Luke and Coony Vestal were to report immediately as soon as they had located the hang-out of Chino Chavez and his gang, and Luke and Coony had left the night before, immediately after eating. But by noon there had been no word from them, so Gunnison saddled up and headed for Middle Valley, intent on lining up the settlers behind his intended clean-up of the valley. As he cut the Long D trail, he bumped squarely into Cherry Derian. Cherry was headed for town and she had a war bag tied behind the cantle of her saddle.

"Going some place, young 'un?" asked Gunnison cheerfully.

"To town is all," answered Cherry.

"Must be figuring on quite a stay I see you got your war bag along. That little settler kid still need a lot of nursing?"

"Yes and no," was the somewhat evasive reply.

Gunnison studied her. There was a change in Cherry. Somehow she was more sober, more subdued. The old sparkle wasn't there, the old frankness. She was reserved and seemed to have withdrawn behind a mask. Gunnison slouched easily in the saddle and built a cigarette.

"Tell papa," he drawled. "Something is bothering you. You're hiding behind a bush on me."

Cherry braided slim fingers through the mane of her pony. "Part of it is that stubborn, thick-headed brother of mine," she admitted slowly. "That is the real reason I'm heading for town with enough spare clothes to stay a while."

"You mean you and Al had a squabble?"

The dark, curly head nodded. "I thought that after a little absent treatment, he wouldn't take me so much for granted."

"Shucks," protested Gunnison, "on any man who would take you for granted."

She flashed him a swift, inscrutable glance. "I've just about come to the point where I believe that all men are soft-headed," was her tart rejoinder. "Well, I'm on my way. Should you wish to get in touch with me, my address will be the hotel."

She shook her reins and her pony moved on.

"Hey! Wait a minute," Gunnison called. "You haven't told me what you and Al squabbled about."

"I know it," she said over a slim shoulder. "And I'm not going to."

And so she left him, puzzled and wondering. As he watched her ride away, the sun glinted on her bared, valiant little head.

When Gunnison reached Joe Spicer's cabin in Middle Valley, he saw that a number of settlers were present, engrossed in some kind of spirited argument. All were sullen, some obviously angry.

"What's wrong, Joe?" Gunnison asked of Spicer. "Another raid last night?"

"No," Spicer responded. "Nothing like that. But Leif Erickson has surrendered to Collingwood. Sometime yesterday he paid Collingwood his price of fifteen dollars an acre for the quarter-section he'd settled on. The boys are wild. I don't like it myself, for it means a break in the solid front we were trying to preserve. It makes it that much harder for us to bring Collingwood to the original terms. There is another angle. You remember Knute Jorgenson, who Haggerty killed in that shootout in the Midnight? Well, Jorgenson and Erickson were related. Leif Erickson married Jorgenson's sister. On that basis, you'd have thought him the last man in the world to come to Collingwood's terms. The boys are having a tough time swallowing this setback. They're talking about running Erickson out of the valley, but I think I got them talked out of that. But I can tell you this much. Leif Erickson is going to be a friendless man from here on out."

Gunnison recalled Leif Erickson, a bulky, square-jawed, level-eyed man, one he would have taken as a fighter. "Wonder where he got the money?" he murmured thoughtfully. "He never struck me as being overly prosperous."

"We're all wondering the same thing," said Spicer. "But he must have had it, for there is no mistake about the deal. By the way, I hear you had a close call in town yesterday, and only got out of it by some mighty fast and straight shooting."

"And luck," Gunnison added dryly. "That's what I came over to see you about. For a time I've been counseling a sort of waiting game in this thing, giving Collingwood and his crowd rope enough to hang themselves. It's been the wrong hunch. I learned my lesson yesterday. I was plenty lucky to come out of that with a whole skin. The point is, if Collingwood and his crowd would try that on me, they'll try it on you or Andy Killian or Ed Lutz or anybody else they figure to be standing in their way. It is plain enough now that there is only one answer. We clean them out before they clean us out. Are you settlers willing to join up and go after them?"

"Are we!" exclaimed Spicer. "And how! The boys would bust if they didn't have a chance to strike back pretty quick. What's your scheme?"

Gunnison gave it to him, and they discussed details for the next hour. Then he headed for town. If he didn't find Henry Marsten in town, he intended to ride right on out to the Dollar Ranch. For he wanted one more talk with Marsten, before flinging down the glove that could mean bloody warfare all along the Blue River.

On his way to town a train wailed its whistle downvalley, then came up behind and passed him, a freight loaded with ties and rails and other construction supplies. As it rolled by, the engine rocked with what seemed almost a swagger of arrogance. The chill purpose in Gunnison's eyes deepened.

The first person Gunnison saw when he hit town was the man he was looking for, Henry Marsten, just coming out of Miles Letterman's store. Gunnison cut his pony quickly across the street, dismounted, and tied. "A word with you, Henry!" he called.

Marsten looked harried, grouchy. "What do you want?"

Gunnison told him curtly: "We're going to clean this valley of Chavez and his crowd and all like them. The other boys and me just want to know if you're backing Collingwood's hand far enough to shoot at us."

"I am not!" snapped Marsten. "I'm backing no man's hand that far. I'm entitled to my own ideas of what is good for this Blue River range and what ain't. I'm with Collingwood in this feud with the settlers, or rather . . . make it that my sympathies are with him against the sod-busters. Now don't tell me over again that the railroad brought them in on a deal they ain't prepared to keep. I've heard that story enough and I don't give a damn, either way. All I'm interested in is keeping sod-busters off this range for they're like a plague of katydids. Once they get on a range, they spread to hell and gone. But I'm not about to start shooting at anybody. In fact, I'm sick and tired of all the ruckus. All I want is to mind my own business."

Here was a different Henry Marsten than had been apparent for the past month or two. Evidently someone had been going over the cattleman with sharp spurs, the effects of which still rankled. Gunnison had to grin slightly. "That's all I wanted to know, Henry."

Gunnison went on along the street warily. He wasn't walking

into any more gun traps, not if he could prevent it. As he neared the hotel, he saw something to amaze him. Sitting side-by-side on the porch were Cherry Derian and Kate Marsten. They were talking and laughing in friendly enough fashion with a tall, keen-eyed young fellow in store clothes—Rex Desmond, the rumpled, foot-sore drifter who Gunnison had befriended. But this was a new Rex Desmond. His clothes no longer looked rumpled and disheveled. He was clean-shaven, well-groomed, and he gave Gunnison a friendly smile as he approached.

"Pleasant town, pleasant people, Gunnison," he said. "And I am very glad to see you. In fact, I've been hoping you would show up. For I need a witness to a bit of business I think you will enjoy being in on. If you ladies will excuse me . . . ? I have something in my room I must get."

As Desmond hurried into the hotel, Cherry Derian made a face at Gunnison. "You would come along and take that so pleasant young man away from Kate and me."

"Didn't mean to butt in. But it is his idea to leave you, not mine. Kate, I just had a talk with your father. He seems to have sort of changed his mind on some things."

"He definitely has," said Kate. "I saw to that. He told me I was a spoiled, unreasonable brat, but I didn't mind as long as I got results. That . . . that affair yesterday almost finished me. You mustn't ever take such risks again, Vike."

Gunnison laughed. "I had no choice. But I'm glad you were afraid for me, Kate."

"Kate will have to get toughened up like me," said Cherry, a hard, bright note in her voice. "Any woman is a fool to worry over a man."

Gunnison looked at Cherry gravely. What the devil had come over this girl, this whole-hearted, sincere little comrade of better days? He couldn't tell, by looking at her, for she met his glance with a cool, almost defiant calm. "I forgot to tell you this morning along the trail, young 'un," he said gravely. "I'll tell you now. Things were pretty fast and savage in that ruckus yesterday. But I remember you running out into the street, trying to warn me. That was pretty fine. You might have been hit. If I forgot to thank you, I thank you now."

"I'd have done as much for . . . ," began Cherry, but somehow her voice seemed to tie up in her throat.

Just then Rex Desmond returned and Cherry seemed vastly relieved. "The sheriff's office, my friend," he said to Gunnison. "The estimable guardian of the law is there at the moment, I believe, as is another individual we are both interested in. Come along."

Gunnison didn't get this at all, but he went along. The door of Buell Hess's office was shut, but at Desmond's crisp knock, Hess growled a summons. Gunnison and Desmond went in, and Gunnison was a trifle startled to see that it was Abel Collingwood who was with Hess. Gunnison looked around warily. "Just what is this, anyhow?"

Hess and Collingwood were plainly startled themselves. "What's on your mind?" Hess demanded. "We're busy."

"Our business won't take but a moment or two," said Desmond, a crisp note coming into his bantering tone. "I have a warrant here I wish you to serve."

Desmond drew a folded paper from his pocket as he spoke. Hess took it, unfolded it, and began to read. He stiffened, his eyes stuck out, and he swallowed with difficulty. Then he turned to Desmond, blustering: "I got no time for damn' fool jokes. You can get into trouble with the law, mister, faking up a warrant."

"No fake," said Desmond, and now a strange air of authority seemed to pulse through him. "That warrant is perfectly legal, as you will see, if you care to read the signature of His Honor,

Superior Judge Macklin, at the bottom. Yes, it is very legal. Serve it."

Abel Collingwood, aside from his bleak, black stare at Vike Gunnison, had paid little attention to the argument until Desmond mentioned the name of the superior judge from whose court the warrant had been issued. Now he swung his dark glance at Buell Hess. "What's this all about?" he rapped. "Who is that warrant for?"

"It's about plenty," blurted Hess. "And the warrant names . . . you."

"Me?" Collingwood hit his feet as though shot. "What sort of stupid farce is this?"

"No farce," said Desmond. "Perhaps I had better explain. I am Rex Desmond. I am from the office of General Manager John A. Lassiter, of the Midland and Southwestern Railroad. There is only one specific charge in that warrant, misappropriation of funds. But I stand ready to back several charges against you in the interest of the railroad, and of others, Mister Collingwood. Within the past day or two, you accepted from one Leif Erickson the sum of twenty-four hundred dollars in payment for the quarter section of subsidy land this said Leif Erickson settled on. That constitutes a breach of faith with the railroad and with Mister Erickson. The original price agreed upon between the railroad and the settlers in Middle Valley was one dollar per acre. On behalf of General Manager Lassiter, I'm commissioned to ask you, Collingwood, just what you intended doing with the overage in the amount of twenty-two hundred and forty dollars?"

Vike Gunnison, hardly able to believe his ears, was tight and alert, watching every move of Abel Collingwood and of Buell Hess. He saw a dozen emotions flash their betraying message across Collingwood's face, and by the time this amazing Rex Desmond had finished his cool speech, there was but one left: a trapped bluster.

"You're crazy as a loon!" exploded Collingwood. "I never accepted any such amount from Leif Erickson. I accepted just one hundred and sixty dollars, as the agreement called for."

"It was quite simply done," said Rex Desmond. "I loaned it to him to . . . ah . . . bait the trap, shall we put it?" Desmond's voice changed to a deep note of contempt. "Collingwood, you're a cheap crook and you're caught. Sheriff, serve that warrant. Arrest that man."

Buell Hess had been doing some fast thinking. There was no doubting the legality of this warrant or the portent behind it. Abel Collingwood was no longer a power along the Blue River range. And Buell Hess was never one to hitch his fortunes to a fading star. He had tied in with Collingwood in the first place because he figured that Collingwood and the railroad represented a power that could do more for him than could the scattered elements along the Blue that might rise in opposition. Now, it seemed, Collingwood was not the railroad so much as he was just plain Collingwood, a crook trapped and cornered by the very railroad he was supposed to represent. Hess was looking out for Hess and he switched sides quickly.

"This warrant seems valid, Collingwood," he said importantly. "You're under arrest."

No more bitter irony could face any man than that which now faced Abel Collingwood. He cursed savagely at his erstwhile deputy. "You witless fool! You can't arrest me."

Hess's long, horse-like face darkened. He had taken a lot of abuse and contempt from Collingwood at one time or another and had been wary about striking back, but now the shoe was completely on the other foot. He grabbed Collingwood by the shoulder and spun him around. "You're under arrest, I say. And another sneer out of you and I knock your teeth out with a gun butt. Go easy. I'm taking your gun." Hess jerked a small, compact, lethal-looking gun from Collingwood's hip pocket.

"Very good, Sheriff," said Rex Desmond. "Lock him up. The courts will take care of him later. And now, Gunnison, you and I are heading for Middle Valley to spread the good news among those settlers."

They went out, and Vike Gunnison still felt like he was in a dream. "I don't . . . I can't savvy . . . ," he stuttered.

Desmond laughed. "From the outset the railroad has never meant to do anything else but shoot square and honor its agreement with the Middle Valley settlers. It was the belief at the central office that Collingwood was doing this on his own. But one of those breaks that generally manage to upset the best plans of the shrewdest crooks took place. You see, we maintain a legal staff to take care of all legal actions and complaints without bothering the general manager with such details. It turned out that a member of that staff was just as crooked as Collingwood and in cahoots with him on his scheme. So, when the settlers sent their legal representative, a man named Reese Bagshaw, to complain to the general manager, his complaint never reached our Mister Lassiter, but was headed off by this crooked individual in the legal department. Then, one day, a letter came in to Mister Lassiter's office, addressed simply to the general manager. It told in direct language what was going on along the Blue River, and in very concise terms told of the possibility of bloodshed if something wasn't done to stop it. Mister Lassiter was very much impressed and put me on the job of running the matter down. I managed to corner and trap Collingwood's confederate in the legal department and wring a confession from him. Then I set out after Collingwood. I was comparatively new in the employ of the railroad and Collingwood had never heard of me before. So I drifted into this valley casually, asking questions all along the way. The day I first met you I had already seen this settler, Leif Erickson, gotten his story, and loaned him the money to make that deal with Collingwood that would be the final clincher in the case against Collingwood. I had that warrant with me all the time."

"But . . . what was Collingwood's scheme in putting the pressure on the settlers the way he did?" asked Gunnison. "I don't see. . . ."

"Basically," Desmond broke in, "I got it all in the confession from Collingwood's confederate in our legal department. In case the settlers met Collingwood's demand of fifteen dollars per acre, he would remit one dollar per acre to the central office and pocket the balance, which in the Erickson case alone amounted to two thousand two hundred and forty dollars. It would have been much larger with other settlers who controlled, say, an entire section. Collingwood and his confederate stood to clean up a small fortune had the settlers met their price. On the other hand, if the settlers refused to meet that price, Collingwood figured to evict them in the name of the railroad and seize control of the land himself, which, with the improvements already put in by the settlers, is of very real and large value. It was an ambitious scheme by a pair of ambitious crooks, and it could have paid off big, had it succeeded. But thanks to that letter I spoke of, it fell apart."

"If it is any of my business . . . who wrote that letter?" asked Gunnison.

Desmond smiled. "A very charming young lady . . . Miss Cherry Derian."

"Cherry!" exclaimed Gunnison. "She would, that smart little rascal."

Gunnison looked toward the hotel porch, but neither Cherry nor Kate Marsten was in sight now. So, at Desmond's request, they headed for the livery barn, where Desmond rented a buckboard, and then the two of them headed out of town for

Middle Valley, to spread the good news among the settlers and put Leif Erickson right in the eyes of his fellows.

Back in the sheriff's office, Buell Hess had taken a bunch of keys off a wall peg and had unlocked a door at the rear of the office. Beyond this door lay a short, narrow hall. At the far end was another door, of heavy oak and bound with iron. Beyond the door lay the jail. "All right," said Hess to Abel Collingwood. "In you go."

"Listen, Hess," said Collingwood desperately. "You don't mean this. You know you don't. Hell, we're in this together, man."

"No go, Collingwood," said Hess. "That warrant named you, and I'm arresting you and locking you up."

Collingwood lost control of himself. "You dirty double-crosser. You were willing to go along with me while everything was rolling fine. Now you think you can let me drop. Well, you can't. I'll tell them plenty. I'll incriminate you."

"How?" Hess's smile was mocking. "All I've done is chase the Vestal boys for a shooting scrape. And I can start running Chino Chavez and his crowd out of the valley. That's doing my duty. And who can incriminate a man for doing his duty?"

"Your duty!" Collingwood spat. "Your duty don't mean a thing to you where a few lousy dollars are concerned. Why you cheap coyote. . . ."

Hess shouldered him roughly into the little hall. "Shut up! I've had enough of your sneers and abuse. Another word out of you and I'll gun-whip you silly."

Wild, desperate decision formed in Abel Collingwood's eyes. He smashed Buell Hess a short, savage punch in the face, knocking him back against the wall. Before Hess could recover, Collingwood had snatched one of the sheriff's holstered guns. Then, as Hess lurched back to attack, Collingwood shot him through the body twice. Buell Hess died swiftly, victim of his own folly. Collingwood raced back through the office and out into the street. A saddle pony was at a nearby hitch rail, dozing in the sun. Collingwood tore loose the tethering reins, hit the saddle, and sped out of town.

IX

Joe Spicer could hardly believe his ears. He looked at Vike Gunnison, then at Rex Desmond. "You mean then," he blurted, "that we don't have to fight eviction and that all we have to pay is the dollar per acre first agreed upon?"

"That's right," said Desmond. "The railroad never intended that you pay any more. It was Collingwood's scheme alone to hold you up for fifteen an acre, or evict you. Collingwood is under arrest, now, and I am in charge. I want you to spread the word, Mister Spicer, that the railroad is honoring its pledges."

"And explain to the boys how Leif Erickson helped Desmond get the deadwood on Collingwood, Joe," put in Gunnison. "Leif did a sweet job of avenging the death of Knute Jorgenson."

A wide grin spread over Spicer's tired face. "This is wonderful. This is great. This is a dream come true."

Gunnison happened to look out along the town trail. He stiffened. Back there, a rider was tearing toward them, a slim little rider with a curly head all shining and wind-tossed. "Hold everything," he said. "Here comes Cherry Derian, and she wouldn't be riding that way if something hadn't gone wrong."

Cherry seemed to see no one but Gunnison. She brought her foaming pony to a rearing halt. "Vike!" she cried. "Collingwood has escaped. He shot Buell Hess to death, and escaped."

Gunnison whirled to Desmond and Joe Spicer. "Things were going too smooth for us," he said. "Anything can happen now, with Chino Chavez and Collingwood in cahoots. There's no time to waste. We've got to go after that crowd. Joe, spread the word. Organize the settlers and get them to town as quick as possible. And Joe, send men to the Elkhorn and the Wagonwheel after Andy Killian and Ed Lutz and their boys. Desmond, you'd better go with him to explain the set-up and as an authority for the railroad. I'll be waiting for you in town. Cherry, your bronc' is going to have to carry both of us back to River Junction."

Cherry nodded. "Scramble up," she panted.

Cherry's pony wasn't very big and didn't like the added weight of Vike Gunnison behind the saddle, but Cherry stood no foolishness from it, and they made fair time back to River Junction. Cherry explained as they rode: "There were two shots, muffled. Kate and I heard them plainly from inside the hotel. We ran out, just in time to see Collingwood racing out of town on a pony. Nobody seemed to understand exactly what had happened, but Miles Letterman investigated and found Buell Hess lying shot to death in the hall that connects the sheriff's office to the jail. And in Hess's pocket was a warrant for Abel Collingwood's arrest. From that we were able to guess what had taken place. I came after you, right away. The roustabout at the livery barn said you and Mister Desmond had rented a buckboard and headed for Middle Valley. When will this terrible killing stop?"

"It will probably get worse before it gets better," said Gunnison grimly. "But there will be only one answer, for the decent elements of the valley are on the march."

River Junction was seething with excitement when they rode in. Miles Letterman was forming a posse before his store.

"We've had a big plenty, Vike," he said. "We're going after Collingwood and all his crowd. And when we clean them up, we're going to dynamite every bridge and culvert under that railroad, tear up rails, and burn ties. The damned thing has brought nothing but hell and trouble to us."

"Take it easy, Miles," Gunnison said. "There's lots of things you don't understand. It isn't the railroad, it's just Collingwood. Oh, we're going after him. Before long the Middle Valley settlers will be here, and Andy Killian and Ed Lutz with their crews. This is a clean-up drive. So keep your shirt on. An hour or two one way or the other won't affect matters much."

At the back of his mind, Gunnison was wondering what had happened to Luke and Coony Vestal. They should have reported by this time and definite news of the whereabouts of Chino Chavez and his renegade band was vital. He was still wondering when Shad Guthrie showed up, looking mysterious.

"Luke and Coony," Shad muttered. "They're back in the sage, waiting to report. They got Chavez located."

"Go get 'em," ordered Gunnison. "Tell 'em they got nothing to worry about any more. Hess is dead and there is no charge against them. Rustle!"

Shad sped away, and within ten minutes was back with the Vestal boys, bursting with questions and information. Gunnison said: "All that's happened can be explained later, boys. The sheriff's dead and Collingwood is a fugitive. Where is Chavez? That's the big thing."

"Up at Hunger Gap," said Luke. "Him and his crowd are holing up with Collingwood's construction gang. Last place we ever thought they'd be. But we tried every other possibility, and then Coony suggested Hunger Gap, just on a hunch. So we took a prowl and sure enough, there they were."

"From what I hear, Collingwood headed west, toward the gap," mused Gunnison. "It ties in. With luck we'll round up the whole crowd there."

Settlers began pouring into town, armed and eager to prove themselves in the eyes of the cattlemen. Ed Lutz and his crew pounded in. Then Andy Killian and his boys. And behind the

Elkhorn outfit came Rex Desmond, dusty and disheveled again, but with his eyes eager and cool.

About that time a startled yell sounded upstreet. A man had lurched into view. He was white with dust, except for his bared head, which was matted and stained with the ominous darkness of blood. He shambled with weakness when he walked. It was Henry Marsten. He collapsed when they got to him. Somebody produced a bottle of whiskey, which brought reasonable coherency to the cattleman.

"He's got Kate . . . he's got my girl!"

Vike Gunnison was on his knees, supporting Marsten. "Get it clear, Henry," he gritted. "You mean Collingwood has . . . ?"

Marsten nodded. "After Collingwood killed Hess . . . and got away . . . I figured the best place for Kate and me was home. She didn't want to go, but I made her come with me, in the buckboard. Out . . . out along South Fork, where the trail runs close to the river, Collingwood poured into the road. He had a gun and he cut loose at me without a word." Marsten's right hand touched his torn, bloody scalp. "He . . . he creased me . . . knocked me out. Next thing I knew, I was laying there in the trail, alone. The buckboard was upset. One of the team was dead, shot through the head. The other bronco was gone . . . and Kate was gone. I . . . I headed for town. That skunk . . . that Collingwood . . . he's run off with my Kate."

Gunnison's face was icy when he stood up. "The last straw," he said tonelessly. "Collingwood will never live to face any court. It's lead or a rope for him. We're going to ride, boys."

X

Hunger Gap was a bleak, rocky defile some five miles long, running between the somewhat precipitous southern flank of Battle Peak and an upflung shoulder of gray, basalt rock. Through this defile plunged and roared the waters of the South Fork of the

Blue River. Here was the toughest construction obstacle of the whole line and here the railroad had massed men, equipment, and materials.

Steel-snouted drills and tons of dynamite had torn a great, gaping raw scar along the flank of that basalt cliff. Stubborn rock fighting equally stubborn men, and slowly, inexorably losing. On the flat just below the gap a small siding had been thrown together, holding a line of jerry cars to house the construction crew. A boxcar, plastered with red signs, stood on another short siding. Those signs read—**Dynamite**. A few small, raw-boarded shanties stood here and there, to house tools and equipment and to offer shelter and a rough desk for the surveying crew to spread their maps and figure their gradients and levels.

Ordinarily, at this time of day, the gap would be all clamoring with the sounds of industry and work. But now, as Vike Gunnison looked down upon it from the flank of Battle Peak, the place lay strangely still. Few men were in evidence and one of these stood beside a jerry car, as though on guard. Even at the distance, Gunnison could identify him as Black Mike Brady, the foreman bully boy he had whipped in the Midnight. And now, even as he watched, there came a sudden rush of men from the jerry cars. Black Mike tried to hold them back. He began swinging heavy fists, knocking some of the men down. But the rush was too much for him. They rolled over him and left him there, and went pelting along the track, back toward River Junction. Here, some quarter of a mile along, they bumped into a crowd of armed, grim-faced men, under the charge of Rex Desmond and Andy Killian.

"Road's closed, gents," twanged Andy Killian. "Where you boys think you're going?"

A clean-shaven, brown-faced youngster in laced boots and corduroys spoke up. "We're getting out of a dirty mess. We hired on with the railroad to run grades, blast rock, lay rail beds, and build track. But we want nothing more to do with a bunch of half-breed gun-toters, or with that skunk of a Collingwood. Hell! We thought he was a right guy. But do you know what? He's brought a girl into that camp, a girl with her hands tied. And he's holding her there, him and that Chavez and that crowd. I don't know any of the whys and wherefores, but I know I want nothing more to do with this set-up. Me and these boys are leaving the country."

"No need of that," spoke up Rex Desmond. "I'm from General Manager Lassiter's office. Collingwood is out, a fugitive from the law. We're after him, these other men and I. As soon as that little chore is done, I'll want you men back on the regular job. And I promise you, there'll be no more trouble. So stick around."

Up on the flank of Battle Peak, Vike Gunnison watched the pell-mell exodus of the construction gang with calculating eye. "That means that Collingwood and Chavez are down there, all right," he said to Luke Vestal, who was at his elbow. "Those jerries know a scrap is coming up and they want none of it."

"Yes," Luke agreed. "If it wasn't that they had Kate Marsten down there, it would be simple enough to clean them up. We'd just pump rifle slugs into that car of dynamite until it went off. As it is, Vike, looks kinda like we're stalled."

An Elkhorn cowboy came clattering around the slope. "The boss sent me to report, Vike," he said. "That flock of jerries you saw pulling out are dropping Collingwood cold. They were going to leave the country complete, but that feller Desmond told 'em he was going to take Collingwood's place, soon as the house cleaning was over. He's persuaded them to stick around and go back to work when things are straightened out. They're all burned up over Collingwood bringing Kate Marsten in. And the boss wants to know if you got any scheme figured out yet."

L. P. Holmes

Gunnison shook his head. "Not yet. It would be simple if it wasn't for Kate being down there. But we don't dare do a thing that will endanger her. Collingwood is smart, like any other wolf. That's why he grabbed Kate. With her for a hostage, he's got us with our hands tied. This is going to be tough."

A man appeared down there by the jerry cars. He wore chaps and a huge sombrero, one of Chino Chavez's men. The lock of Luke Vestal's rifle clicked. "A long shot," muttered Luke. "But I think I can make it. How about it, Vike?"

"No." Gunnison shook his head. "Let's see what he's up to."

The fellow seemed busy over something in his hands. Then he held a stick high. On the end of it fluttered a bit of white. And he started swaggering down across the flat toward the river's edge.

"Looks like he's wanting to parley," said Coony Vestal. "I'd like to parley him with a slug in the ribs."

"Don't try it," said Gunnison sharply. "I'm going down there."

"You keep out of sight," warned Luke Vestal. "Don't you let 'em lure you into the open, Vike. Nothing those rats would rather do than pot you from ambush."

"I'll take care of that," promised Gunnison.

He went down the flank of the peak on foot, sliding from one brush clump to another, keeping handy rock outcrops in line between himself and the clutter of the construction camp. Presently the moist breath of the tumbling waters of South Fork came up to him, and he ended up behind the shelter of a clump of sour willow.

"All right!" he called, pitching his voice so it could be heard above the rumble of the stream. "What do you want to talk about?"

The answer came, thinly mocking. "About things of sense, *señor*. We are leaving shortly. We go out by way of the old Indian

100

trail through the gap. And if you or anyone else should try and stop us, *señor,* it would be verry bad for the *señorita* we have with us. It would be a pity, *señor,* for harm to befall anyone so beautiful. You hear me, *señor?*"

"I hear you!" Gunnison called down. "Go on. You know that the world isn't big enough to hide a single one of you if any harm is done Miss Marsten. That's a promise for you and all the other coyotes."

Gunnison heard the renegade laugh. "This is no time to call names, *señor.* You should listen well, for we do not talk again. As I say, we shall ride out over the old Indian trail. The *señorita* will ride in the very middle of us. And should but one shot be fired at us, or any attempt made to stop us, the *señorita* will die very swiftly. All guns among us will instantly be turned upon her. We are desperate men, *señor,* and we will do as I say. Make no mistake about that."

Gunnison was thinking fast. "And suppose we agree. What guarantee will we have that Miss Marsten will be turned loose, unharmed?"

Again came that mocking laugh. "As to that, *señor,* my good leader, Chino Chavez, and *Señor* Collingwood will decide. Now I must be getting back. For shortly we leave. I warn you once more. Make no mistake, *señor.* We will not hesitate to act if we must. The life of the *señorita* is in your hands. That is all, *señor.*"

Gunnison went back up the slope as he had come down, never exposing himself. A cold, still rage was burning in him. Collingwood and Chavez held the aces, and Gunnison knew that they would not hesitate a second in doing just what the renegade had told him they would do. Men who would raid and burn and murder helpless settlers in the black of night would not hesitate over one more murder. Collingwood would know that to be taken would mean a hang noose about his throat. For, whatever kind of worthless sort Buell Hess might have been, he had still been sheriff when Collingwood shot him down. That, too, was murder. And Collingwood, if taken, would hang for it.

When Gunnison got back to Luke and Coony Vestal and told them, they cursed tonelessly. "The dirty rats," raged Coony, "what I wouldn't give to get in the middle of them, with both guns blazing!"

Gunnison's head jerked up. "That's it!" he exclaimed. "That's our one chance. I wonder. . . ." He whirled on the Elkhorn cowpuncher who had brought Andy Killian's message. "Go back and tell Andy to send three men up here . . . to replace Luke and Coony and me. Hurry up! We've got no time to waste."

The cowpuncher spurred away.

"What you got in mind, Vike?" asked Luke Vestal.

"You boys know the country north and west of Battle Peak pretty well, don't you?"

"Well as anybody in these parts, I reckon. Why?"

"Try and imagine yourself in Collingwood's boots. And in Chino Chavez's place. Say the set-up was the same for you as it is for them. Now then, once you'd got plumb past Hunger Gap, which way would you turn, figuring to get clear? What part of the country would you head for? Knowing, of course, that a big bunch of damned mad and tough men were on your trail."

"Just one place," said Luke. "I'd keep heading west until I hit the Cinnabar Roughs along Cinnabar. Then I'd turn due north, skirt the Choctaw Rim, and scatter to hell-and-gone across the old reservation country up there. That's plenty wild and broken country up there and smart, trail-wise *hombres* could keep an army running in circles all through there."

"You call my thoughts to a word, Luke." Coony nodded. "Was a man to turn south from Hunger Gap or keep on west past the Cinnabar Roughs, he'd bump into civilized country all along the way."

"Then," said Gunnison, "our job is to head 'em off. It will mean tough riding. For we'll have to cover more country than they will. But it's our best bet, if we make it."

As soon as the three cowpunchers showed up, Gunnison told them: "Just sit tight, boys. They'll be pulling out pretty quick, over the old Indian trail through the gap. Let 'em go. They've got us where the hair is short for now. But I'm working on a scheme I think will pay off. All right, Luke, Coony, we've got no time to waste."

Gunnison knew that at the distance, the renegades could not identify those who came and those who went from the flank of the peak. Three men had ridden out. Now three were riding back. Maybe the same three, for all the renegades could tell. That was the effect he wanted. As he left, Gunnison saw tiny figures of men lead tiny figures of horses from a willow copse along the river. The renegades were ready to start.

XI

"I'm taking Luke and Coony Vestal," said Gunnison. "And I want Billy Daniels and Slim Jeffers of the Elkhorn, Charley Gear and Buck Ryan of the Wagon Wheel. If we can't do the job, then a hundred men wouldn't help." Gunnison was facing the assembled group of riders and settlers. Those who understood, realized that Gunnison had picked men noted for their cool courage and their ability with a rifle or a six-gun. "We're heading for my Oxbow ranch first, where we switch to fresh bronc's. Then we line out along the North Fork. We'll beat that crowd to the Choctaw Rim. From then on, it's up to us."

Someone tugged at Gunnison's elbow. He turned to see Al Derian. "I'm going with you, Vike," said Al quietly.

"I thought you didn't take sides in things that didn't concern you," said Gunnison curtly.

"This concerns me," said Al. "I'm not as blind as I was."

Gunnison's manner mellowed. "Good enough, Al. Glad to have you along."

Now it was Rex Desmond who faced him. "I'll tag along, also, if you don't mind, Gunnison."

Gunnison shook his head. "You'd only hold us back. This will be the toughest kind of a ride."

Desmond's eyes narrowed slightly. "I'm going along. You see, I happen to have a very great admiration for Miss Marsten. Yes, Gunnison . . . I'm going along."

Gunnison hesitated, then shrugged. "If you fall behind, we won't wait for you. We can't afford to. On that basis . . . come along."

"I won't fall behind," said Desmond grimly.

Desmond borrowed a horse from Andy Killian and they were ready to go.

"I'd shoot some men around to the south of Hunger Gap, Andy," said Gunnison. "Just in case I'm guessing wrong and the renegades try and fox us by turning south. I don't think they will, however."

"OK, Vike," said Andy. "Good luck. If you do run into them, give 'em hell for all of us."

After that it was ride, roaring across the flats to the east of Battle Peak, fording North Fork, and racing up Oxbow Creek to Vike Gunnison's headquarters. Here saddles were switched to fresh horses. While this was going on, Gunnison took Rex Desmond into the ranch house. "You've got to have riding clothes for what's ahead of us," he said. "You can't buck a tough trail in those kind of clothes. They'd be ripped off your back inside of five miles. You and me are about of a size. Jump into some of my spare duds."

When they were in the saddle again, Rex Desmond appeared just another cowpuncher. Gunnison led the way up North Fork Cañon. He rode hard, remorselessly. Time was an element, a vital one, distance something to be conquered. There was no mercy on horse or rider. They slashed through cat-claw thickets; they swam their horses across the foaming waters several times as they switched back and forth from one side of the cañon to the other. They scrambled over boulders, edged along savage, precipitous cliffs. There was no waiting, no stopping. And when, at last, they topped the rim of the rock-bound basin where a huge spring formed the headwaters of North Fork, and Vike Gunnison looked around at his followers, the first one he saw was Rex Desmond. Desmond was looking at him, a hint of a grim smile on his lips.

"You win, Desmond," said Gunnison.

From there on the going was a little better until they picked up the eastern end of the Choctaw Rim. Here were brush and rock slides, with now and then a great boulder that had fallen away to crash down on the low slope. Through this treacherous tangle they drove on, horses laboring and foaming, riders whipped and clawed and beaten by the tenacious brush. But they kept on, while the hours and the miles flew away.

In time the Choctaw Rim began to curve more and more to the north, while due west the afternoon haze was laying blue shadows across the wild tangle of country that was the Cinnabar Roughs. Nowhere could be seen a single moving object except the high, far speck against the sky that was an eagle, hunting along the curving majesty of the Choctaw Rim.

Gunnison called another brief halt. "We've either guessed right or we haven't," he said tensely. "We'll know before long. Luke, you and Coony head out and see if you can locate them. We'll be waiting for you up yonder where that big slide runs out into that patch of tamaracks. Remember, the whole thing will depend on surprise. Don't let 'em guess you're around, whatever you do."

"Trust us," said Luke. "Come on, Coony." The two brothers

spurred away.

"Those boys know what they're doing," drawled Slim Jeffers. "They're regular panthers in the brush."

"Something for you to remember, Desmond," said Gunnison. "The railroad cut across a point of the Vestal boys' range. Collingwood promised to pay them for it. He never did."

Rex Desmond nodded. "That will be taken care of."

They went on, Gunnison setting a more leisurely pace. They moved into little groves of tamaracks and the country began narrowing in. Now they were heading due north and Gunnison came to a stop at the foot of the big slide. "The rest of you wait here," he said. "I'm doing some prowling afoot."

Here was the rough mouth of a pass, which split the Choctaw Rim and the Cinnabar Roughs. It was through this natural gap that he figured the renegades would head, and it was here that he had planned the showdown. What he wanted to know was if, by some chance, the renegades had already passed. Moving cautiously, so as to leave no trace, he cut clear across to the edge of the Cinnabar Roughs and back. He saw neither sign nor track of horses anywhere. No riders had gone through.

Back with the others, Gunnison settled himself to wait. The hours went on. The sun was low and getting lower out past the Cinnabar Roughs, which wasn't too good. Darkness would upset his plans fatally. When, he fretted, would Luke and Coony get back?

When the Vestal brothers did return, they came so silently they were there before anyone could guess at their approach. Their black eyes were burning with excitement and triumph.

"We guessed right, Vike," exulted Luke. "They're headed this way, not two miles below. They ought to hit here just about at sunset. By the way they're riding, they figure they've put it over on us. They're not hurrying a bit now."

"Honest men do get a break now and then," said Gunnison.

"All right, Slim, Buck. Take all the horses well back around the rim. We tackle this chore on foot and we can't risk a giveaway by having one of the bronc's whicker. We'll wait for you."

Slim Jeffers and Buck Ryan rode away, leading the rest of the horses. For the benefit of the others, Gunnison pointed. "There is a string of little narrow meadows running north out there. A natural way through for a bunch of riders. We split up, half and half, on each side of the trail. When they come between us, we hit 'em from both sides. We've got to clear those closest around Kate Marsten and not make a mistake."

Slim and Buck were soon back, and then Gunnison placed his forces. There was a spot in one of those meadows where a tongue of tamarack thicket came in on each side, with only a space of some fifty feet wide separating them. Gunnison sent Slim Jeffers, Al Derian, Buck Ryan, Charley Gear, and Rex Desmond to the far thicket. With himself he kept the Vestal boys and Billy Daniels.

"When we break from this side, you come in from the other, boys," he said. "Now lay low and don't make a move or a sound." To Luke and Coony and Billy Daniels, Gunnison said: "We've got to get Kate Marsten out of her saddle ahead of any possible chance of lead. There's too much chance of her getting hit."

"We'll do it," said Luke Vestal. "You watch."

XII

The tamaracks stood in spaced, solemn beauty, quite still under the misty hush of sunset. The hovering eagle, seeing nothing to disturb it, drifted on leisurely wings toward some distant roosting place. Smoky blue shadows stole in, thickening in gentle layers. Then sounded the muffled thud of hoofs and down at the lower end of the long, narrow meadow riders moved into view. In the lead were Chino Chavez and Abel Collingwood.

Others straggled after them in an uneven column. In the very center of that column rode Kate Marsten. She was not tied to the saddle in any way, but there was a hunched, hopeless look about her somehow, like one despairing. Right behind her rode a hulking brute of a renegade, with beady eyes in a broad, animal-like, pockmarked face. Those beady eyes were fixed on Kate Marsten's shoulders, on the blonde glory of her bent head. Vike Gunnison, peering through the lacework of the tamaracks, knew where his first lead would go.

Chino Chavez and Abel Collingwood were talking as they rode. Chavez seemed gay, cheerful, but Collingwood's face was dark and drawn and sullen, full of desperation and the persistent rage of one who had made great plans and had had them fall apart about his ears. They came on steadily. Apparently Luke Vestal was right about their attitude. These men figured that they had completely outsmarted, outdistanced any pursuit.

Now Chavez and Collingwood were passing. Now Kate Marsten was even with the thrusting points of the tamaracks. And with a deep breath swelling his chest with cold purpose, Vike Gunnison burst from cover. Even as he hit the open, Gunnison was shooting. He was shooting at the hulking brute directly behind Kate Marsten. He saw his man lurch and topple.

Gunnison's first shot seemed to open the door of an inferno. From both sides of the trail guns were roaring and crashing. Gunnison, driving straight for Kate Marsten, found Luke and Coony Vestal and Billy Daniels bounding along beside him.

Kate's head had snapped up, her eyes wide, almost unbelieving. Then Gunnison had her, dragging her from the saddle. "Run!" he rasped. "Into the tamaracks!"

As Kate sped away, Gunnison saw a renegade stand high in his stirrups, gun poised to chop down at the fleeing girl. Gunnison threw desperate lead. There were others who saw the same threat and shot to head it off. Luke and Coony and Billy

Daniels, and someone else from the other side. The renegade, laced with lead from both sides, melted out of his saddle. Then Luke was looking for Collingwood and Chavez. Apparently the suddenness of the attack had left the minds of these two a little numbed. They might have ridden for it and made it to the far end of the meadow, but they had no way of knowing whether more guns might not be waiting for them up there. So, like desperate, cornered wolves, they were trying to shoot their way out.

Right beside Gunnison, Billy Daniels cursed and went down, a leg buckling under him. Coony Vestal had a gun shot out of his hand, mangling a finger, filling his wrist and forearm with spattered splinters of lead. But Coony kept at work with the other hand and got a slug in Chino Chavez. The renegade leader sagged, grabbed at his saddle horn with both hands, and Luke Vestal blasted him squarely with both guns.

Vike Gunnison was looking past Chavez. He was looking at Collingwood and it seemed to him that Collingwood's glance met his, just a split second before Gunnison shot him. The lead seemed to craze Collingwood. He spurred straight at Gunnison, cursing thickly. Gunnison shot him again at a distance of fifteen feet, and barely side-stepped the terrified and riderless horse as it plunged past.

Then, somehow, it was all over. Distant points of crashing told of two or three of the renegade band that had somehow escaped the hail of lead and were fleeing in blind panic. But the rest were down, there in the still twilight, in this virgin little meadow that had never before known the crash of guns and the crimson stain of deadly conflict.

Gunnison's first thought was for Kate Marsten, and he hurried in the direction she had gone at his order. Then he stopped abruptly. She was there all right, but not alone. Rex Desmond stood beside her, supporting her with an encircling arm. Kate was saying: "Somehow, Rex . . . I knew that you would come after me. I know that I prayed that you would."

Gunnison went softly away.

XIII

The morning sun was shining across the hotel porch in River Junction. Vike Gunnison came stalking along the street. His face was slightly drawn, his eyes a little sunken from lack of sleep. As he mounted the hotel steps, Kate Marsten and Rex Desmond came out on the porch.

"At last!" cried Kate. "Now I have a chance to thank you, Vike."

Gunnison grinned. "No thanks necessary. It was a pleasure."

"How are Coony Vestal and Billy Daniels?" Kate asked.

"Fine as frog's hair," Gunnison told her. "The doctor was able to save Coony's finger and Billy's leg will be good as new in a month or so. Those boys aren't kicking. They figure we got off mighty cheap at the price."

Kate was watching Gunnison's expression curiously. She said, without looking back: "Rex, please leave me and this old leather-pounder alone for a while."

Desmond smiled and went into the hotel. Kate stepped closer to Gunnison. "Do you wish me luck, old fellow? It was . . . one of those things. The first time Rex Desmond ever looked at me, I knew. And so did he. We're going to be married in a scandalously short time."

"That's great, Kate," said Gunnison quietly. "He's tops, Desmond is . . . a four-square man. I was hoping it would be that way."

"For shame! And all the time I thought you were in love with me."

"No you didn't," said Gunnison. "You knew better. And you knew you weren't in love with me. But you just like to boss men around . . . and I wouldn't boss."

Kate laughed, then sighed. "No more. I'm a very humble woman, now. I don't want to boss anyone. I just want to be bossed and protected from now on. I'm very happy, Vike."

"I'm very glad, Kate. Be a good wife, and the happiness of the world will fall into your lap."

Her lovely eyes misted. "You . . . you're mighty sweet, Vike Gunnison. And as one old friend to another. . . ." She rose on her tiptoes and kissed him. Then she said, very softly: "Cherry, bless her heart, is in town."

Kate turned and hurried into the hotel. Gunnison built a cigarette. Strange, how relieved he felt. He had rather dreaded his next meeting with Kate. He was afraid she might have felt under some obligation to him for his part in her rescue. Well, she did, no doubt, but she was being sensible about it, and he was mighty glad for her and Rex Desmond.

Gunnison went up the street and down. He met men who shook his hand, men who seemed to have a new optimism, a new enthusiasm. But he couldn't locate the person he was looking for. And, finally, a strange depression settled upon him, so he sought his mount and headed for home. Come to think about it, Cherry had acted rather queer the last couple of times he had met up with her. Ever since that shoot-out he had had with Chino Chavez's three renegade followers, there in the main street of River Junction, she had changed, seemed to have turned hard and distant, with a barb on her tongue. Moodiness came over him as he rode, a queer hurt pulling at him inside. He had built a lot of dreams about a certain black, curly head and it was going to hurt him all the rest of his life if he had to let go of those dreams. Women, he mused, were supposed to be able to read a man through and through. Well, that was all a lot of guff, for apparently they couldn't.

He reached North Fork and let his pony idle across the ford, and when it took to tossing its head, he loosened the reins and let the animal stop and drink of the crystal waters splashing under foot. And then, as he rode out the other side, there was Cherry Derian, sitting her saddle easily, waiting for him. There was a small, remote, guarded look about Cherry, somehow. Like she had a part to play and was going to play it if it killed her.

" 'Morning," she said with a rather obvious attempt at her old brightness.

" 'Morning. Thought you were in town," said Gunnison grumpily.

"I was. But decided I'd go home and make up with brother Al. I hear the old scoundrel was rather fine in that showdown with Chavez and Collingwood."

"He was. It just took Al a little time to see the light."

Silence fell, a trifle strained and uncomfortable. Then Cherry shook her reins. "Let me know when congratulations are in order, won't you, Vike."

"Huh?" Gunnison stared at her. "What congratulations?"

"Why . . . ah . . . you and Kate."

"Me and Kate? You mean, Rex Desmond and Kate, don't you? They're going to be married pretty *pronto,* you know."

Cherry swayed a little in the saddle and her face went white. "Rex Desmond . . . and Kate?"

"Sure. Seems like it was love at first sight. So Kate was telling me a little while ago."

Cherry's face was a mixture of emotion. She said in a tight little voice: "I'm really sorry, for you, I mean, Vike. I . . . I know how you felt about . . . Kate."

"Sorry for me! Say, look here, young 'un, what's biting you, anyhow?" Gunnison squared around in his saddle to look at her more directly. "I thought you were a smart little monkey. Me, I'm tickled to death for Kate and Desmond. He's a mighty fine man and Kate, well, now that she's come down to earth, she's pretty fine herself. But if you mean, you figured I felt that way about Kate Marsten . . . why you little blockhead, I thought you knew better."

Cherry was clinging to her saddle horn with both small, gloved hands. One moment she looked as though she were going to faint and fall right out of that saddle, the next she colored hotly, seemingly revivified by a wild rush of spirit. Then she began to laugh. She laughed until she rocked back and forth in the saddle.

"What's so darned funny about everything?" growled Gunnison warily.

She looked at him with brimming eyes. "I . . . I'm laughing at a f-fool named Cherry Derian," she gasped. "And now, I think I'll be getting home."

"No you won't," asserted Gunnison grimly. "I got something to tell you, something I been trying to get up courage to tell you for a long, long time. But you won't ever be serious. I know I'm just a roughneck saddle-pounder. I know I killed two men right in front of your eyes, which is enough to turn any good woman against such a man. But I didn't go hunting that fight, Cherry. You know I didn't. I had to kill those two wild ones or they'd have killed me. And . . . aw, well, I was sort of hoping you'd maybe forget in time about that incident and give me the benefit of the doubt."

Cherry looked around at the sunlit sky and addressed the whole world. "And the man had the nerve to tell me I was a blockhead," she murmured. Now she switched her glance to meet Gunnison's eyes and he saw to his amazement that the old Cherry was back, with that faint, elfin-like smile pulling at her lips and her dark eyes filled with the old mischief. But there was a tremulous softness there, also, which gave Gunnison nerve to go on.

"I'm wondering," he mumbled, "I'm hoping. . . ."

"You said that before, clumsy," Cherry mocked gently. "Can't you say what you mean . . . ?"

Gunnison turned desperate. He spun his bronco close to her, reached over, lifted her bodily from the saddle, and swung her over in front of him. "Listen, young 'un, from as far back as I can remember, I've been in love with you. Every time I look at the sunrise I see you. Every time I look at the sunset, I see you. I see your face in the stars, I hear your voice in the wind, and if you don't tell me you'll marry me, I'll ride the loneliest trail for the rest of my life any man ever faced. . . ."

That strange, blind, breathlessness was in Cherry's eyes again. "Vike," she whispered, "don't say that unless you mean . . . every word of it."

"Mean it? Of course I mean it. Can't you understand that I love you, young 'un?"

Her arms went about his neck. "Vike, darling! Oh, my dear . . . my dear . . . hold me tight. Don't ever let me go, not ever."

Of course, he did let go of her, after a while. He even swung her over and dropped her into her saddle again. She was very lovely, lovelier than anyone he had ever seen or ever would see.

"You're a brute," she charged. "I'm all mussed up."

"You're a regular little hellion," he retorted, grinning. "Happy?"

"Of course, silly. Happy enough to bust. And Vike, you've really been in love with me . . . all the time?"

"All the time, young 'un. Even when I've felt like pulling your ears or giving you a paddling to teach you manners. Which has been more than once and will probably happen again." But he tempered this with a look that made Cherry's singing heart turn completely over.

Down in the valley an engine whistle sent mellow echoes rolling. Cherry twisted in her saddle and looked down that way. "I don't hate the railroad any more, Vike," she said softly. "I don't hate anything or anyone. I only hope that everyone can be just half as happy as I am. But, of course, they can't. No one could. Vike . . . I've always loved you, too." Her voice was like a caress.

He reached over and took her hand. "Come along, sweetheart. We'll go tell brother Al all about it."

★ ★ ★ ★ ★

DOOM PATROL

★ ★ ★ ★ ★

I

Judge Henning finished speaking. Buck Comstock, standing up to receive his sentence, surveyed the judge with cool, sardonic, contemptuous eyes. Judge Henning would not meet Buck's eyes. At no time during the trial had he met Buck's glance. And as he had rendered the sentence, he had looked past Buck, over Buck's head.

For a long second after the droning voice of the judge died away, the courtroom was dead still, so still that when old Bill Morgan cleared his throat wrathfully, the sound was like a thunderclap.

Sheriff Brood Shotwell stepped up and took Buck by the right arm. Spike St. Ives, Shotwell's number one deputy, moved up on the other side.

"That's all," growled Brood Shotwell. "Come on, Comstock."

Buck shrugged, turned, and walked between them toward the side door of the courtroom, which led across some forty feet of yard before reaching the jail.

Buck twisted his head and looked out over the crowd in the courtroom. He saw Bill Morgan, Johnny Frazier, and Bud Tharp pushing their way along as though to intercept Buck and his two guardians before they could reach that side door. The intention of these three was plain in their eyes and attitudes.

"No go, Bill!" called Buck sharply. "It wouldn't work, anyhow. Don't start anything."

"I'll do my best, Buck," answered Bill Morgan. "But I want

to state here and now that of all the cheap, crooked, low-down farces ever pulled under the name of law, this is the worst. I thought that damned, squint-eyed rooster up there was a judge."

Everybody in the room heard Bill. He spoke as he usually did, in rumbling tones that would carry a hundred yards in the teeth of a high wind. Judge Henning's pursed mouth tightened. He whanged his gavel on his desk.

"There will be no remarks against the dignity of this court!" he shrilled. "I'll have you cited for contempt!"

"That's the right word!" bellowed Bill Morgan. "Contempt. I got plenty of that for you and all the rest of the mealy-mouthed crowd connected with this travesty. Just try and cite me for anything, you weasel-eyed buzzard. Try and have me arrested. I'm in a shooting frame of mind right now, and the first *hombre* that touches me gets blowed in half at the belt buckle. That's cold turkey. Eat it or choke over it, whichever you please."

"Bill!" yelled Buck. "Will you shut up?"

Bill Morgan subsided with a growl. A lot of people in the courtroom were talking now. Some were angry at Bill; others were nodding their heads in approval. A tipsy cowpuncher, standing just inside the main door of the courtroom, yipped shrilly: "That's tellin' 'em, ol' lobo! That's tellin' 'em, you ol' tarantula. An' if you need help at smoke-rollin', jest you call on littl' Smoky Rawlins. He'll be with you . . . till hell freezes. Yes, sir . . . that's me . . . Smoky Rawlins. An' I don't like judges or sheriffs any better than you do."

This brought a laugh. The tension lessened. Buck, realizing that neither Bill nor Johnny Frazier or Bud Tharp would do anything foolish, let his eyes fix on Leek Jaeger and Frank Cutts, who stood near that side door. Leek Jaeger, squat and burly, was rocking back and forth on his heels and toes, a habit of his when pleased. His block-jowled face, perennially unshaven, was drawn to a mocking grin, while his eyes, little and deep-set and of the dull, brutal color of old lead, were squinted with triumph. Frank Cutts, once a gambler, still affected the immaculate dress of his former calling. His thin, pale face was a graven mask, but in his black eyes also glinted triumph.

Buck Comstock's eyes went over the two men swiftly and came to a startled halt on the girl who stood between them. It was the first time in his life Buck had ever seen her. Yet, for some reason, sight of her gave him a distinct shock. She was a pretty girl, not over twenty, a girl with wide, grave, dusky eyes, crisp black hair, and a softly crimson mouth. The color of her skin was that of remarkably pure, richly tinted old ivory. She was slim and dainty in a close-fitting traveling suit of dark brown material. Just before Buck and his two guards came opposite the little group, Leek Jaeger leaned over and murmured something in the girl's ear. The girl's eyes sought Buck's face and she seemed to shrink slightly.

Buck looked at her coolly, met her glance squarely. Then Brood Shotwell kicked the side door open, and Buck was outside, under the shade of a clump of cottonwoods.

Buck would have liked to linger under those cottonwoods. Where he was going, there wouldn't be any trees. On a nodding branch tip, gay in black and gold, an oriole piped its rich notes.

"Hurry up," rasped Brood Shotwell. "I want to get you safe behind bars again, Comstock. Some of those salty pals of yours might get wild notions if we stand out here in the open too long."

Two more steps and the jail door clanged behind Buck.

Almost immediately the door opened again. Brood Shotwell and Curt Wallace, a slender young lawyer in store clothes, came in. Curt Wallace stood looking miserably at Buck. His sensitive face was now wreathed in gloom. "Buck," he said, "this is hell. I don't know what to say. It's all my fault. I made a mess of things. As a lawyer, I'd make a good sheepherder."

"Not your fault, Curt," said Buck quietly. "You did everything any man could do. But things were stacked against me. Forget it."

Curt shook his head. "I'll never be able to forget it . . . not as long as I live. Twenty-five years in Pinole. My God, Buck, do you realize what that means?"

Buck's smile was bitter. "Afraid I do, Curt. That sentence was equivalent to a rope around my neck, only I'll be a damned sight longer dying. And did you see how old Henning enjoyed it? He sure rolled those words over his tongue."

"I'm not supposed to listen to you jaspers run down Judge Henning, you know," objected Brood Shotwell.

Buck laughed softly, but there was a harsh sound in that laugh, like the breaking of ice. "If you stick around me, you'll have to, Brood," he said. "He's a shyster, with a rotten mark on his soul. And he's not alone."

Brood Shotwell's heavy brows drew down. "Meaning what, by that crack?"

"Forget it," said Buck wearily. He crossed to the narrow bunk against the far wall and sat down, fumbling absently for the makings in his shirt pocket.

"I'm going to keep on fighting, of course," said Curt Wallace. "I'll go clear to the governor."

Buck shrugged. "Wouldn't do any good, Curt. Besides, my money is gone. I'm broke."

"Damn the money!" cried Wallace. "This is for principle."

Sheriff Brood Shotwell looked at his watch. "I ain't got time to stand here while you jaspers talk in circles. If you got anything real important to say . . . say it, and then we'll get out of here. I got to make arrangements to start Comstock traveling toward Pinole first thing tomorrow morning."

Young Curt Wallace steadied to a grave dignity. "Somewhere in this mess are some filthy fingers and some lying tongues, also some crooked motives. I'm sticking with the proposition until I uncover some of those things. When I do, this country is going to see a shakedown they'll date time from." He shook hands with Buck. "Keep your chin up, Buck. Twenty-five years is a long time for a bunch of snakes to keep entirely out of sight. And I'll be waiting with a club for the first head that shows."

They went out. The door closed, and Buck was once more alone. Suddenly he realized just how much alone. Beyond these four walls he had friends, but there was nothing they could do. This thing was about settled. Twenty-five years. A little of Buck's iron self-control slipped away from him. He shivered. Twenty-five years in Pinole Penitentiary. If he lived that long, he would be over fifty when he got out. He'd be an old man, with the best of life gone by, all his hard work, his ambitions, his purpose in life shot to hell, thrown away, wasted. Buck Comstock knew how a trapped animal felt. And now that it was all over, somehow the whole scene lay fairly clear before him. Looking back, he could see how cunningly the net had been woven and drawn about him, and he knew that as long as he lived he would never forget the look of satisfaction on the faces of Leek Jaeger and Frank Cutts as he passed them on his way out of the courtroom.

The afternoon waned and died. Dusk came in and the shadows in the jail thickened to blackness. Through the single narrow, barred window, Buck could see the stars winking out. Buck had always liked to watch the stars. Many a night he had lain in his soogan, looking up at them, watching their slow wheel. There wouldn't be any stars in Pinole. Even their ageless brilliance could not penetrate stone prison walls.

Deputy Spike St. Ives came in with Buck's supper. He carried the tray in one hand, a ready gun in the other. St. Ives had little imagination, but he was a cautious, suspicious sort. From the crook of his left elbow hung a lantern.

Buck, forestalling the cadaverous deputy's warning command, moved over to a far corner, while St. Ives deposited lantern and tray of food on the bunk. Then St. Ives retreated to the door while Buck crossed to the bunk and ate.

"Looks like this is the last night you'll have to bother with me, Spike," Buck drawled mockingly.

St. Ives grunted. "Damned glad of it. I never did like to wet-nurse a killer."

Buck's eyes narrowed, but he said nothing more. You got nowhere arguing with a fellow like Spike St. Ives. Only, thought Buck sardonically, it was strange to be called a killer by a man who packed at least six notches on his gun.

Just as Buck finished eating, two more men came in. They were Brood Shotwell and Leek Jaeger.

"All right, Spike," said Shotwell. "You can mosey along. Run along out to Long Barn and see if you can locate that Mex *vaquero* . . . the one they call Concho. Slim Bradley swears that Concho knows where that Oregon bronco of his went. Bring the Mex in, if you can find him. I want to question him."

St. Ives nodded and went out. Buck Comstock, sitting on the edge of the bunk, was strung, tight and cold. He had never imagined that he could hate any man as he hated Leek Jaeger. Even in that tumultuous moment when he had faced Ben Sloan through smoke, he had not known hate. He had gone for his gun and turned lead loose on Sloan merely because of the instinctive prompting of the oldest unwritten law in the world— self-preservation. But he had hardly known hate, even at that time. With Leek Jaeger, it was different. From the moment he had first laid eyes on Jaeger, some two years before, he had hated the man. It was something instinctive, something that had leaped into life, full-blown and savage, with the first meeting of their eyes. That hate had grown with the years.

Buck spoke to Brood Shotwell. "If you've brought this coyote in here so he can gloat, Brood, you're less of a man than I thought."

"He's got something to tell you," explained Shotwell, "some kind of a proposition to make."

"I want no dealing with him," rasped Buck. "I wouldn't trust him an inch in broad daylight."

"Wait a minute, Comstock," said Jaeger. "I know you hate my guts. That's your privilege. But remember, twenty-five years is a long time. You'd be a bigger fool than I think if you weren't willing to make a trade that'll cut that time to maybe five years. Think that over."

Buck sat very still, his thoughts racing. What was Jaeger up to? What sort of a scheme was going on in that bullet head? What sort of a trade could Jaeger possibly manipulate that would reduce the sentence from twenty-five to five years? Buck's first impulse was to tell Jaeger to go to hell. He choked it back, however, for another idea came to him, an idea that sent the quick, white flame of hope burning through him. He fenced cautiously. "You're just making talk, Jaeger. You may figure you're the he-wolf in this neck of the woods, but you don't rate big enough to cut any part of that sentence."

"I wouldn't be here tonight if I wasn't sure of my ground," said Jaeger curtly. "If you want to listen to my proposition, say so. Otherwise, I'll be on my way."

Buck got up, began pacing back and forth across the inner end of the jail room. His eyes, narrowed and hidden in the shadows that lay above the ragged circle of the lantern's light, were burning with a strange and reckless glint. He was thinking of just two things right now. One was that Brood Shotwell had not locked the jail door. The other was that, if Leek Jaeger proved he could reverse that twenty-five year sentence, it would be as much as an admission that the whole trial had been framed and that Jaeger was more than a little afraid of events that might pop up in the future. Buck Comstock came to a savage, relentless decision. "All right," he snapped. "Let's hear your proposition, Jaeger."

"I won't mince words," said Jaeger. "I can use that Cotton Valley range of yours, Comstock. With you heading for Pinole tomorrow, I could go ahead and grab it, regardless. That would raise a stink, of course, but I reckon I could live it down. I don't like trouble any more than the next man, so I'm willing to make a bargain with you. Sign that Cotton Valley range over to me, and I'll see that twenty years is taken off that sentence. There it is, straight up and down. Take it or leave it."

"And after I signed over that Cotton Valley range what's to prevent you from letting me be dragged off to Pinole and forgetting all about me?"

Jaeger shrugged. "You'll just have to take my word for that."

Brood Shotwell spoke: "Maybe you don't realize it, Leek, but the talk you've made just now throws a nasty smell over my office, over Judge Henning, over the whole organization of law and order on the Twin Buttes range. Me, I don't like it."

"You'll have to lump it then, Shotwell," said Jaeger bluntly. "Let me see. Three months from now you come up for reëlection, don't you? Kind of like your job, don't you? Well, go out and see who controls the votes in the Twin Buttes country. You'll find that I do. Now then, Comstock . . . what's your answer?"

"This," said Buck.

Ten feet he covered in one terrific, diving plunge—a long, lean, hurtling projectile. Whipping out ahead of him was a leaden fist backed by muscles of rawhide power. His fist caught Leek Jaeger squarely in the face, pulping his nose, smashing his lips. Jaeger, in falling, crashed into Brood Shotwell, and the two men went down in a tangle. Buck, already on his way to the door, kicked out at the lantern, which smashed on the bunk.

There was a gust of smoke, then a spreading ball of spattering flame, some of which dropped on Brood Shotwell's pant legs. Shotwell, fumbling wildly for his gun, felt the bite of that flame and started slapping madly at it. This instant of delay was all that Buck Comstock needed. In another second he was out of the jail and running.

He whipped about the corner of the old adobe courthouse, reached the street. Several saddle mounts were tied to a handy hitch rail. Buck did not hesitate. He swung into the nearest saddle and lifted the bronco to a wild run.

By the time Brood Shotwell could put out his burning pants and drag the dazed and bleeding Leek Jaeger away from the spreading flames inside the jail, Buck Comstock was clear of the town of Twin Buttes and racing into the far, free night.

II

The Twin Buttes range was made up of three distinct and separate valleys, roughly parallel and running from north to south. North of them stretched an area of broken, tangled *malpais* country, from the center of which rose two jagged buttes, scarified by wind and weather. These two buttes, known locally as East Butte and West Butte, were the basis of the name of the town of Twin Buttes, which lay at the head of the westernmost valley. Buck Comstock, speeding out of the southern end of Twin Buttes' single street, turned east and set the horse to a long, ground-eating run. Buck had spent a lifetime in the saddle and he knew horses. This one he had grabbed was a good one, fresh and full of fire. Buck felt vaguely that he knew this horse, that he recognized its gait, that he had ridden it before. He fingered the horn, passed a hand over the bucking rolls. There, on the face of the rolls, was smooth, cold metal set into the leather, metal shaped like a star. Then Buck knew. This was Bill Morgan's big, bald-faced sorrel.

Buck smiled tightly. No matter what else might be laid to his door, good old Bill would never accuse him of horse stealing. The fact that Buck had, by chance, grabbed this bronco for a getaway would tickle Bill to death. Also, Buck knew this was a horse to rely on; he had little fear that he would be overtaken even if Brood Shotwell should manage to follow his trail. For Bill Morgan's bald-faced sorrel was known the length and breadth of the Twin Buttes range for its speed and bottom and staying power.

On Buck's left, jagged and lonely against the starlit sky, loomed the bulk of East and West Buttes. Buck reined gradually toward them, with the idea of skirting the *malpais* country. This would take him well above the J Bar C headquarters, which lay midway across Timber Valley, the first of the three valleys.

Under the drumming hoofs of the sorrel, the miles rolled swiftly back. Soon the horse began breasting a long, rolling slope, where scattered, stunted sage began to take the place of the grassland of the valley. The slope topped a sort of tableland, barren and rocky, and, when some two miles of this had been covered, Buck's trail dropped off into the wide and flat center valley, the richest of the three. This was Coyote Valley, and here lay Bill Morgan's spread, the Circle Star, Bud Tharp's Rafter T, Johnny Frazier's Lazy F, and, far at the southern end, Old Man Addis's outfit, the Stirrup Cross. Beyond the fertile reaches of Coyote Valley and across another sage tableland lay Cotton Valley in the center of which Buck's own little spread, the Half Moon, was situated. South of Buck's spread, Cotton Valley ran out into free government land, which lacked water, so that it was only of tangible grazing value in the late winter and spring. The northern portion of Cotton Valley was held by the Wineglass outfit, which had been Ben Sloan's spread. But now that Ben Sloan was dead, it was problematical as to who would eventually own the Wineglass.

Again, before Buck Comstock's eyes, a picture took form, carved indelibly on the retina of his mind, a picture he had seen many times during the past month. It was of Ben Sloan, hatchet face set in a killing snarl, eyes red with blood hunger, crouched in deadly belligerency as he dragged at his guns. Then the tragic finale of that picture—Buck's gun leaping into his hand, coughing heavily in report, jarring and rearing in recoil. Ben Sloan had lunged forward on his face, the startling wonder of death in his staring eyes. For that they had called Buck a killer. For that they had dragged him to jail, tried him, and sentenced him to twenty-five years in Pinole Penitentiary. But now he was free once more, at least for a time—a fugitive from law, but free.

The sorrel halted, heaved a gusty sigh, and stood tossing its head. Aroused abruptly from his thoughts, Buck saw before him a corral and the heavy bulk of feed sheds and ranch buildings. It startled him for a moment. Then he laughed softly, relaxed, and patted the sorrel's neck. The horse had come home. This was the Circle Star, Bill Morgan's spread.

The place was silent. It seemed almost deserted until Buck caught the pale gleam of light in a single window of the ranch house. Buck twisted in the saddle, looking back the way he had come, eyes and ears straining. There was no sound of pursuit, no sight of any moving thing. Buck dismounted and prowled up to the ranch house, peering guardedly through the window. A grim smile flickered over Buck's face. In that room, sprawled at ease on his bunk, lay fat, rotund Bones Baker, the Circle Star cook. Bones held a magazine of lurid romance in both tense fists and, by the light of the lamp on the chair beside his bunk, was reading avidly.

Buck rapped softly on the window. Bones jerked upright, stared around. Buck tapped on the window again. Bones unearthed a .45 Colt from under his blankets, pushed open the window, and leaned out.

"Who's there?" he demanded belligerently. "If any of you gol-darn' grub-spoilers are aiming to play a trick on me, I'll hash you up with a couple of slugs."

"It's Buck Comstock, Bones," drawled Buck. "Can I come in?"

Bones's jaw dropped, his eyes bugged out. "Huh . . . who? Buck Comstock. How the hell? Sa-ay, you're supposed to be in the jug."

"I know. But I made a break for it, won free, and jumped that big sorrel of Bill's. The bronc' brought me straight here. I got to make a hide-away somewhere, Bones. I'll need grub and some blankets . . . and a couple of guns. How's chances?"

Bones flung the window wide. "Gosh Almighty, boy, you shore can. Climb in here. Gollies, I'm glad to see you. I heard they gave you twenty-five years for killing that pigeon-toed tarantula bug, Ben Sloan. I figgered I'd seen the last of you in these parts, Buck. And I was feeling plenty bad about it . . . plenty. You bet you can have that grub and blankets. You can have anything I got." Bones wrung Buck's hand tightly. "You had any supper?" he demanded eagerly.

"Yeah. I'd fed before I had my chance for a break. Don't waste any time throwing that pack of blankets and grub together, Bones. Shotwell is pounding along my trail, back there somewhere. He'll end up here eventually, and I want to be a long time gone by then."

Bones caught up the lamp and waddled out. In five minutes he had a flour sack of grub and a couple of blankets ready. He made another short journey, and came back with a pair of gun belts, heavy with hardware. Under one arm he had a rifle.

"Here y'are," he puffed. "These are Bill's spare belt guns and one of the half dozen or so rifles laying around the house. I'll rustle you some cartridges."

Ten minutes after he had arrived Buck was ready to leave. In addition to the grub, blankets, guns, and ammunition, Bones had given him an old sombrero and a short, warm jacket. As a final thought, Bones threw in a slicker. Then he helped Buck lug it all down to the corrals.

"Better keep right on traveling on that sorrel, Buck," advised Bones. "Bill won't mind a bit. He kinda thinks a lot of you, cowboy."

"They don't come any better than Bill," said Buck. "But I don't want that sorrel. Known too well in these parts. See if you can find me a old saddle while I catch up some ordinary-looking nag."

Bones got the saddle, and Buck cinched it on a well-built Grullo, an Indian horse carrying a brand no white man could decipher. Buck tied grub, blankets, and slicker behind the cantle, slung the rifle in the boot under the stirrup leather, then turned to Bones.

"Listen close," he said. "I don't want you to forget a word of this, Bones. I want to see Bill. I want to have a long talk with him. But I can't afford the chance of sticking around here. He'll have to come to me. Tell him I'll meet him tomorrow night around midnight at Indian Spring. Don't forget."

"I won't," Bones promised. "How you fixed for money? I got about twenty bucks here you can have."

Buck jabbed the fat cook affectionately in the stomach. "Thanks. I don't need money. I need friends. I got one in you. So long, Bones."

Bones Baker listened until the sound of the Grullo's hoofs had died away. Then he started automatically to unsaddle the sorrel, but stopped almost immediately.

"Nope," he muttered. "That won't do. Brood Shotwell is liable to come ramming in here hellity-larrup any minute, and I don't want him to think Buck has been here. I'll just leave this nag stand here as is."

As an afterthought he looped the reins about the saddle horn. Then he went back to the ranch house and squatted in the doorway to listen and wait.

A half hour later, coming down on the ranch from the west, there sounded the rising clatter of speeding hoofs. Bones nodded wisely, returned to his room, and sprawled out on his bunk once more.

He heard those racing hoofs speed to a halt outside the door, then a clamor of voices, among which he recognized Bill Morgan's heavy rumble and Brood Shotwell's cold, clipped tones. Then Bill Morgan yelled: "Hey Bones! Wake up and come out here."

Bones went to the door, magazine in one hand, lamp in the other. He stood in the open doorway, yawning hugely. "Hi, Bill. What you want? What's all the excitement?"

Brood Shotwell stalked up out of the darkness with Bill Morgan behind him. "You been awake all evening?" demanded Shotwell harshly.

"Yep." Bones nodded. "Been thinking of turning the light out and getting some shut-eye, but this story was so gol-darn' exciting. . . ."

"Seen or heard anybody ride up?" cut in the sheriff impatiently.

Bones shook his head. "Not until you jaspers came in. Why? You looking for somebody?"

"Oh, no," Shotwell growled caustically. "I'm jest ramming around through the dark making love to the squint owls. Come alive, you tub of lard. You damned shore you didn't hear or see anybody ride in here besides us?"

"I said so, didn't I?" retorted Bones. "Gol blast it, just because you're sheriff, Brood Shotwell, is no sign you can go around calling folks names, regardless. Maybe I am kinda plump, but I can kick your teeth out if I get mad enough."

"There's a horse down at the corrals, Bill Morgan's big sorrel," said Shotwell coldly. "That bronc' was stole off the street of Twin Buttes by Buck Comstock. Now it's out here. You mighty shore Comstock didn't ride that bronc' in here?"

Bones stared at the sheriff in amazement. "You must be loco. I heard this afternoon that Buck Comstock had been sentenced to twenty-five years in Pinole and that you had him locked up tight in your jail in town. Now you try and tell me he rode Bill's sorrel out to this ranch. What kind of a joke is this?"

"Joke be damned," spat Shotwell. "Comstock made a getaway tonight and rode that sorrel out of town. The bronc' is here. Comstock must have rode it in."

Bones seemed to be trying to get all this news straight in his round, close-clipped head. He opened his mouth and closed it two or three times. He gulped, then shrugged. "This sure is news to me," he asserted stoutly. "If Buck Comstock rode that sorrel into this ranch, he sure must've come in awful quiet. I never heard nothing. I never saw nothing. I didn't even know the bronc' was here. I tell you, I ain't seen hide nor hair of a soul since Dave Wagg rode by just before suppertime and told me Buck had been cinched for twenty-five years. That's all I can tell you. Don't chaw on it if it hurts your teeth."

Brood Shotwell cursed savagely, furiously, stamping back and forth.

A cowboy came hurrying up from the dark. "Say, Brood," he called, "did you notice how the reins on that sorrel bronco are tied? That horse ain't been dragging those reins. They're looped over the horn."

"What of it?" snapped Shotwell. "That don't mean anything."

"I wonder." The cowboy shrugged. "It could mean that somewhere between here and town, Comstock got off that bronco, turned it loose, and dodged out on foot. He might have cut north into that *malpais* country around the buttes."

The idea caught with Shotwell momentarily. Then he shook his head slowly. "Not likely. Comstock was raised in the saddle. He wouldn't give up a perfectly good bronc' to do his traveling on foot, least of all when he'd know I'd be after him."

Bill Morgan spoke, in his deep, rolling tones: "In this case he might. It would be just like Buck, knowing that sorrel was my pet bronco, to use it only as long as he absolutely had to, and then turn it loose to come home. Still, the darned chump ought to know I'd've given him that bronco or all the broncos I own, if they'd help him get away."

Shotwell whirled on Bill Morgan, scowling. "That kind of talk. . . ."

"Listen, Brood," cut in Morgan. "You know damned well how I stand in this mess. I'm for Buck Comstock, all the way. And I don't give a tinker's damn who knows it. I hope he gets away, clean. I hope you founder yourself before you catch him. And if I thought that by blowing your head off, right here and now, it would make Buck sure to get away, I'd be more than likely to chance it. I guess that's plain enough."

Shotwell cursed and whirled toward his horse. "We're going back and take a look at that *malpais* country!" he yelled to his posse. "Come on!"

In a surge and creak of saddle gear, they were gone, pounding back the way they had come. But Bill Morgan remained with Bones, who was looking out into the night with a twinkle of satisfaction in his eyes. Morgan, however, was moody and scowling.

"Why the devil did that darned chump of a Buck turn that bronco loose to come home?" he wondered. "He could have kept the sorrel and welcome. Me, I've got a good idea to throw a saddle on a spare bronco, take the sorrel, and cut around into that *malpais* ahead of Shotwell and his posse. If Buck's up there afoot, he won't have a Chinaman's chance."

"Don't you worry none about Buck," murmured Bones softly. "Buck's been taken care of already."

Morgan fixed alert, eager eyes on his cook. "Then . . . ?"

"Yup." Bones nodded. "Buck was here. He rode the sorrel in. I gave him some grub and blankets and guns. He took that Grullo Injun pony. He's to hell and gone over in Cotton Valley by this time."

"Come inside while I kiss you, you fat, old fox," boomed Morgan. "Come inside and tell me all about it."

In the seclusion of the cook's room, Bones told his story, while Morgan listened eagerly.

"So Buck hightailed it out on the Grullo," Bones ended. "And the last thing he told me was this. You're to meet him at Indian Spring around midnight tomorrow. He said he wanted to have a big powwow with you. And he said for us to clam up and say nothing to anybody else. There you have it, boss."

"Indian Spring," muttered Bill Morgan. "I'll be there. You bet. Bones, I think I'll give you a raise in wages."

"You will like hell," retorted Bones. "I didn't help Buck out for pay. I did it because I like him, because he's my good friend. Why, when Dave Wagg told me that orrey-eyed old pelican of a Judge Henning had given Buck twenty-five years in Pinole, I was all busted up. I couldn't swallow my evening grub. And when I laid down and tried to read to get my thoughts straightened out, I couldn't even see the print. Honest Bill, I was fair blubbering, thinking of a high-class boy like Buck Comstock, due to put in twenty-five years in Pinole. Was I glad when he showed up, free and ready to ride? Mama!"

"That whole trial was a farce, Bones," said Morgan. "They railroaded Buck cold. The jury was hand-picked, ten out of the twelve were J Bar C men. The other two were Toad Black and Duke Younger. Buck didn't have a chance. Leek Jaeger and

Frank Cutts pulled the strings all the way. I'm no fool. I could see that."

"Well" said Bones slowly, "I don't know nothing about that. But I do know this. Buck Comstock would never have pulled a gun and cut Ben Sloan down if Sloan hadn't gone for his gun first. Buck ain't the kind to kill unless he has to . . . in self-defense. So it must have been self-defense when he rocked off Ben Sloan."

III

About midafternoon of the following day Bill Morgan cinched his silver-mounted hull on the big sorrel, slung a canteen to the horn, stuffed a couple of sandwiches into his slicker roll, and rode leisurely south through the center of Coyote Valley. He stopped for a time at both the Rafter T and the Lazy F, where he held short confabs with the respective owners, Bud Tharp and Johnny Frazier. What he told these two left them with musing smiles on their faces.

Traveling on south, Morgan pulled in at the Stirrup Cross just at sundown. There he ran into a distinct surprise. Old Man Addis stood in front of the ranch house, engaged in heavy argument with none other than Leek Jaeger and Frank Cutts. Bill Morgan's eyes narrowed slightly, then became bland and innocent, as he drew up before them. He leaned over and rested his forearms across his saddle horn in a lazy slouch. He nodded. "Howdy, gents."

Old Man Addis looked flustered. He was a narrow-faced old fox, with thinning, sandy hair, a ragged, tired-looking mustache, and pale eyes under bleached brows. Frank Cutts showed no change of expression on his coldly set features, but Leek Jaeger scowled openly at Morgan's arrival.

"Kind of a long way off your range, ain't you, Morgan?" said Jaeger.

Morgan shrugged. "Not near as far off as you are, Jaeger. What happened to your phiz? You look like a mule kicked you."

Jaeger, his blocky face swollen and bruise-blackened from the terrific blow Buck Comstock had given him the night before, cursed savagely. "Shotwell was telling me that you made some pretty long talk last night," he complained.

Bill Morgan lifted his eyebrows. "Suppose you talk a little plainer. I don't know what you're driving at."

"He told me you said you hoped Comstock got away, and added that you'd do anything you could to help him."

Morgan shrugged again carelessly. "Yeah, I said that. I meant it, too. Buck Comstock is a good friend of mine. I think a lot of him, and I don't give a whoop who knows it."

"He's a fugitive from law . . . a killer, a murderer," insisted Jaeger.

"Part of that is true, and part's a damn' lie," said Bill Morgan coldly. "He's a fugitive from the law . . . damn' cheap law, I might add . . . but he's no killer and no murderer. Any man who says he is, is a liar."

"I say he is," affirmed Jaeger.

"Then the shoe fits you . . . perfect," drawled Morgan, coldly watchful.

Jaeger's swollen face twisted into a snarl, his right hand began to creep toward the gun at his hip. Old Man Addis, his pale eyes flickering with sudden fear, started to back away.

Frank Cutts caught Jaeger by the arm, swung him partially around. "Don't be a damned fool, Leek," he cautioned. "In the first place, you're acting like a kid. And, in the second, you wouldn't have a ghost of a chance. Trading words like this don't mean a thing. Come on. You and I are all through here. We're riding."

Bill Morgan, a cool, musing smile on his face, watched the two partners climb into their saddles and spur away. Then Morgan looked at Old Man Addis. "What did those two jaspers have on their minds, Tom?"

"Business . . . just a little business," Addis answered testily. "Damn it all, Morgan, you don't realize how heavy-worded you can be sometimes. You had no call to give the lie to Leek."

"I said," returned Morgan coolly, "that any man who says Buck Comstock is a killer and a murderer is a liar. I'm sticking to those words."

"Comstock put Ben Sloan in his grave, didn't he?" twanged Addis angrily. "If that don't make him a killer, I don't know what does."

"A killer," said Morgan, "is a professional, a man who sells his guns, who works to get the edge before rolling smoke, who goes out with deliberate intent to cut a man down. Throwing a gun in self-defense makes no man a killer."

"But the jury decided it wasn't a case of self-defense," argued Addis. "They decided that Comstock went out deliberately to get Ben Sloan . . . and got him."

"That jury didn't go up there to give Buck Comstock a square deal. They were hand-picked for just one purpose . . . to find Buck guilty. They never paid a damn' bit of attention to the evidence."

Old Man Addis threw up his hands. "I ain't got time to stand here arguing all that over again. You got your opinion. I got mine. What brought you down this far, anyhow?"

"I started out with the idea of business," said Morgan crisply. "But I've sorta changed my mind. I don't like the company I found you in, Tom. *Adiós.*"

With that, Morgan swung the sorrel about and started back the way he had come. Old Man Addis stared after him, with his narrow face twisted angrily.

★ ★ ★ ★ ★

Dusk found Bill Morgan halfway between the Stirrup Cross and Lazy F. Morgan had been watching his back trail carefully. When he was sure it was empty, he seized upon the first deep blanket of shadows to turn the sorrel directly east.

The first stars found him crossing Cotton Valley. Leaving that, he pushed up past the long rimrock and out onto the vast reaches of Big Sage Desert. Here he turned slightly northeast and set the sorrel to a steady jog.

Lacking perhaps some fifteen minutes of midnight, Bill Morgan rode up to a dark bulk of jagged rock outcroppings, sparsely blanketed with sage and mesquite. The night was illimitable, vast, silent. For a moment Morgan knew a qualm of worry. Perhaps, somewhere along the line, Buck Comstock might have run into trouble.

Then a cool voice spoke from the darkness: " 'Evening, Bill."

"Buck!" Morgan stepped from the saddle as Buck Comstock, a lean, tall shadow, moved up to him. They shook hands wordlessly. Then Morgan spoke gruffly: "You beat Johnny and Bud and me to it, you long-legged whelp. We were aiming to bust that gol-darn' jail wide open and haul you out by the scruff of your neck. But you beat us to it. I saw Jaeger today. His face still looks like it had been sideswiped by a freight train. How you been making it, kid?"

"Fair enough. I forgot to have old Bones put some extra tobacco into that grub pack, though. I'm going to rob you of all you got."

"Your luck still holds." Morgan chuckled. "I always pack half a dozen extra sacks in my saddlebags. Here, I'll get it for you."

They built smokes, squatted on their heels. "Bones said you wanted to tell me something," Morgan reminded Buck.

"Here it is," Buck said. "Maybe you've been wondering how

Jaeger happened to be present in the jail when I made my getaway?"

Morgan nodded. "That's right, I have."

"Well, here's something that will startle your ears. Jaeger came in there to lay a proposition in front of me. He said that, if I'd sign over my Cotton Valley range to him, he'd see that my sentence was cut from twenty-five to five years. What do you make of that?"

Morgan sat very still. "It just proves that you were railroaded, that there is a weak spot somewhere in the scheme that was cooked up to frame you. And it sounds like Jaeger is afraid it might pop out and raise hell."

Buck nodded. "It proves that and suggests a lot else. Some folks say Jaeger and Cutts bought the J Bar C, fair and upright. Others claim it was euchred from Bob Haley over the poker table Cutts used to run in the Yellow Horse Saloon. Anyway, they got it. In no time at all, they got control of all of Timber Valley. I don't pretend to know how they got it, but they did. I heard that cattle buyer, Ed Fitch, tell Leek Jaeger that if the J Bar C didn't quit stocking Timber Valley so heavy, they'd strip the range. Jaeger laughed and said there was a lot of other range around Twin Buttes that he and Cutts intended to control before they were done. What other range is there, except Coyote and Cotton Valleys?"

"None," observed Morgan. "Go on. You interest me, boy."

"OK. Time was when Ben Sloan and I got along well enough. Then Sloan started turning pretty mean and sulky. I didn't bother him, figuring he'd outgrow it. But he didn't. He grew worse. Finally, one day in town, he accused me of sleepering some of his stuff. I laughed at him and told him he was crazy. He got so he wouldn't even talk to me. Then came that day . . . well, you know what happened. He accused me again of tampering with his stock, and I got mad. I told him he was a damned liar. He went for his gun. It was him or me. I got him. Now I'm dodging the law and Ben Sloan is dead. There's nothing to keep the J Bar C from moving into Cotton Valley. If Jaeger could have bluffed me into signing over my Cotton Valley holdings, it would have been a big help, made it easier for the J Bar C to move in. Let's suppose the J Bar C moves into Cotton Valley. Where does that leave the middle and richest valley of the three, the Coyote range?"

"Right in the center of J Bar C holdings, and sure as hell to be swallowed up sooner or later," Morgan said tersely. "Buck, you've made a picture."

Buck inhaled deeply, his lips grim.

Morgan went on: "They're clever as hell. Ben Sloan always did have an ugly temper. By setting him against you, it was almost a cinch that he'd force a gun play. And it wouldn't matter a tinker's damn one way or the other which of you two got killed. They'd railroad the other fellow for murder, leaving Cotton Valley wide open. Oh, I get it now. I get it."

"Thought you would, Bill." Buck nodded. "It's just like reading signs on a trail . . . easy to figure out if you look at the right marks."

"And the answer to it, Buck, is what?"

"The answer is," said Buck with fierce grimness, "that the J Bar C doesn't get a foothold in Cotton Valley. Once they dig in there, Bill, you and Johnny and Bud can begin counting the days until your finish. It isn't Cotton Valley they really want. It's Coyote Valley."

"Correct," said Morgan. "Go on."

"My range is still my range, even though I am what is known as a fugitive from justice. But the Wineglass, Ben Sloan's old spread . . . well, if Jaeger and Cutts can get hold of that, they've got their foothold. Your play, Bill, is to beat 'em to the Wineglass. What you should do is line it for town first thing tomorrow, get hold of Curt Wallace, and tell him to try to locate the nearest kin of Ben Sloan. When and if he does locate 'em, offer to buy the Wineglass. Between you and Johnny and Bud, you should be able to swing it. And if Jaeger and Cutts try and move in, call 'em. Make 'em show their authority for taking over the Wineglass. For just as sure as you and me are sitting here, they're going to try it."

"Correct again, Buck," Morgan agreed. "I'll do it. I'll have Curt Wallace on the job first thing in the morning. I know Bud and Johnny will see the right of this. They'll back our hand all the way. What started you thinking this thing out?"

"When Jaeger tried that proposition last night," answered Buck. "Most of it hit me all in a bunch, right then and there. That was what made me take such a long chance to break free. I didn't give much of a whoop what happened until that thought hit me."

Morgan stood up. "I'll be drifting. You making out all right?"

"Sure. I can take care of myself. I always was more or less of a nighthawk. I'll probably drop in some night and see you."

"You take it easy," warned Morgan. "You know what a bloodhound Brood Shotwell is. He'll stick after you till hell freezes."

Buck laughed softly. "He'll have to ride faster and farther and jump quicker than he ever did before in his life to get me. By the way, Bill, if a bronc' or two of yours turns up missing every now and then, don't get excited. You'll know who's riding them."

"Help yourself, kid. I'll pass that word to Johnny and Bud, too. Watch yourself. Don't take any long chances. And trust me to start things swinging. So long."

They shook hands again, and Morgan was soon lost in the night. Buck whistling softly between his teeth, went back into the rock outcropping that surrounded Indian Spring, swung astride the Grullo, and lifted the reins. When he turned in that night to get a couple of hours sleep, he was a good ten miles from Indian Spring.

In the chill grayness of the desert dawn, Buck cooked and ate a meager breakfast, saddled the Grullo, and struck out, riding a wide, watchful circle. He was not underestimating the resourceful stubbornness of Brood Shotwell. Shotwell was a born manhunter and had grown old and grizzled at the game. There were few tricks of the trade he didn't know. He was a fox who would bear watching.

Yet, even with the knowledge that Shotwell would be riding and looking and watching all the time, Buck was cheerful. Back there in jail, before the great light had burst upon him, Buck's spirits had been plenty low. It had seemed that he was so hemmed in with the withes and tithes of law, he didn't have a ghost of a show. What was the use? he had asked himself. Everything was set against him; there wasn't a loophole; the case was hopeless. But when his mind had grasped the significance of Jaeger's scheme, he had been galvanized to a new courage, a new determination. He had made his getaway and was now riding the free, open world. He had, through good old Bill Morgan, set machinery in motion that Jaeger and Cutts would find mighty hard to stop. Also, gleaming far out in the future somewhere, still a little indistinct and uncertain, but visible nevertheless, was a star of hope for his own future. When the J Bar C had its hand called, facts that would exonerate him might come to light. A man of twenty-six, with the good red tide of blood running strongly in his veins, knows the value of freedom.

Buck whistled as he rode, welcoming the warm beat of the morning sun. He found a strange and exhilarating satisfaction in watching the sage wrens flit here and there and an occasional jack rabbit scud fleetly away. Noon found him some half dozen miles north of the Wineglass headquarters, and at midafternoon he was less than two hundred yards from the ranch buildings, flattened out on his stomach in a patch of thigh-deep wild oats that fringed the top of a low ridge. In the gully in back of the ridge, the Grullo Indian pony stood ground-reined, rolling its bit ring busily as it grazed.

Buck could hardly have told why he had come to this place. It wasn't the safest thing to do by any means. The far reaches of Big Sage Desert were a much more secure sanctuary for a man who had Sheriff Brood Shotwell on his trail. But Buck was young and restless, and he was eager to be somewhere near the center of the fight. He peered cautiously through the tawny wild oats, watching the ranch buildings below. Except for a single horse, standing ground-reined in the shade of a feed shed, the Wineglass seemed deserted. Buck wondered who the owner of that horse would be. Ben Sloan had only kept two regular riders, picking up three or four more during roundup and branding, then laying them off when the rush was over. These two regulars had been Dave Wagg and Curly Jenkins. Perhaps that horse down there belonged to one of them.

Buck soon saw this was not the case. A hulking, bulky-shouldered figure left the ranch house and sauntered over to the ground-reined bronco. He took something out of the saddlebags, then started back toward the house once more. Buck stiffened, and a growl of fury rose in his throat. He knew that man. All through the long, depressing hours of the trial, that fellow had been one of twelve Buck had watched and about whom he had wondered. The fellow was Toad Black, one of the jurymen who had adjudged Buck guilty of murder. What was Toad Black doing out here at the Wineglass? He had never, at any time, worked for Ben Sloan. Yet he was apparently just hanging around down there, killing time. Maybe he had been sent out to guard the place. Maybe Jaeger had sent him out.

While Buck was pondering this, Black came to a halt beside the ranch house and built a cigarette. As Buck watched him, Black suddenly twisted his head, looked hard out to the west, then ducked swiftly from sight. Buck's glance immediately followed that look Black had thrown. Out there, coming straight for the ranch buildings, some four or five hundred yards distant, was a rider on a white and liver-spotted pinto bronco. It was a slim rider, wearing a white shirt and a new, white Stetson hat. As Buck frowned in his curiosity, the pinto clipped into a little hollow and out of sight.

When the pinto next appeared, Buck got a start. That rider was a woman. No mistake about it. And she was a stranger. No woman Buck knew on the Twin Buttes range, and he knew them all, wore riding breeches, high, glossy Cordovan boots, and a white silk blouse. But this woman did. By the sheen of the material, even at a distance, Buck knew that blouse was silk. Whoever it was, he bet she'd be pretty. She sure made a nice picture on that pinto, sitting her saddle with an easy, straight-backed grace.

Not until she had pulled to a halt before the ranch house and was about to dismount, did Buck remember Toad Black. Then he lunged to his knees. But ingrained caution dropped him flat again. This was no business of his. Maybe she had arranged to meet Black here at the deserted Wineglass headquarters. Yet, somehow, Buck knew that couldn't be true. What decent woman would have anything to do with Toad Black—a big, black-browed, lowering brute of a man with a flat face and horrible, bulbous eyes?

The girl walked into the house, moving with a free, slender grace. She had taken off her hat just before going out of sight, and in that brief glimpse Buck saw that her hair was very dark and that the sun shone on it.

Buck stared at the ranch house intently, squinting. He was of half a mind to throw caution to the wind and go down there. More than once he'd heard stories about Toad Black. Maybe. . . . Buck lunged clear to his feet this time. For carrying up the slope to him had come the thin, high panic of a woman's scream—and there was utter terror in the sound. The next instant Buck was racing down the slope.

IV

Buck Comstock was less than a hundred yards from the Wineglass ranch house when a thought struck him that sent a trickle of ice up his backbone, turned his mouth to a parched, leathery dryness. Maybe this whole set-up was a trap. Maybe he had not been unobserved. Maybe there were other men in that ranch house besides Toad Black, men looking at him over gunsights this very moment. Maybe within the next stride or two a blast of venomous lead would rip his life out. Buck's brain numbed at the possibility. Yet, he realized, if he had been tricked, there was nothing he could do about it now. He couldn't go back. He was in the open. It was farther back to the top of the ridge than to the ranch house. He had to gamble that the scream had been genuine. So he drove on.

Again sounded the forlorn, hopeless, terrified cry. Now Buck knew he hadn't been tricked. There was no falsity, no pretense in it. The mortal fear in that scream was stark, heart-rending. Buck's eyes turned bleak and savage. He raced toward the door. Suddenly a tangle of fighting figures spun through the doorway, out into the white, searching sunlight. The girl seemed incredibly frail in the pawing clutches of that hulking beast, Toad Black. Already he had torn one sleeve completely off her blouse; the white, soft curves of her arm were banded with red and blue where the clawing fingers of Black had bruised her flesh. At this moment he had her by both slim shoulders, trying to drag her close to him. His horrible, protruding eyes and lecherous mouth mocked her as she fought.

A feral, red haze swept across Buck Comstock's gaze and through it he could see but one object—that face of Toad Black. Buck forgot he had guns at his hips, forgot everything but a savage, crazy desire to kill and crush that man with his bare hands. Then he was close behind the struggling girl, looking into the startled eyes of Toad Black. The next moment Buck hit the fellow, his fist traveling right over the top of the girl's dark head. Buck put everything he had into that punch. He knew a wild joy as he felt his knuckles bite into Toad Black's face, felt them split the flesh. Toad Black had let go of the girl as he saw that blow start, throwing up both hairy paws in a futile effort to ward it off. And now, under the lethal drive of the punch, he tottered backward, slammed against the wall of the ranch house, dropped to his knees, and fell over sideways.

Buck swept the startled girl aside with his arm. He lunged forward. Black wasn't out. He was clawing for the gun at his hip. Buck kicked out violently, viciously. The toe of his boot caught Black on the forearm, and the brute's gun flipped harmlessly to one side. Then, his hands clawing and reaching, Buck went for the fellow's throat.

Toad Black still had fight in him. In that big, hulking bulk of his lay a frightful reservoir of brute strength. He warded off Buck's reaching fingers, rolled over with surprising speed, and lunged to his feet. Black's face was a gory pulp from that first punch. His froggy eyes seemed to protrude more than ever. His yellow teeth showed beneath his flattened nose in a simian snarl. With both huge arms clubbed and swinging, he rushed at Buck.

Buck side-stepped and his fist drove out in a rapier-like blow that nearly tore Black's ear off. Black gave a weird, coughing bawl of fury as he staggered wildly, again thrown off balance by the power of Buck's lashing fist. He was like nothing so much as a mad, wounded gorilla. Buck slithered after him and caught him again as he was turning. His knuckles laid Black's left cheek open from temple to chin. Buck knew he had never hit any man so hard in his life, yet somehow, Black kept his feet. It was like battering at something inhuman.

Buck moved in, trying for a clear shot at the point of Black's jaw. And one of the renegade's wildly clubbing fists caught him on the side of the head. The white fire of agony bathed Buck from head to toe, his senses reeling and crazy lights blazing before his eyes. It was as if he had been struck with a post maul. Instinct alone caused Buck to duck. For a reeling moment it seemed as if he had been scalped as another whizzing fist skimmed across the top of his head. Then Black caught him and dragged him close.

Only the utter fury that blinded the renegade at the moment kept Buck from being broken and trampled like a reed. But Toad Black now was like a beast gone mad. He tore and clawed at Buck like a wild animal, and he was snarling bestially. Blood from his split and pulped face drenched both men, and its raw stench was sickening. Strangely enough, this shaking and slamming around had the effect of clearing Buck's tortured head. Buck's rage and fury flared up anew as Black tried for a wicked blow with one knee. Buck twisted his hips aside, suddenly dropped both fists and sank them deep into Black's gross stomach.

He knew, with savage exultation, that those blows had hurt Black—hurt him plenty. He pumped more into the same spot, and Black, groaning and retching, gave ground. Buck swarmed after him, smashing savagely into the body. Black backed, spreading both hairy paws across his stomach in an effort to halt that punishment, which seemed about to tear him in half. Buck switched his attack, drove a ripping left into Black's face. The blow hurled the renegade again against the side of the ranch house. As he struggled to catch his wind, his sagging jaw loomed, fair and open. Power swept up Buck Comstock's lean body, rippled up from his very heels, arcing through straightening knees, narrow hips, and wide, driving shoulders, and the end of that surge of power was Buck's right fist, finding the very point of Toad Black's jaw. The sound was as if a stout board had been split. Black's feet crossed, he spun half around, and dropped with a crash. He lay like a dead man.

Buck staggered back. He himself almost went down. His knees were trembling, his feet clumsy and uncertain. Those few mad moments of furious combat seemed to have drained every atom of strength from him. He stood there, weaving, gulping hoarsely for air, his sweat-filled eyes staring at the crumpled bulk of Toad Black. For the moment he had forgotten about the girl. Then her hand was on his arm, and he turned slowly. She was crying soundlessly, tears rolling down her cheeks. Her lips opened and closed, as though she were trying to say something, but no words came.

Buck shook himself, managed a lop-sided grin. " 'S all right . . . now," he panted. "Everything's . . . all right. That hog . . . won't come back for quite some time. It was like . . . hitting a stone wall. Don't cry, lady . . . you're safe enough now."

Abruptly he realized that she was staring at him, her wide eyes shocked, almost unbelieving. "You," she gasped. "Y-you . . . you're Buck Comstock, the man who . . . who killed my uncle. The man who broke jail."

Now Buck recognized her. This was the girl who had stood between Leek Jaeger and Frank Cutts and had recoiled at the sight of him as Brood Shotwell and Spike St. Ives had led him from the courtroom after Judge Henning had pronounced sentence. The lop-sided grin left Buck's face. Stern gravity took its place. He moved a little apart from her. He nodded slowly. "Yes," he said, "I'm Buck Comstock."

Her hands, trembling a little, were pressed against her lips, while the look in her eyes made Buck shake himself. "Don't look at me like that," he said harshly. "If Ben Sloan was your uncle, I know what you're thinking. You'd be bound to think that. And I can't blame you. Yet, no matter what lies Jaeger and Cutts might have put in your ears, please remember that there are two sides to everything. I'm not as black as they've painted me."

The recollection that he was standing in the open, free to the sight of anyone, came to him. He looked around, searching the distance in every direction. But everywhere the range lay empty, white under the sun. He took another deep, slow breath, and new energy and strength flowed through him.

He turned to Toad Black, who had not moved. With pigging strings taken from his pocket, Buck pulled Black's thick wrists behind him and tied them securely. Then he straightened up and rolled a cigarette.

In all this time he had not looked at the girl again. But now, for a second time, her hand fell on his arm. He looked down at her, his face set and wary. "Well?" He could not keep the harshness out of his tone.

She spoke with simple honesty. "Regardless of what else may have happened, in this you were splendid, Buck Comstock. I want you to know that I thank you . . . sincerely. If you had not come to aid me. . . ." She broke off, shuddering.

Some of the bleakness went out of Buck's face. "Forget it," he said. "Any decent man would have done the same. And now, if you don't mind, I'll be getting out of here. I can't afford to stay here, in the open. I'm taking Toad Black out of here. I got use for that *hombre.*"

He stalked off to the feed shed and got Toad Black's horse. When he returned, Black was stirring. Buck caught him by the shoulder, hauled him to a sitting position. He jabbed a gun in

Black's ribs.

"Get up," he rasped. "You're going with me. Try any fuss and I won't waste a lick of time on you."

Toad Black lurched upright. But there was no fight or truculence in him now. He was craven, shrunken, and a great fear showed in his swollen, blackened eyes. Buck took the lariat from Black's own saddle, dropped a loop over the fellow's head, drew it snugly about his beefy throat, then tied the other end to the saddle horn. He picked up the reins of Black's horse and swung astride it. "March," he ordered. "Right up over yonder ridge."

"Wait!" cried the girl. "I want to talk to you, Buck Comstock."

"Not here," replied Buck. "With Brood Shotwell looking for me, I got to get out of sight."

"Then," declared the girl, "I'll ride over that ridge, too."

Buck did not look back, but he knew she was astride the pinto, following him. This was a mix-up for fair. She had said that Ben Sloan was her uncle. Buck stiffened slightly. If that was the case, then undoubtedly she was heir to the Wineglass Ranch.

V

At the top of the ridge Buck made another survey of the range. All was bland and peaceful and empty. He rode down the other side, to the point where his own horse was grazing, with Toad Black stumbling ahead.

"Lie down," Buck ordered Black curtly. "Lie down and stay there. I'll be keeping my eye on you."

He dismounted, went to his own horse, and slid the Winchester rifle from its boot. Then he turned to the girl, who was watching him inscrutably.

"I'll have to ask you to leave your pinto here and climb back to the top of that ridge on foot, if you want to talk with me," he said. "I've got to keep watch, and I can't let anybody see me."

The girl did not hesitate. She slid to the ground and marched sturdily along beside him as they climbed to the screen of wild oats atop the ridge. When Buck flattened out, she crouched beside him.

"All right," drawled Buck. "Fire away. If I don't look at you, don't think I won't be listening. But I've got to keep watching."

She was silent for a time, and Buck glanced at her questioningly. She was, he thought, even prettier than she had seemed that first time he had seen her. The svelte riding outfit she wore was especially becoming.

"That was a very brave and unselfish thing to do, Buck Comstock, coming to my aid as you did," she said suddenly. "For all you knew, you might have ridden straight into a situation that would have put you back behind the bars. Yet you didn't hesitate."

Buck stirred restlessly. "Maybe if that thought had hit me in time, I wouldn't have jumped in so quick. But hearing you scream . . . well, I didn't stop to think."

Again she was quiet for a long moment. Her voice was not quite steady as she asked a question: "You did kill Ben Sloan, didn't you?"

"Yes," said Buck, meeting her level gaze, "I killed him."

"Mur-murdered him?"

"No! In this country, when a man has to kill in defense of his own life, it isn't called murder . . . and it isn't murder. That is what I did. Ben Sloan came for me, rolling smoke. I did only what any other sane man would do. I shot to keep from being shot. Ben Sloan missed. I didn't. That's the truth, if it was ever spoken."

"The jury. . . ."

"Toad Black . . . that damned animal that was after you . . . he was on *that* jury," broke in Buck.

"I see," she said slowly. "I do see. I-I believe you, Buck Comstock."

There was no particular reason that Buck could see why these words should make him feel good. Yet they did. He turned his head, smiled at her. "That's swell. It means a lot to have you say that, Miss . . . ?"

She colored slightly. "Harper," she said. "Jean Harper. Ben Sloan was the only brother of my dead step-father. Ben Sloan was not really my uncle, except by law. At that, I am the only known living kin of Ben Sloan."

"Which makes you owner of the Wineglass spread," said Buck softly.

"Yes. I had no idea that Ben Sloan owned any property . . . nor any idea where he was, for that matter. I didn't even know if he was still alive. Then Mister Jaeger got in touch with me and had me come here."

"And now he wants to buy the Wineglass spread from you," Buck added flatly.

She looked at him keenly. "How did you know?"

Buck laughed. "Because that would be exactly in line with what he's scheming to do. How much did he offer you for the place?"

She hesitated, then her lips tightened. "I don't know that I should. . . ."

"Of course," conceded Buck. "Forget I asked that. Let me give you a little advice, though. Get the help of some reliable cattleman on the proposition before you sell. Or else Jaeger and Cutts will rob you blind. Go have a talk with Bill Morgan or Johnny Frazier or Bud Tharp. They'll give you a good square estimate on what you should get for your spread."

The girl stared thoughtfully at the ground, her smooth brow corrugated in a frown. "What," she demanded suddenly, "would you say the Wineglass Ranch is worth?"

"Not a cent less than twenty thousand dollars," answered Buck.

"Twenty thousand dollars!" She stared at him aghast. "Why Mister Jaeger only offered six thousand. And I thought that was an awful lot of money."

"It is, until it's applied as a price against the Wineglass. Then it becomes robbery. I don't know exactly how many cattle are packing the Wineglass iron, but I've got a reasonable idea, and I know the kind of range it is and what the possibilities of that range are. You wouldn't be getting a cent too much at twenty thousand."

Buck twisted around and looked back down into the hollow at Toad Black. The renegade was lying flat on the ground, making no move to get away.

"I suppose you're wondering why I wanted to come up here and speak to you," said the girl, "when you admit that you . . . well, came off victor in a shooting scrape with my uncle."

"That's right." Buck nodded. "I am."

"I'll tell you," she said in sudden decision. "At first it was pure impulse, I suppose, born of the fact that you saved me from that beast. Now . . . there is something about you, Buck, Comstock, that invites confidence. I suppose I should hate you, fear you, despise you, if only for the memory of Ben Sloan. But I don't. After all, Ben Sloan was little more than a name to me. You . . . you were terrific down there. And I must talk to someone. You see, I do not trust either Mister Jaeger or Mister Cutts."

"Good girl," drawled Buck. "You got savvy. Go on."

"Even from the first, it seemed strange to me that Jaeger and Cutts . . . total strangers . . . should go to the trouble of having me traced, so that they could notify me of this inheritance. When I first met them, I did not feel any more confident about them. And, even though six thousand dollars seems an awful lot of money to me, there was something about Jaeger when he made the offer . . . an eagerness, a greedy eagerness and a filmed cunning in eyes . . . that I did not miss. I asked them to take me out to the Wineglass to look the place over, but both he and Cutts always had some excuse to keep me away from it. One of their arguments was that you were on the loose. They would have had me believe that you were some terrifying dragon who might eat alive any woman you met. But their excuses were not very convincing. And today I managed to slip away from the J Bar C while both Jaeger and Cutts were in town. I met a cowboy out on the range and asked him how to get to the Wineglass. You know what happened then."

"It fits in with the rest of the picture perfectly," mused Buck softly. He looked directly into the girl's questing, measuring eyes, and he spoke crisply. "Miss Harper, I know Leek Jaeger and Frank Cutts a lot better than you do. There's neither truth nor honor in either of them. They'd double-cross their own mothers . . . or skin a flea for its hide and tallow. You're staying at the J Bar C. Leave there right away. Go into town and stay at Joe Lester's hotel. If you intend to sell the Wineglass, let a competent lawyer handle the deal for you. I can recommend Curt Wallace. He's young, but he's square and he's no man's fool. If you think you'd like to hold onto the Wineglass and operate it, get in touch with Bill Morgan and ask his advice. They don't come any better than Bill, and he knows the cattle business both ways from the ace. If you follow his advice, you can't go wrong. And Bill would be more than glad to help you out."

The girl stared thoughtfully out into the distance. She nodded slowly. "Thanks, Buck Comstock. I'll do as you say. Now I'll be riding. As I said before, I *should* hate and fear you. But, somehow, I don't. And thanks again . . . for what you did down there at the ranch."

"If you want to do me a favor," drawled Buck, "say nothing to anyone about any of this."

"Of course." She nodded. "I understand. Good bye."

Shortly before midnight, Buck Comstock was again on the prowl. On foot, he was reconnoitering the Circle Star. Well back from the ranch house, out on the empty range, two ground-reined horses stood, while in the dew-wet grass beside them lay Toad Black, firmly trussed, hand and foot. The Circle Star ranch house was dark. Finally Buck reached Bones Baker's window, where he knocked softly at the glass. Bones roused and the window slid up. "That you, Buck?" he asked guardedly.

"Right, Bones. Let me in. I want to talk to Bill."

In another minute the three of them were gathered in the cook's room. Bones hung a blanket over the window before lighting his lamp. "I got news for you, Bill," said Buck.

"That goes double, kid," Morgan said. "I got news for you. You remember that girl that was with Jaeger and Cutts in the courtroom? Well, she's. . . ."

"Ben Sloan's heir," Buck finished, with a grin.

Bill Morgan stared at him. "How the hell did you find that out?"

"Had a long talk with the lady, in person, today," Buck drawled. "Listen while I spin it."

He told the story of the afternoon's happenings in brief, terse words. "So I told her to get loose from Jaeger and Cutts and stay in town at the hotel," he ended. "I told her to let Curt Wallace handle her affairs and to call on you, Bill, for advice. She promised she would. Tomorrow you ride right into town and have a talk with her."

"I'll do it," Morgan agreed. "But you . . . if you ain't got the damnedest knack of bumping into things I ever saw."

"What did you do with Toad Black?" asked Bones eagerly.

"Take him out and kill him?"

"Hardly." Buck chuckled. "Dead, he wouldn't be worth a plugged dime to anybody. Alive, he can be made to talk. I've got sense enough to know that I can't keep on dodging Brood Shotwell forever. Some way or other, I've got to clear myself, according to law. If I can prove that some member of that jury . . . Toad Black, for instance . . . was approached by Leek Jaeger or Frank Cutts and was paid or bribed to vote me guilty, then the whole trial can be thrown out and I can get a new shake. But I can't go on dragging Black around with me, not while I'm on the dodge. I've got to leave him somewhere in safe keeping. How about it, Bill? Can you take care of him for me?"

It was Bones Baker who answered. "You bet. Bring him in, cowboy. I'll keep him in my spud cellar. How about it, boss?"

Bill Morgan grinned and nodded. "Think you can handle him, Bones?"

"Handle him?" snorted Bones. "Wait and see. He tries getting ructious with me and I'll pin his ears back five times a day. I'd enjoy currying that *hombre* down with a pick handle."

Bill Morgan went out with Buck to bring in the horses and Toad Black. Bones swore in sublime amazement as he viewed Black's face. "Holy hen hawks!" he exploded. "You must've had a rock in each fist, Buck."

"It's a wonder I didn't bust my hands all to hell and gone," admitted Buck. "He was tough. He took a lot of slapping before he went down. OK, Bones. He's all yours."

Bones pulled his big six-shooter out of his blankets. "Starting now," he proclaimed, "one Toad Black disappears from the world of men. March, you pug-ugly blister, and do exactly as you're told. Else you'll think all hell and half of purgatory is crawling up your frame."

VI

Jean Harper knew a sense of relief when she got back to the J Bar C ranch house and found that Jaeger and Cutts had not yet returned from town. There were several of the J Bar C cowpunchers down around the corrals, but she managed to keep her left side toward them, so they would not see that her right arm was bare, that a sleeve had been torn from her silk blouse. She did not stop at the corrals to leave her pinto; she knew someone would take care of the animal even if she left it in front of the ranch house. She could not afford to have questions asked as to what had happened and why her blouse was torn that way. Hence her relief on finding the ranch house empty as she hurried to the room that had been given her by Leek Jaeger. There she stripped off the offending blouse, wadded it up, and thrust it into a far corner of one of her traveling bags. She took a cold bath, and viewed with shudders of repugnance the darkening bruises on the soft flesh of her arms and shoulders where the craving fingers of Toad Black had touched.

Yet, right after this wave of repugnance, came a warm and truant thrill. She was thinking of Buck Comstock, of the flaming, thrilling ferocity of him as he had beaten down Toad Black. She could hardly understand this thrill. By all rights, she should fear Buck Comstock—fear and hate and despise him. He had killed her uncle, Ben Sloan. He admitted that. He had been judged guilty by a jury and had been sentenced to twenty-five years in a penitentiary. But he had broken jail, and was a hunted man now, an outlaw.

In the world in which Jean Harper had lived, all these things would put a man so far beyond the pale that no decent person would give him a kind thought. This, however, was a different world, out here in the far-flung cattle country. It was a different world entirely, where men and their acts were gauged and measured by another set of standards. Out here, apparently, if a man killed another in self-defense, it left no stain upon him. Dimly, for there was still much for her to learn and unlearn about this Western world, Jean Harper could perceive something of the spirit and elemental reasoning of the cattle country. Already it was affecting her, opening her eyes, widening her perceptions. In one thing, of course, there was no difference between the world she had known and this one she now lived in. Men were the same. Some were honest, some dishonest; some good, others bad; some brave, and some cowardly.

It had, Jean Harper decided, taken a lot of courage for Buck Comstock to do what he had done, to disregard his own danger entirely and leap to the aid of an utter stranger. That very act might have cost him his liberty, even his life. But he had not hesitated. Surely no man who would do that could be vicious or unprincipled. Her eyes shone warmly as she pictured those terrible moments. What a literal tiger Buck Comstock had been as he smashed Toad Black into insensibility. She could see him now as he had been just before she left him—the lean, hard, muscular brownness of his clean-cut face and jaw, the alert, cool clearness of his gray eyes, which crinkled at the corners when he smiled.

She wondered now about all those personal things she had told him—a total stranger, met for the first time in her life. Of course, impulse had had something to do with that—impulse born from the emotional hurricane she had been through. Yet there must also have been some instinctive realization of honor and trust in his make-up. It was all very strange and bewildering. At the moment, Jean Harper was not exactly sure that she knew the reason for her confidence in him.

It was after dark when Leek Jaeger and Frank Cutts returned from town. Jaeger was plainly out of sorts, but Cutts, whatever his feelings were, masked them behind that cold, set gambler's face of his.

Jean had already eaten. She came into the room just as the two partners were finishing their meal. At her entrance, Leek Jaeger's head jerked up and his eyes held a real impact as they reached her.

"I understand you took a long ride this afternoon," he growled. "I thought I told you not to."

Jean drew herself up coldly. "As your guest, Mister Jaeger, I fail to understand either your tone or your meaning. Are you trying to say that I am subject to your orders?"

Hot blood rushed to Jaeger's heavy face. It took a very obvious effort on his part to swallow the words that were on his lips and substitute less offensive ones. "I didn't mean that the way it sounded, Miss Harper," he blurted. "Only, you're here as a guest of Frank and me and, naturally, we feel a responsibility for your safety. You don't know the kind of country this is, or the kind of men in it. You shouldn't go on long rides alone."

Frank Cutts nodded. "Leek is right, Miss Harper," he said in his cold, measured tones.

Standing at the edge of the lamp glow at that moment, Jean Harper was a decidedly handsome picture. She had donned a soft, gray dress, a simple thing of flowing lines that brought out the cool, clean slenderness of her. Her dark, erect head was touched with glints of dusted gold by the lamplight, and there was quick color in her cheeks.

Cutts, looking at her, knew a sudden stirring of his pulse. For a brief second the practiced curtain of his eyes was lowered and something from the cold core of the man leered out. "No," he said, his voice less chilly and brittle than before. "We wouldn't want anything to harm you."

"You can rest your fears," said Jean. "I can take care of myself. I rode out to the Wineglass headquarters."

This shot told. Both Jaeger and Cutts stiffened. "Yes?" murmured Cutts.

"Yes," the girl retorted. "And I have decided that I do not care to sell the ranch. Instead, I am going to operate it."

"You!" ejaculated Leek Jaeger. "You operate the Wineglass spread?" He leaned back and laughed. "That's foolishness."

Angry lights danced in Jean Harper's eyes. "Mister Jaeger, I distinctly resent your words and your tone. Anyone would think that you had some kind of authority over me. You haven't. None. You make it impossible for me to remain in this house any longer. The first thing in the morning I am removing to town, to the hotel."

She turned then and swept out of the room. In the distance of the house, the room to her door closed emphatically.

Frank Cutts looked at Leek Jaeger in swift anger and disgust. "Sometimes I wonder how in hell you ever got as far in the world as you have, Leek. You got brains, but there's times when any man would doubt it. You sure made a mess of that."

"I don't see it," objected Jaeger. "I only. . . ."

Cutts spread his hands in exaggerated weariness. "You never admit you're wrong. But you've been wrong in a couple of ways, lately. The first blunder was in trying to proposition Buck Comstock that night in jail. You spread our hand right in front of him, showed him every card. Comstock is no fool. That's another mistake you always make. You think nobody can see through your deals but yourself. But Comstock did. He made a desperate play at a getaway as soon as you had spread your sign. He got away. And he's got friends, powerful friends. You can bet he's seen some of them, talked with them. Why have Morgan and Frazier and Tharp all sent out calls for extra riders? They're not branding or rounding up. I know the answer, and so do you. And it's your fault."

"All right. All right," snarled Jaeger. "Let it go at that. I dragged my rope on that play. But this damned girl. . . ."

"You've made her mad. Once she leaves this house, there'll be a lot of other people talking to her. Maybe some of Comstock's friends will talk with her. Maybe they have already, seeing that she's decided she doesn't want to sell the Wineglass. What's the answer?"

"I'll bite," said Jaeger. "What is it?"

Cutts stood up, took a turn about the room. "All my life I've gambled," he said. "I never dodged the stakes, no matter how high they went. And whenever I picked up a hand and decided to back it, I backed it to the limit. I'm backing this hand we hold. I'm going to play it to the limit. I'll bet as long as my chips last. And then I'll bluff. In other words, the thing we've worked and planned to do is going to be done. Possession of the Wineglass is vital. We've got to have it. That girl has got to change her mind. She's going to change her mind."

"That won't be as easy as it sounds," Jaeger said. "She ain't got that haughty chin for nothing. And she'll be leaving us in the morning."

"No, she won't," said Cutts softly.

Jaeger jerked his head up, staring at Cutts. "Go on," he purred.

Cutts spoke in low, swift tones. When he had finished, Leek Jaeger sat motionlessly, his heavy features set, his little, leaden eyes staring and unwinking. Presently he cleared his throat with a harsh, rasping sound. "That will mean all of our chips go on one hand," he said thickly. "Hell will split wide open if there's any kind of a slip."

"There won't be any slip," said Cutts. "Not if you'll keep your mouth shut and let me handle this. No man ever made a plan work if he stopped halfway. And no plan ever works as smooth as it first figures out. But we still hold high cards if we got nerve to back 'em all the way."

Jaeger nodded abruptly. "Fair enough. I'll go you."

A minute later a knock sounded on the door of Jean Harper's room. "This is Cutts, Miss Harper. Could Mister Jaeger and I see you for another minute? Leek is sorry he spoke as he did, and we have another proposition to make you on your ranch."

Jean was of two minds for a moment. Somehow her distrust of the two men had grown tremendously since her meeting with Buck Comstock. At the same time, anything additional that she might learn of their scheming might prove useful later. There could be no harm in listening to what they had to propose. She opened the door.

"Very well," she said. "But I want no more insults from Jaeger."

"There'll be none," promised Cutts.

He walked beside her, and somehow it came to Jean that there was something of the prowl of a jungle animal in the stride of Frank Cutts. At the door of the dining room, he stepped aside to let her enter.

There was Leek Jaeger, holding a colorful Navajo blanket in his hands, examining some of the figuration. As she entered, Jaeger looked up with what was plainly meant for a placating grin. He held the blanket out to her.

"Here's a peace offering, Miss Harper," he said. "Please accept it with my compliments."

Jean, a trifle taken aback, was nonplussed for a moment. She hesitated, then stepped forward, her hands outstretched. "Thank you, Mister Jaeger. This is kind of you."

At that moment, with a move that was lightning fast for one of his bulk, Leek Jaeger threw the blanket over her head. From behind, the arms of Frank Cutts dropped about her, tightening like steel bands. A moment later, blinded, half smothered in the folds of the blanket, Jean Harper was helpless, arms and ankles tightly bound, the blanket pulled tightly against her mouth to stifle any outcry.

VII

For three days, Buck Comstock passed no word with any human being. He spent most of his time well back in the vast shelter of Big Sage Desert. He never camped twice in the same place. Each tiny fire he built for cooking spread its ashes where no ashes had lain before; each time Buck lay down to sleep his blankets covered ground never touched by blankets before. Long hours each day he spent with a pair of binoculars, which had been given him by Bill Morgan, studying the surrounding country, alert for every foreign movement or sign of riders. Twice he saw riders, and each time, leading them, was a man on a big, white horse. Buck knew that horse. It belonged to Brood Shotwell.

Shotwell was a stubborn, tenacious manhunter, but now he was up against a fugitive who knew every corner of his territory, who took genuine pleasure in laying false trails and blotting out the real ones. At no time did Shotwell come even close to finding Buck.

Out there in the desert, Buck had plenty of time for thought. In that solitude and stillness, Buck's concentration became such that he saw the scheme of Jaeger and Cutts with steadily growing clearness, and his conviction as to their ultimate purpose became certain. Not all of his thoughts, however, moved about this one subject. With increasing frequency, Jean Harper intruded into his cogitations. It gave him a strange, warm pleasure to think of her. Again and again, he lived over those momentous minutes after he had heard her scream at the Wineglass ranch house. It seemed that he could feel again the impact of his clenched fists against Toad Black's brutal face and gross body. He felt a savage satisfaction in the knowledge that he had beaten and punished Black. And he remembered Jean

Harper as she had looked, standing there beside him, her hand on his arm, right after Toad Black had gone down to stay.

He could feel the warm seep of blood into his bronzed cheeks as he recalled the truant impulse of that moment. Somehow, he had wanted to take her into his arms, to comfort her and quiet her, much as he would have a frightened, weeping child. But she had recognized him then and drawn away from him, with a look of horror in her eyes. Yet, before she had left him, she had shown remarkable common sense, had viewed the death of Ben Sloan with an open mind, and had seemed to understand the provocation that lay behind the fatal gun play. After that she had talked with him, really confided in him, and had agreed to accept his advice. And when she had left him, it was almost as a friend, agreeing to tell no one that she had met him out there at the Wineglass headquarters.

These memories gave Buck a measure of satisfaction during the lonely hours of his exile. And out of them came an ever growing desire to see and speak to this girl again, this girl with the ebony hair and the enchanting slimness. He must, at least, get some news of her.

So it was that, in the thick, warm dusk of the third day, Buck rode cautiously down upon the Circle Star headquarters. As before, he left his pony well back from the buildings and went in on foot. Abruptly he halted, crouched low and still, there in the darkness. In front of the Circle Star were many horses and men.

Buck's mind raced. Who could they be and what were they here for? Had something happened to Bill Morgan? Or maybe Jaeger and Cutts had already started their invasion of Coyote Valley, and these were the riders of the Coyote Valley ranches gathered to organize for battle. Either way, Buck had to know what it meant. His heart and his interests were bound to Bill Morgan and the rest, and he had to be in on it, too, if it was coming to open range war. Daring decision took hold of him. He circled the house, a noiseless, low-crouched shadow.

Buck knew the Circle Star ranch house. On the blind side of the house he tried two windows, found the second partially open. With slow, steady pressure, he pushed the sash up enough to wriggle through.

Once inside, he pulled off his boots, then felt his way through two rooms. On the far side of the second was a door with lines of yellow light across the top and bottom. Buck crept close to it, pressed his ear to the door, and listened. Voices were speaking beyond that door.

Buck recognized Brood Shotwell's cold, heavy tones: "This range has gone nuts, I tell you, Morgan. First the trouble with Comstock. Now Toad Black has disappeared, complete, and that Harper girl has vanished into thin air. God knows what will happen next. Damned if I'm not beginning to get spooky myself."

Bill Morgan answered him: "Toad Black don't count, Brood. He was only a drifter, anyhow, not worth the powder to blow him to hell. Probably, realizing that he shared responsibility for the damnedest legal farce I ever heard of, or you, either, and fearing that retribution might catch up with him, he just simply hightailed it out of the country."

"You mean that Comstock trial?" challenged the sheriff.

"I mean exactly that. You've grown old and gray, Brood, dealing with the faults and meanness of human beings. You can't look me in the eye and tell me that Buck Comstock got a square shake in that trial."

"My office ain't concerned with that angle of law enforcement," Shotwell said. "I'm not worrying a lot about Toad Black's disappearance. It's the girl that's got me fighting my head."

"That is plenty serious," agreed Morgan. "You can't find a trace of her?"

"Not a trace. According to Jaeger and Cutts, she left the J Bar C first thing Tuesday morning, saying she was going to stay at the hotel in town. Somewhere between the J Bar C and town she just vanished into thin air."

"How did the word get out?"

"Leek Jaeger came into town Wednesday with the idea of having another talk with her about the Wineglass. When he asked for her at the hotel, Joe Lester thought he was crazy. Jaeger insisted she'd left the J Bar C Tuesday morning, saying she was going to stay at the hotel. Joe Lester said she hadn't showed up. Then Jaeger came to tell me about it. I've been ramming up and down, back and forth, ever since. I've had posse men riding everywhere. But there ain't a sign of her that we can locate."

"That's bad," said Bill Morgan. "Plenty bad. In this country, we don't bother women. Somebody will get their neck stretched for this."

"You're telling me!" exploded Brood Shotwell. "Listen, Morgan, in running my office I try to play the game as impersonal as possible. I don't show sympathies one way or another. But I don't mind telling the world that right now I'm just an ordinary man who's madder than hell. If I can get my hands on the polecat who ran off with that nice girl, I'll forget all about my star and just take him to pieces with my own bare hands. So far, I've been trying to pick up Buck Comstock's trail. But Comstock can run around plumb loose, for all of me, until I find that girl. There's been some talk made. . . ."

Shotwell broke off, as though reluctant to say anything more, but Bill Morgan gave him no chance. "Go on, Brood. What is this talk?"

"Well," grunted Shotwell, "some folks are hinting that maybe it was Comstock who met up with her and packed her off."

It was Bill Morgan's turn to explode. "I want somebody to

make that crack to me!" he roared. "I'll drive their lying words right back through their teeth with a Forty-Five slug. Don't tell me you're big enough a fool to believe that?"

"I'm not," said Shotwell. "I slapped one jigger down already for telling me that must have happened."

"Who was he?"

"Duke Younger. I'm not exactly soft in the head about Buck Comstock, after the fool he made of me in his getaway, but I've seen too many men shoved all the way to hell by people blaming them for everything that happens after they get into one jam with the law. Buck Comstock might be a smoke-roller, but he's not the sort to harm any woman."

"Brood," said Morgan, "there's been two or three times lately when I was ready to brand you as a knothead. I'm apologizing for the thought."

Shotwell laughed harshly. "Being a sheriff ain't all gravy, Bill. Lots of times you have to do things you ain't no way crazy about. I'm human, same as anybody else, though there's folks who'll try and tell you different. Well, long as you can't help me about that girl, I'll be dragging on."

"I'll pass the word to my crew, Brood. I'll keep 'em riding and looking. Should they stumble across anything at all, I'll see that you're notified *pronto.*"

"Thanks, Bill. That's fair enough."

The tramp of spurred heels sounded heading to the front of the house. Shortly after came the concerted pound of hoofs, vanishing out toward the west.

When Bill Morgan and Bones Baker returned to the room where Bill had talked with Brood Shotwell, they froze in amazement. There, sitting in a chair, was Buck Comstock.

"W-where in hell," stuttered Bones, "did you come from?"

Buck jerked his head. "In there. I heard what Shotwell had to say about the disappearance of Miss Harper. Bill, why the devil didn't you go into town Tuesday like I told you to? Then you'd have found she hadn't showed up. And whoever ran off with her wouldn't have had a day's start?"

Buck was bleak of eye, his face grim and forbidding.

"I did go in, Buck," replied Morgan quietly. "I spent all of Tuesday morning in town, waiting for her. When she didn't show, I figured maybe she had changed her mind about leaving the J Bar C . . . at least, leaving it right away. I came home then, not giving it more than a second thought."

"Sorry, Bill," said Buck. "Only, that news . . . sort of knocked me for a loop. That's bad, Bill . . . her disappearance. There's only one answer."

"Jaeger and Cutts, you mean?"

"Exactly. She must have told them that if they wanted the Wineglass, they'd have to jump their price. She might have told them she didn't care to sell, that she intended to keep the spread. I wouldn't put it past either of those polecats to have locked her up somewhere to try and make her sign the Wineglass over to them."

"I can see the possibility, all right," said Morgan.

"One more thing, Bill. So far, we've been waiting for Jaeger and Cutts to make the first break. We've been set for a counter-punch, you might say. It ain't getting us anywhere. What do you say we walk in swinging?"

"If you can pick out a decent angle of attack, I'm willing."

"Good enough. Bones, you still got Toad Black?"

"Yup," said Bones. "I got him. He made one try to break loose, so I whapped him with a frying pan. He's a good dog now. He gets right down on his shins and starts praying when he sees Bones coming down into the spud cellar."

"You hang onto him. Bill, you and me are heading for town."

"Now?"

"Now. Duke Younger will be hanging around there, most

likely, lapping up liquor. I want him. I'm going to get him. Then I'm going to make him and Toad Black talk. If I have to, I'll burn the truth out of them with hot branding irons. I'm tired of dodging and ducking and hiding out. Long as it was only myself to consider, I didn't mind it so much. But now those damned rats are fighting Jean Harper. And I'm going to get to the bottom of this thing and find that girl. I'm not going to sit back and let time tell the story. I'm going to jam the truth right out into the open. Coming with me, Bill?"

In answer, Bill Morgan lifted his gun belts down from a wall peg and buckled them on.

It was 9:00 p.m. when Buck Comstock and Bill Morgan rode up to the outskirts of Twin Buttes. They reined in, just short of town.

"You ease around and leave your bronco out back of the hotel, Buck," said Morgan. "I'll go straight in and locate Younger. When I've found where he is, I'll meet you in the alley between the hotel and Pete Allen's store. Then we can figure how to get hold of him."

Morgan had no trouble in locating Younger. He was standing at the far end of the bar in the Yellow Horse Saloon. Drinking with him were Leek Jaeger and a man who was a stranger to Morgan. This third man was of average height, compact and wiry of build. A long, livid scar ran across the left side of his face, reminder of a wound that must have been deep enough to shatter the bones of his jaw—for the lower half of his face was queerly drawn and puckered, giving a pointed, rodent suggestion to his mouth. When he spoke, his words carried a strange, whistling sibilance. He was dressed in average range togs, but he carried two big guns, slung low and tied down. Something in the way he stood and moved told Morgan the story. Here was a gunman, if he had ever seen one.

Morgan edged up to the bar, spoke or nodded to various acquaintances, ordered and downed a short whiskey. He let his eyes play along the bar and saw that Jaeger and his two companions were looking at him.

Jaeger called along the bar in affected friendliness: "Come and have one on me, Bill! I want you to meet a friend of mine."

Morgan elbowed his way over to the three. "Four whiskies!" Jaeger called to the bartender. "Bill, meet Whistler Hahn. I reckon you've heard of him. Whistler, this is Bill Morgan."

Bill Morgan had heard of Whistler Hahn, all right. Few men in that section of the country hadn't. Whistler Hahn was proof to the old adage that a bad reputation travels farther than a good one.

Morgan shook hands with him. "Glad to know you, Hahn."

They downed their drinks. "What do you think about the disappearance of Miss Harper, Bill?" asked Jaeger.

"I don't know what to think." Morgan shrugged. "I can't understand why any man would be low enough to run off with a girl like that."

Duke Younger smirked crudely. "Me, I only saw her once. That was across the courtroom. But I must say it would be a lot easier for a man to run off with her than with a lot of battle-axes I've seen. She sorta warmed a man's eye." He brayed with laughter at his own idea of humor. Duke Younger was tall and lank, with high, narrow shoulders. His face was long and horsey, with loose lips and a looser chin. His eyes were pale and evasive.

"I still say," drawled Morgan quietly, "that any man who would run off with a helpless girl like that is about fifty degrees lower than a rattlesnake. I can understand men fighting men, but when they start fighting women, they cease to be men."

It seemed to Bill Morgan that Leek Jaeger's bull neck was just a trifle redder than usual.

Jaeger switched the subject glibly. "I hear you're building up your crew, Bill. If you could use another man, here's one." He jerked his head at Duke Younger. "Duke just hit me for a job, but I told him I was full up. Then you came in, so the idea occurred to me that you might use him."

"That's right," said Younger. "How about it, Bill? I can't live on my income forever." Again he brayed with laughter.

Bill Morgan managed to curtain the distaste that he felt for this fellow. "I might use you at that, Duke. I came into town tonight to see Charley Fournier, who had kinda half promised he'd sign on with me. If he does, I'll be full up. If he doesn't, you can have the job, Duke. Stay here for a while. I'll let you know."

When Bill Morgan left the Yellow Horse, he went down the street, cut across and back to Pete Allen's store. Here he paused for a moment, building a cigarette, his eyes busy up and down the street. Then, with a few quick strides, he had ducked into the alley between the store and the hotel.

"Any luck, Bill?" came Buck Comstock's voice.

"Best in the world." Morgan chuckled. He told swiftly of meeting Jaeger and the other two in the Yellow Horse, and of Younger's request for a job. "Does it make sense to you, Buck?" he ended.

"Plenty," was the terse reply. "Younger is Jaeger's man. Always has been. Jaeger wants a spy in our camp, Bill. And he's trying this trick to get one. You're hiring Younger, of course?"

"Sure. Just long enough to get him out to the ranch, where I'll jam a gun in his ribs and send him to help Toad Black hold down the spud cellar."

"You do that, Bill. And I'll be out there waiting for you. So Jaeger has brought in Whistler Hahn, eh? The tide is building up, Bill. One of these days the dam is going to bust wide open and there'll be hell and sudden death spread all over this range. Well, you go get Younger, and I'll drift out to the Circle Star.

See you later."

Bill Morgan headed again for the Yellow Horse, while Buck slid cautiously back along the alley and out into the open beyond. He crossed to where he had left his bronco. He picked up the reins, threaded them about the animal's neck, and reached for the stirrup.

There was the faintest of sounds behind him. Then a hard object was jammed against his spine and a cold voice reached him—Brood Shotwell's voice.

"Too bad, Buck. But reach high. You shouldn't have been fool enough to come this close to town."

VIII

The surprise and swiftness of the attack by Leek Jaeger and Frank Cutts left Jean Harper dazed, almost stupefied. Before she could even think of struggling or putting up a fight, she had been overpowered, tied hand and foot, and any outcry she might hope to make had been effectually stifled by the blanket about her head and shoulders.

She lay on the floor, a slim, helpless bundle, trying to gather her wits and hang on to the little thread of courage still in her. What was the meaning of this? What plan had these two treacherous, cowardly brutes? She could feel the wavering madness of hysteria tugging at her throat. It strained at her lips, and those lips parted. But the scream was never uttered. Somewhere in her being, a whisper of courage reached out and strengthened her jangled senses. That whisper grew until it was a live current. It cooled the fire of dread in her. And she relaxed, the slim lines of her body softening. Muffled though her head was in the blanket, she could hear Jaeger and Cutts talking.

"Go get the horses, Leek," said Cutts. "I'll keep watch here. And if any of those 'punchers down at the bunkhouse ask questions, pass it off that we're riding to town with the girl. They might not care if they did know the truth, but you never can tell. Some of them might talk. Hurry up."

Jean heard Jaeger departing. A door slammed shut. Momentary silence settled. Then Cutts stepped close to her. "If you play the game and do as you're told, you won't be hurt," he said. "But if you get obstreperous, you'll be calmed down in a hurry."

She heard him leave the room. For a moment the wild thought of escape came to her. It left as soon as it came. Those bonds about her wrists and ankles were drawn cruelly tight. Soon Cutts came back, and she could tell that he was anxious and restless, for he paced the floor nervously, back and forth, back and forth. Jean heard a match snap as he lighted a cigarette. Then, even through the blanket, she could smell the tobacco smoke.

A distant door slammed again and footsteps echoed. Then came Jaeger's voice, exultant: "Couple of heavy poker games going on down at the bunkhouse. Nobody is interested in what we do. I don't believe they even heard me get the horses. Everything set? Come on then. You grab her feet."

Hands settled on Jean's ankles, under her armpits. She was lifted and carried, her body swaying as the two men walked. A current of cool air touched her hands and wrists, and she knew she was out of the house. She heard a horse stamp and snort gustily. She was lowered to the ground. Someone was fumbling at the rope about her ankles.

Then came the voice of Cutts again, smooth and suave, but deadly cold: "You're going to be put on a horse, tied in the saddle. You haven't a chance of getting away. Use an ounce of common sense and you'll be all right."

Her ankles were freed and she was lifted into a saddle. Her ankles were tied once more, this time to the cinch rings. Then the horse beneath her began to move.

Jean had no idea where that long ride took her. There were various turnings and twistings, which, if intended to muddle her so she would have no idea of her destination, were entirely unnecessary. In time, her wrists and ankles became numb. Her back ached, her shoulders cramped. But courage held her in full and comforting grip now. Defiance lay in her heart. She'd show these two renegades that even a lone, helpless girl could not be bluffed or bulldozed.

The ride came to an end at last. The horses were pulled to a halt.

"I'll go on ahead, Leek," said Cutts. "I can wield the verbal whip better than you can. He may kick over this some, but I pack enough guns to make him knuckle. I'll be back as soon as I can."

Another wait ensued. Somewhere in the far distance a coyote wailed to the stars. The horses shifted and stamped restlessly about and Leek Jaeger quieted them with harsh, tense tones.

Finally Cutts came back. "Everything is set," he explained. "And there is just the set-up we want. We'll leave the horses here. Help me get her off."

Ankles freed once more, Jean was lifted to the ground. Her feet felt dead from stricture; she would have fallen if the two men had not supported her, one on either side. Half carried, half dragged, Jean was taken forward.

A low voice hailed out of the darkness, a whining, crusty voice. Cutts answered.

Jean's feet stumbled over a threshold. Board floor was under her now. She knew she was beneath a roof again. She was crowded through two more doorways. Then her knees struck the edge of a bunk. She was pushed down upon it.

"Behave yourself and I'll take that blanket off you and free your wrists," said Frank Cutts.

The door was shut. The blanket was lifted away, and in

another moment her wrists were free. Jean lay as she was, looking about her. The room was not over ten feet square, barren and empty except for the bunk on which she lay and a couple of old, rawhide-backed chairs. Leek Jaeger stood with his back against the closed door. Frank Cutts stood beside the bunk. He smiled, only with his eyes and without the slightest mirth. Cold purpose and rampant cruelty were in that smile.

"I don't suppose," he drawled, "that you have the least idea where you are, Miss Harper. That is as it should be, of course. I can tell you one thing. Here you'll stay until you decide you're willing to listen to reason."

Jean lifted herself on one elbow. Her dark eyes flayed both of the men with scorn; her red lips curled in contempt. "If by reason, you mean listening to you two scoundrels offer to buy or steal my ranch," she said, "then I'll be in this room the rest of my life. What a fine pair of cowardly, lying, underhanded curs you are."

This outburst startled the two men. Plainly they had thought that they would have only a frightened, cowering girl to deal with, one who would be only too glad to bargain for her freedom. Instead, they quailed under the scorn of a regal, flaming-eyed beauty.

Leek Jaeger would not meet her eyes, but looked here and there, while shifting uneasily about on clumsy feet. Cutts was the first to recover. And for the first time, the cold mask of his face broke in a sudden spasm of anger. Right then Jean Harper knew that of the two, Frank Cutts, immaculate dresser and ex-gambler, was by far the more dangerous of the two.

"Have your say, you little fool," he grated. "We'll let you cool your heels in here for a day or two. If that doesn't bring you to your senses, we'll try sterner methods. All right, Leek, take that lamp."

They backed out of the door, and the portal closed, leaving

Jean in utter, Stygian blackness. She heard the click of a padlock. Steps moved away. Silence settled in. Then, and only then, did Jean turn downward on the blankets, bury her head in her arms, and give way to her feelings.

It must have been half an hour later that she sat up, mopped her eyes dry with the backs of her hands. Those tears had done her a lot of good. Her head seemed clear now. She settled back for a period of thought. There was no use in being stampeded by this set-up. Reason told her why she had been carried off in this manner. Jaeger and Cutts wanted the Wineglass Ranch and seemed ready to go to any lengths to get it. Yet, for the moment, she was safe enough. There was only one thing to do and that was be philosophical about it. Jaeger and Cutts could run their bluff only so far.

She got up and moved about the room, feeling her way. In one of the four walls of her cubicle was a window, with the glass broken from the sash in several places. Exploring fingers told Jean that this window had been solidly boarded up from the outside, though the cracks were wide enough to let in the cool, moist breath of the night. She stood there by the window for a time, letting those currents of sweet air play over her face and throat. In the distance she heard a cow bawl plaintively.

Obviously her prison was a ranch house, but just which one it was, or where it might be, Jean had not the slightest idea. She left the window, felt her way to the door, and found that it gave not the slightest when she threw her weight against it. Escape was out of the question.

Jean went back to the bunk and stretched out upon it, staring with wide eyes at the invisible ceiling above. Lying there so still, her nostrils picked up a scent reminiscent of a grocery store, of uncooked bacon and onions, of flour and dried fruit. Her prison, evidently, at one time had been a storeroom for provisions. What chance for rescue did she have? Very little in the immediate present. And strangely enough, at this moment, the figure of Buck Comstock swept into her consciousness. Even there, alone in the dark, a tide of warming blood swept into her cheeks. Why, along with the thought of possible rescue, had she also thought of Buck Comstock?

It was ridiculous. At this moment Buck Comstock was hiding out, a fugitive from justice. He could do nothing toward a rescue, even if he should learn of her disappearance. And, for that matter, why should he bother to risk himself to free her? They had met only once, talked but a little while. They were, to all practical extents and purposes, still virtual strangers. A forlorn loneliness descended upon her. It took a real effort to stay the tears. In the end she slept, though restlessly. Once or twice she moaned a trifle, like an infant plagued with dreams.

She awoke to the realization that someone was in the room with her. A vague half light permeated her prison room. Against the cracks of the boards over the window the bright gold of sunlight lay. Another day had come.

Frank Cutts stood over her. There were dishes on one of the chairs. The rich, heartening aroma of fresh coffee was in the room.

"Your breakfast," said Cutts as he saw her eyes open. "I'll talk with you while you eat."

She was hungry enough. Her slender body was too vigorous and sturdy not to call for sustenance. She got to her feet, stifled a yawn. Somehow, she was not in the least frightened. It must have been the fact that, outside, the sun was shining.

"I haven't the slightest desire to talk with you, Mister Cutts," she said quietly. "I will enjoy my breakfast more if you leave me to myself."

Again the cold mask of Cutts's self-control slid aside. He grabbed her by the arm. "You'll talk . . . or wish that you had," he gritted. "Once and for all, get it out of your head that I'm just bluffing. I've handled your kind before, and I can do it again."

She pulled away from him, drew up the other chair, and began to eat. She ignored Cutts.

But he refused to be ignored. "Get all this," he rasped. "If you know what is good for you, you'll do business with Leek Jaeger and me. We want the Wineglass Ranch. We're going to get it, one way or another. You have one chance to get out of this, with money in your pocket and the right to look other people in the eye. I think you know what I mean."

Jean's eyes were devastating as they flamed at him. "You contemptible rat!"

He laughed then harshly. "Jaeger and I will pay you seven thousand dollars for the Wineglass . . . our final offer . . . and not one cent more."

"If you offered seven million, you couldn't have it. And I can tell you this, Mister Frank Cutts, I haven't been in this range country very long, but there are a few things I've figured out. My disappearance is bound to be noted, sooner or later. Men will search. In the end, they will find me. And no matter what has happened to me, I know what the temper of those men will be. You and your fellow rat, Leek Jaeger, will be hanged."

Cutts stood very still. Jean did not know it, but her last words had hit Frank Cutts at the weakest part of his armor. Once, years before, Cutts had seen a man lynched. He had never forgotten that picture. It had stayed with him with such maddening constancy that at times he had felt that it was prophetic of his own end. The horror of that thought had become a mania with him.

Jean was too busy with her food to notice the tiny beads of cold sweat that grew on the renegade gambler's forehead, or see how sudden pallor swept over his face. Cutts cursed harshly, whirled, and stamped out of the room. The lock clicked behind him.

IX

It seemed to Buck Comstock, as he felt the double impact of Sheriff Brood Shotwell's voice in his ears and the gun against his spine, that a complete panorama of his life spread itself before his eyes. He saw it all, the hard work, the hardship, the danger. He saw its triumphs and despair, its highlights and drab shadows. He saw what he had been through in this present crisis, the vision of freedom and its meaning to himself and to his friends. And he foresaw what the future would be—behind the walls of Pinole.

Buck dropped the reins, let go of the stirrup. His hands began to lift. "All right, Brood," he said wearily. "You got me." Then he whirled, leaping. His right hand lashed out and down. It was the most desperate chance he had ever taken in his life. For no intelligent reason, it worked. That clawing right hand smashed fully upon Shotwell's gun, locked the spurred hammer back. With the same move, his left forearm blocked out, striking the sheriff across the throat like a bar of iron while Buck's left foot was driving in and lifting, cutting Shotwell's feet from under him.

Shotwell went down. Buck twisted the gun from his startled grasp, then dropped on one knee, the gun reversed and pressing against Shotwell's side. "Quiet," Buck murmured. "Sorry, Brood, but I had to pull this. I'm not going to Pinole. You'll bury me first."

Shotwell gagged and choked a bit from that forearm blow across the throat. When he spoke, his voice was quiet and even: "You're only making things worse for yourself, Buck. You can't keep away from me for ever."

"I'm going to try," said Buck harshly. "Damn it, why did you

have to come along now. I've got nothing against you person-
ally. I don't want to hurt you. But if I don't keep you quiet
some way, I won't be ten feet from town before you'll have the
alarm out. And I can't afford to be chased tonight. I've got
business to do."

"That," said Shotwell with a thin, mirthless chuckle, "is your
problem to figure out."

Buck scowled down at the sheriff, and then, in his dilemma,
came a thought that brought him crouching even lower and put
a vibrant eagerness into his voice. "Brood, when you were out
at the Circle Star tonight, talking with Bill Morgan, I was in the
next room, listening. No, Bill didn't know I was there. I'd
sneaked in by a window. But I heard what you said. There's
been several times, Brood . . . particularly in the past month or
two . . . when I doubted you. But by what you said to Bill Morgan out at the ranch tonight, I've decided different. I think,
Brood, you're square, deep down. I'm going to gamble that
way. I want you to ride out to the Circle Star with me now.
There's going to be something out there worth listening to, and
I want a bona-fide witness to hear it. After you've heard that,
I'm going to leave it up to you, what you do with me. If you still
want to bring me in, then I'll come quiet, and you can lock me
up and send me to Pinole. I give you my word on that, Brood."

For a long moment Shotwell was silent. "That," he said
slowly, "don't make sense. But your word is good with me,
Buck. I'll go with you."

Buck caught him by the shoulder, lifted him to his feet.
"Here's your gun, Brood," he said simply. "Go get a bronc'. I'll
meet you on the trail."

Slowly Shotwell holstered his weapon. He was staring queerly
at Buck through the darkness. He nodded. "I'll meet you," he
said.

A few minutes later they were riding swiftly across Timber

Valley, across the sage tableland beyond, and finally down into Coyote Valley to the Circle Star headquarters.

Bones Baker answered Buck's knock. He stared in wordless amazement as Buck and Shotwell walked into the ranch house. He saw that both Shotwell and Buck wore guns. Here were sheriff and fugitive, yet they came in side-by-side in apparent friendliness.

Buck grinned at the look on Bones's face. "Whistle," he said, "before you explode, Bones. Big doings tonight. You still got Toad Black in safe keeping?"

"Y-yup," stuttered Bones. "I-I got him."

"Toad Black!" Shotwell whirled and stared at Buck.

Buck laughed. "That's right, Brood. He's here. I'll produce him in a minute. He's one of the two who are going to speak some of the words I brought you out here to listen to. Think hard, Brood, and you'll begin to get the drift."

Shotwell thought hard, grunted, and said nothing.

Buck went to the outer door, listened a moment, then nodded. "Bill and Duke Younger will be here in a minute. I can hear their bronc's. Brood, you go in that room and shut the door. Just listen. I don't want Black and Younger to know you're around."

Shotwell, frowning and thoughtful, went into the other room and shut the door.

Two minutes later Duke Younger stepped into the ranch house. There was a wild, scared look about him. He had his hands in the air, his gun was gone, and Bill Morgan was herding him unceremoniously along. At sight of Buck, Duke Younger seemed to wilt.

Bill Morgan kicked out a chair with a stern command. "Sit there. And not a move, Younger. Else it will be your hard luck."

Younger sat down and clasped sweating hands on his knees. Buck took off his guns and handed them to the still bewildered

Bones Baker.

"Hold these, Bones. Shut and lock that outer door . . . and bring Toad Black in here."

At the mention of Toad Black, Younger caught his breath in a distinct gasp. A moment later Toad Black shuffled in, looking more uncouth and animal-like than the last time Buck had seen him. Black's eyes went straight to Buck, and a plain glint of fear showed in them.

"Fair enough," drawled Buck. "Bill, you and Bones just listen and look on. Don't interfere. I'll handle this thing. Black!" His voice took on the crackle of ice. "You ready to open up and do some talking?"

Toad Black licked his lips. "Talkin'?" the renegade blurted. "What kind of talkin'? I don't know what you mean."

"Yes, you do. I want the truth about that verdict of guilty that the jury brought in against me. Who fixed that jury?"

Black looked startled, then sulkily stubborn. He shook his head. "I don't know nothin'."

The sound of Buck's right hand, palm flat and open as it struck Black's face, was like a small report. Black staggered back, feeling of his face, an involuntary curse breaking from his lips. Buck followed him, stood with his feet spread, shoulders loose and ready, fists tightening into knots of rawhide.

"You know plenty," Buck lashed. "You know that somebody fixed that jury, gave them instructions to vote me guilty, no matter what the evidence. And you're going to tell us all about it, now! Else the beating I gave you last time will be a picnic to what I'll hand you now. Better believe I mean business, Black. My liberty and my life are at stake. If you think I'm not going to fight for them, you're crazy. I'll beat you down. I'll butcher you with my bare fists . . . but, by God, you're going to talk."

Buck Comstock seemed to have gained in stature as he spoke. The set leanness of his face was so marked that it was ridged, almost sharp of angle. His gray eyes held the raw, cold spark of newly cut steel. An air of savage mercilessness settled over him.

Toad Black's bulging, frog-like eyes moved over Buck, pausing but a breath on Buck's face. He spoke to Bill Morgan. "I'm your prisoner here," he blurted. "You going to stand for this?"

Bill Morgan shrugged. "Buck is playing this hand. And I'm backing him."

Toad Black licked his heavy lips, lips still puffed and bruised from his last set-to with Buck Comstock. A sudden, stubborn, hot rage flared up in him. "I'll see you in hell before I say a word!" he snarled.

Buck wove in. Toad Black threw his left arm up in a gesture of defense and clubbed his right at Buck's face. Buck went in under the blow and slashed a savage fist to Black's body. That punch wrung a gasp of agony from Black. And it seemed to touch off, in one wild explosion, a charge of damned-up dynamite in Buck. He swarmed all over his man, rocking his bullet head back and forth with ripping, merciless fists, switching his attack to Black's body as the renegade's hands went up to shield his bruised face, then battering back at Black's face as the body punishment dragged Black's guard down. Black had tried a few wild blows, none of which seemed to have the slightest effect on the savage man before him. Now he seemed intent only on shielding himself from that merciless barrage of punches, which rocked him and tore him and beat the blood from him.

Bill Morgan and Bones Baker watched the conflict with cold, measuring eyes. Duke Younger watched it, also, but his face grew more pallid and sweating with every blow, and his loose mouth shook and slavered in fright.

Abruptly Toad Black gave up backing away, and charged in—a bull of a man gone berserk. But, instead of swinging his fists, he set himself and kicked out and upward, driving a booted foot at

Buck Comstock. That kick would have crippled Buck and dropped him cold had it landed squarely. But Buck twisted to one side and took the impact on the thigh of his left leg. Even so, he nearly went down, for the blow whirled him completely around and drove him the width of the room. He came up with a crash against the wall. Black, blubbering an animal-like cry, charged after him.

Buck's left leg was almost paralyzed. He staggered out of the line of Black's rush, set himself on his sound leg, and smashed Black a blow to the face that rocked him on his heels. Then Buck became a madman. Half hopping, half dragging his left leg, he went after Black like a fury. His punches became faster, the sounds of his fists upon impact louder. Black began to wobble and stagger. He gave back and back until a wall stayed any farther retreat. There Buck cut him down in an avalanche of blows. Toad Black's knees buckled. He slid toward the floor. On his knees, he wavered for a moment. Then he fell, face downward, gasping and twitching.

Buck turned. His bitter, savage eyes fell on Duke Younger. "You're next," he panted. "I'm not through with that stubborn bastard. Soon as he can stand on his feet, I take up where I left off. Between now and then, I work on you, Younger. Get on your feet, you crooked rat."

But Duke Younger did not stand. He cowered down in his chair, licking his trembling lips. Buck started across the room toward him, steady on his feet now that the paralysis was leaving his left leg. There was something utterly certain, utterly remorseless in that advance of Buck Comstock. It was like the steady onward sweep of a storm cloud, filled with white lightning.

Duke Younger's nerve collapsed. "No!" he gasped. "No! Don't hit me. Don't hit me. I'll talk. That jury was fixed. Every man on it got a hundred dollars, cold cash. I got it. Black got it.

We all got it. The jury was fixed, I tell you."

Bill Morgan gave vent to a long sigh, as though a vast relief had come over him. He whirled on Duke Younger, fixed him with a cold, penetrating eye. "Who fixed that jury?" he demanded. "Who gave you that hundred dollars?"

Younger looked around like a trapped animal. He gulped, licked his lips, and hesitated. Buck Comstock slithered forward, with his flinty fists loose and swinging, his eyes glittering and implacable. "Better talk, Younger," he gritted. "You'll not be given another chance."

Duke Younger caved. "Jaeger," he gulped hoarsely. "Jaeger and Cutts. They bought that jury. They passed out the money. They told us to vote guilty . . . no matter what the evidence."

Buck drew a long breath and turned. Toad Black was up on one elbow, glaring at Younger. Buck stepped over to him.

"That right, Black?" he asked, his voice silky soft with menace. "Is Younger telling the truth?"

Toad Black stared up at Buck through eyes filmed and smeared from the punishment he had undergone. Now that old fear came into them again. It was as though he knew that Buck Comstock would always stand over him like this; that no matter what he did, Buck Comstock would always beat him down, drive him to the floor, a sodden, quivering hulk. He nodded. "Younger's right."

Buck went swiftly to the inner door, flung it wide. "All right, Brood!" he called. "Come on in."

There was a strange look on Brood Shotwell's face as he stepped into the light. A vast, burning contempt flamed in his eyes as he glanced at Toad Black and Duke Younger. His glance went on to Buck. He put out his hand.

"Shake, Buck," he said curtly. "I'm sorry I've been part and parcel to such a rotten deal. From the first, I've suspected something along this line, but I had no way of proving it, nor did I imagine it was as raw as it proves to be. Whether you choose to believe it or not, my intentions had been that after you were safely in Pinole, I was going to do a lot of investigating on my own to bring out proof of the crookedness my better sense told me was in that trial. But I had to make a show of going through with my official duty. I might also add that the night you made a getaway . . . and tonight, in town . . . I could have been a little faster in all ways, if I had tried real hard." A slow, grim smile came over his face.

Buck understood. "I'm apologizing for all the hard thoughts, Brood," he said simply.

"That goes for me, too," murmured Bill Morgan.

"And here," chirruped Bones Baker.

Brood Shotwell's smile broadened, but was wiped swiftly away as he looked once more at Younger and Toad Black. "Can I have these two rats, Buck?"

"They're all yours, Brood." Buck nodded. "I'm done with 'em. I got what I wanted out of them. What do you intend doing with them?"

"First, they go to town and face Judge Henning. They'll tell him exactly what they told us tonight. After that, I'm liable to take a quirt and cut my initials in 'em."

Buck frowned slightly. "Remember what Jaeger told you, Brood, the night I made a break for it? I don't want you to jeopardize your job. And with election three months away. . . ."

Sheriff Brood Shotwell made a short, fierce gesture. "I've been sheriff in this neck of the woods a long time, Buck. I like the job. I'd like to keep it. But if keeping it means I've got to sell out on square-shooting and honesty, I don't want the office. While I wear this star, it's going to be kept free from tarnish. If, three months from now, the Twin Buttes range decides they want a different sheriff, let it be that way. I'll still have some self-respect. And I reckon, in this life, that's the main thing. All right! Black! Younger! Get on your feet. We're traveling."

"Miss Harper?" Buck asked. "Have you found any line on her yet?"

"Not yet. I admit that thing has got me fighting my head. I don't know just what to think," Shotwell admitted.

"She must be somewhere," Buck said gravely. "She couldn't have just vanished into thin air. Why not try searching every ranch house on the Twin Buttes range?"

Shotwell gave Buck a long and searching look. "That," he admitted slowly, "is an idea with possibilities. I was dumb not to think of it myself. Tomorrow I'll have to act on that suggestion."

"One more thing," said Buck. "I can circulate as free as I please now?"

"For all my office will have to say about it," said Shotwell quietly, "you can come and go as you please, Buck. Technically the law would have to clear you first, by due process. We'll forget that, this time. *Adiós,* gentlemen. You . . . Black and Younger . . . march!"

X

Judge Henning, awakened from a sound sleep, was irascible and nervous when he opened his door and was confronted by Sheriff Brood Shotwell and his two cowed and sullen prisoners. At sight of the three men, the judge's eyes popped wide, and then filmed with a queer, almost frightened wariness. Brood Shotwell, watching him closely, did not miss that last expression.

"Sorry to root you out this time of night, Judge," said Shotwell. "But these two buzzards've got something to say that I want you to hear."

"This is no time to bother me with anything of the sort," snapped the judge testily. "I'm weary. I need my sleep. You can bring them around tomorrow, Sheriff."

"I've brought them tonight," said Shotwell decisively. "And you're going to listen to them. You can," he added sarcastically, "sleep late in the morning."

The judge tried to meet the boring impact of Shotwell's glance, but failed. His eyes dropped and he stepped aside. "Very well. Very well," he agreed crustily. "If you insist. But see that it is kept down to essentials. I'm in no mood for lengthy conversation."

Shotwell herded his prisoners in and closed the door. "All right, Younger, speak your piece. If you think you can clam up because Buck Comstock isn't here to work on you, forget it. I'll take on where Buck left off and do equally as good a job."

Judge Henning started. "Did you mention Comstock . . . Buck Comstock? Where is he? Have you found him?"

"We'll come to that later, Judge," said Shotwell dryly. "Speak up, Younger."

Younger shifted his feet nervously, stared at the floor. "W-well, Judge . . . Leek Jaeger and Frank Cutts paid me and Black and the other ten of the jury one hundred simoleons apiece to turn in a guilty verdict against Comstock. But, Judge,"—and here a frantic, pleading note came into his voice—"us boys didn't realize. . . ."

"Shut up!" rasped Shotwell. "Well, Judge, did you get that? Did you hear him say that Jaeger and Cutts bought that jury for twelve hundred dollars, so that Buck Comstock would be convicted and railroaded to Pinole? Now what've you got to say?"

The judge had gone pallid. Sweat was starting on his forehead and his eyes blinked wildly. "W-why, bless . . . gracious me," he stammered. "I-I don't know what to say."

"While you're getting your breath," snapped Shotwell with definite contempt, "listen to Black. All right, Black. Is Younger telling the truth?"

Toad Black, smart enough to know that he was definitely hooked, and viciously intent on dragging everyone else he could into the mess, leered savagely as he nodded. "Sure, he's tellin' the truth. But that ain't news to this bleary-eyed old crane of a judge. He knew that trial was fixed, all the time. He knew the jury was bought. And I been wonderin' how much Jaeger and Cutts paid him to slap twenty-five years on Comstock. Me, I took the money they offered. But it wasn't necessary. I've always hated Buck Comstock's guts. I'd have voted him guilty, anyhow. But don't let that old skunk fool you, Shotwell. He's in this as deep as anyone else. Look at him and you can see I'm right."

"That's a lie!" shrilled the judge. "Why, that leering scoundrel, I'll have him up for contempt. I'll sentence him to Pinole for the rest of his natural life. Why. . . ."

"Save your breath, Judge," advised Shotwell curtly. "You're all through sentencing anybody to anywhere."

Judge Henning sank into a chair, his head in his hands. Confession of his perfidy and knowledge of its enormous effect was written all over him. Sheriff Brood Shotwell's eyes were very, very bleak. He turned to Younger and Black. "You two," he stated, "are traveling. I don't care where, long as it is far enough away. To hold you and prosecute you for perjury would cost too much time and money. So I'm giving you a floater. But get this right. If I ever see either of you within a hundred miles of Twin Buttes, after you walk out that door, I won't arrest you. I'll. . . ." His hands slid to his gun suggestively. "Git!" he barked flatly.

Younger and Black, startled at their release, knowing that Shotwell meant exactly what he said, disappeared into the night.

The sheriff shut the door and turned back to Judge Henning. "Well, Judge," he said coldly, "I guess it's your turn to talk. And I reckon you better talk plenty."

The judge did not look up. He sat there with his head in his hands, hunched shoulders shaking as though with palsy. "They had me under their thumb," he quavered. "I had to do it . . . or they would have made a pauper of me. Every cent I had in the world is tied up. . . ."

"Tied up where?" demanded Brood Shotwell.

The judge shook his head. He seemed almost on the verge of a stroke. He was shuddering and giving vent to gasping, whimpering moans. The man was far gone in the depths of utter cowardice and despair.

Brood Shotwell's eyes glittered with contempt. "Before morning, you'll prepare written authority declaring that past farce was no trial. You'll dismiss the charges against Buck Comstock and you'll give the reasons why. I'll be in to see you tomorrow morning. And I want those papers ready and in order. I'll admit there are a lot of shorthorns in this neck of the woods, but there are a lot of mighty good and square men here, also. If I should let out all the truth about that trial, it might go plenty hard for you, Henning. I'm not calling you Judge. You're not worthy of the name."

At this moment a dark, low-crouched figure stole away from the side of the judge's house, circled a cautious way down to the center of town, and finally slipped into the Yellow Horse Saloon.

When, a minute later, Brood Shotwell stepped out into the night, all was still, except for his horse, which stood, patiently ground-reined, rolling its bit ring now and then. The sheriff took up the reins and walked downtown, leading the horse behind him, heading for the livery barn at the far end of the street. A great weariness, a vast disillusionment lay over Brood Shotwell. In all the years he had been in office, where he had seen the mean, leering, naked souls of wayward men paraded many times, he had never come across such a befouling condition as now faced him. The dignity of the law had always meant much to Brood Shotwell. The manner in which it had been defiled in this case made him almost physically sick.

He put up his horse and went to his room. For a long time he was unable to sleep. In the end, weary nature took its toll. Hours later, not long before dawn, a faint, muffled report echoed dimly through the chill hours. The sound did not awaken Shotwell, although it disturbed him enough to make him turn over and sigh deeply, before sinking back into heavy sleep. A dog barked fitfully, but even that did not rouse the weary sheriff.

Shotwell was up and about again at sunrise. He was grim of face and eye. His nod was curt to the greetings of several townspeople he met on the street. He saw the Widow Jenkins, who eked out a meager living for herself and her three children by doing odd jobs of housework about the town, hurrying on her way to Judge Henning's cottage, where, three times a week, she cleaned and scrubbed. Shotwell thought of Judge Henning as he had last seen him, the night before, a hunched, palsied wretch, stammering out the admission that he had defamed his high office. That picture had been with Shotwell all night long, and it was not a pretty one.

Spike St. Ives, Shotwell's deputy, came across the street. "What's the job today?" he asked.

"The girl, of course," stated Shotwell. "We've got to find that girl."

"Comstock," said St. Ives meaningfully, "will be getting plumb away if we don't do something about him."

"No matter." Shotwell shrugged. "Right now the important thing is to locate Jean Harper. As far as Comstock is concerned. . . ."

He broke off sharply, for, echoing down the street, came the shrill, high scream of a terrified woman. Whirling toward the sound, Shotwell and St. Ives saw the Widow Jenkins rushing out into the middle of the upper end of the street, tossing her arms and shambling about hysterically.

Shotwell and his deputy raced for the spot. The street behind them filled swiftly with an excited crowd. By the time Shotwell reached the Widow Jenkins, she was on her knees in the dusty street, her apron thrown over her head while she rocked back and forth, moaning. Shotwell caught her by the arms, dragged her to her feet, and shook her.

"What's wrong, ma'am?" he asked. "What scared you?"

Her eyes were rolling, her chin sagging. "The judge," she quavered. "Judge Henning . . . blood. . . ."

Shotwell turned to St. Ives. "Take care of her." Then he darted across to the judge's cottage and leaped through the open door. He stopped, dead still.

In one corner of the room was a small desk and chair. In a crumpled heap beside the chair lay Judge Henning. A dark pool of blood had formed under his prone head. It took but a moment to find out two things. The judge was stone dead—and had been for hours. He had been shot through the head. Scattered papers, all of them blank, lay on the floor. A bottle of ink had overturned on the desk and spread its crooked, black stain. Some of the ink had run down the slant of the desk top and dripped onto the floor.

Sheriff Shotwell turned slowly to the door, where men were crowding through. "Get out, boys," he insisted harshly. "This is a job for the coroner. Somebody has shot Judge Henning. Send the word to Doc Pollard."

Two hours later Shotwell and St. Ives mounted horses in front of the livery barn and rode out of Twin Buttes. They rode alone, taking no posse with them. Two miles from town they met up with Leek Jaeger, Frank Cutts, and Whistler Hahn, heading for town at more than a leisurely pace. The three men pulled their mounts to a rearing halt in the middle of the trail.

"What's this about Judge Henning being shot?" demanded Jaeger. "Any truth to it?"

Shotwell nodded. "He's dead. Somebody killed him late last night. Doc Pollard said he'd been dead for hours when the Widow Jenkins, who did housework for the judge, found the body this morning."

"But who in hell would have wanted to plug Judge Henning?" blurted out Jaeger.

"I'm trying to figure that out myself," said Shotwell quietly. "At present, all I know is that somebody did."

"More than one criminal the judge has sentenced has had it in for him," said Frank Cutts coldly.

Leek Jaeger jerked around in his saddle. "By hell!" he exclaimed. "I'll bet that's the answer."

"What is?" rasped Shotwell.

"Comstock . . . Buck Comstock. He'd be feeling that way toward Judge Henning. I tell you, Shotwell, you better. . . ."

Shotwell cut him short with a curt laugh. "Suppose we lay off that kind of talk, Jaeger, until we know. You seem to me to be a little too ready in your accusations against Buck Comstock. You've made talk Comstock was the one who ran off with Jean Harper. Now you got him murdering Judge Henning. And you backed the charge of him murdering Ben Sloan. Better go slow, or some of those accusations will have a kick-back, and a damned hard one at that."

Quick anger twisted the face of Leek Jaeger. "Do I have to remind you again, Shotwell, that election is only three months off?"

"No!" snapped Shotwell. "You don't. But I'm telling you this much. No matter what happens at that election, for the next three months I'm going to be sheriff . . . all the way."

Jaeger would have made another retort, but Frank Cutts threw up his hand. "Shut up, Leek. You had that call-down coming. Shotwell's doing all right. You got any line on Comstock, Brood?"

"I might have," said the sheriff, looking Cutts hard in the eye. "I may locate him today. You'll hear about it if I do. Come on, Spike. We've got work to do."

Brood Shotwell rode south for the entire length of Timber Valley, with Spike St. Ives jogging silently along at his elbow. Shotwell was grimly thoughtful. St. Ives rode with his lank figure in a crouching slouch, his narrow face inscrutable and expressionless. Not for several miles did St. Ives speak. Then he stirred restlessly.

"Just where the hell are we headin', Brood?" he asked.

"I want to check up on something concerning the disappearance of Jean Harper," answered Shotwell. "Something is rotten around this range, Spike. Something smells to high heaven. And I think the answer to the whole mess will come when we locate Jean Harper and have a chance to talk with her. So . . . I'm going to run down a little idea this morning."

St. Ives shrugged, said nothing more, and built a cigarette.

Now Shotwell reined to the east. They left Timber Valley and crossed the barren sage land beyond, to come down into the southernmost reaches of Coyote Valley. Out there, dead ahead, stood the headquarters of the Stirrup Cross. Spike St. Ives stirred in his saddle again.

"Hell! You don't think Old Man Addis knows anything about the disappearance of the girl, do you?"

Shotwell shrugged. "All I'm thinking is that I ain't been figuring deep enough or in the right line. But I'm starting to now."

They came down in front of the Stirrup Cross ranch house, and Old Man Addis came out to meet them. Addis looked seedy, worried. His manner and voice were querulous. "What brings you down here this morning, Shotwell?" he inquired. In the words and the tone was a vast uneasiness.

Brood Shotwell's eyes narrowed as he dismounted. "I'm looking for Jean Harper, Addis," he said. "I got to thinking that she might be hid out in one of the ranch houses somewhere on the Twin Buttes range. So I'm going to search 'em all. I'm starting with this ranch house."

Addis went white as a sheet. He began to shake. "I-I didn't want them to bring her here," he pleaded. "I told them not to. But damn 'em, they did. I'm not party to this thing, Shotwell. I couldn't help myself. I knew this would happen."

He began wringing his hands in a manner which reminded Shotwell of how Judge Henning had caved. How far did this cesspool of deceit and corruption reach? Who next would he find to be another tool of greed and fear? Shotwell wondered. "We've found the answer to one of our problems, Spike," he said over his shoulder. "Come on. Get out of your saddle and help me search this ranch house."

Instead of obeying, Spike St. Ives whipped out a gun. Coldly he leveled it—at Sheriff Brood Shotwell—and pulled the trigger. Shotwell staggered, coughed, and went down. Even as the sheriff struck the ground, a rifle snarled wickedly from the head of the low slope above the ranch house. Brood Shotwell, his senses blurred and fading, managed by terrific effort to pull himself up on one elbow. Through the darkness that was closing in across his eyes, he could dimly see a compact group of riders, lashing down the slope and he could hear the mutter of speeding hoofs.

XI

When Sheriff Brood Shotwell rode away toward Twin Buttes with Duke Younger and Toad Black, Buck Comstock closed the door of the Circle Star ranch house and turned to Bill Morgan and Bones Baker, with a grim smile on his lips. He began rubbing his thigh where Toad Black's treacherous kick had landed.

"Well," he drawled, "it worked. I knew that one of those two would cave. Younger always was a yellow dog. And when he spilled it, Black saw there was no use playing the clam. Bill, I'm a free man. Do you realize what that means?"

"I realize plenty, kid," said Bill heartily. "Shake. Bones, you generally have a bottle hid out. Go get it. We're going to celebrate this with a drink."

"I'll bring two bottles," vowed Bones enthusiastically. "Me, I feel like going on a binge. Buck, I'm shore tickled pink over this. Sit down and rest that laig of yours where Black kicked you. Dog-gone his crooked soul, I wish I'd batted him a little harder with my frying pan the other day."

Bones got his bottle and they had their drink of celebration. "Getting Brood off your trail doesn't mean you're plumb clear of trouble, Buck," said Morgan. "Jaeger and Cutts will be after your scalp. Don't forget that."

"And I'll be after theirs," Buck answered quietly. "The picture grows clearer and clearer all the time, Bill. We've got those skunks in the open now. And we know for certain what they're after. I'd bet a leg that they're behind the disappearance of Jean Harper."

"Shouldn't wonder," concurred Morgan. "They seem to be in back of every other piece of dirty work. I'd give a lot to know what became of that girl."

Buck's jaw stole out. "The first thing I intend to do is to run that trail down. For all we know, she may be hid out somewhere in the J Bar C ranch house, or in some other ranch on this range. She's around here somewhere. I feel it, somehow."

"Common sense narrows the whole thing down pretty well," observed Bill Morgan dryly. "We know she's not in this house. And we know she wouldn't be at the Rafter T or Lazy F. Bud Tharp and Johnny Frazier don't shape up that way, Buck."

"Hell," said Buck, "I know that. But I'm going to have a

good look at the Wineglass again, and they might even have brass enough to hold her down in my cabin. Anyway, I'm sure going to look around."

"How come you didn't mention the Stirrup Cross?" put in Bones Baker. "There's a ranch house down there, you know. Or don't you figure Old Man Addis would . . . ?"

Buck snorted contemptuously. "Old Man Addis is a cantankerous old pelican, but he wouldn't. . . ."

Bill Morgan jumped to his feet, took a quick turn up and down the room. "Wait a minute. Wait a minute," he rumbled. "That reminds me. Buck, you remember the night I met you out at Indian Spring? Well, I was pretty careful not to lay a straight trail out there, so I left here in the middle of the afternoon and rode kind of here and there and yonder to mix up my sign. About sundown I poked into the Stirrup Cross. Jaeger and Cutts were there, talking to Tom Addis. None of the three of them seemed overjoyed at sight of me, and Jaeger and I got in a little word fuss over you. Funny part of it was, Addis sided with those other two polecats. At the time, it struck me as powerful funny, but afterward I forgot it. But now," he added meaningfully, stopping his pacing and staring at Buck shrewdly, "if you're going to search ranch houses, I wouldn't overlook the Stirrup Cross."

Buck's eyes gleamed. "Keno. We'll have a little look through the Stirrup Cross. And then we'll tackle the J Bar C."

Morgan nodded slowly. "That last listens like quite a chore, Buck. It'll take more than a couple of men to put that over."

"I reckon maybe Bud Tharp and Johnny Frazier might be interested," said Buck. "That will make four of us."

"We'll take along some of the crews, too," said Morgan. "A dozen of us won't look too many when we hit the J Bar C. You get a good night's sleep in a real bunk tonight. We'll get under way first thing tomorrow morning."

The following morning, with Bill Morgan and two of the Circle Star crew, Buck rode south to the Rafter T, where they put their plan before Bud Tharp. Bud, short and broad, was explosively happy over Buck's exoneration by Brood Shotwell.

"Brood is square," he said. "Most likely, he's beginning to see through a lot of crooked stuff. Shore, I'll go along with you boys. And I'll throw a couple more 'punchers into the gang."

At the Lazy F they met with a similar welcome. Johnny Frazier, tall and keen-eyed, with a soft, lazy drawl, showed enthusiasm for the scheme. "Even," he said, "if we don't draw a lick of luck, it'll be a lot of satisfaction in showing Jaeger and Cutts that we got suspicions which we ain't afraid to back up. Me, I'm going to enjoy this."

When they left the Lazy F, they had mustered ten men. Buck, leading the pack, set a steady pace for the Stirrup Cross. Just short of the crest of the low slope above the ranch house, Buck went on alone to look over the scene. Immediately he saw and identified Brood Shotwell and Spike St. Ives, riding down on the ranch headquarters from the west. Neither Shotwell nor St. Ives saw Buck, apparently being intent on the ranch buildings. Buck turned and waved up the rest of his party.

"I guess Brood is out to do a little searching on his own, Bill," he said. "Remember, I suggested it to him last night."

"Yeah," affirmed Morgan. "Looks like we had our ride down here for nothing. Brood can take care of this joint, all right."

"Wait a minute," advised Buck. "I'm interested enough in this to find out what Brood learns."

They saw Shotwell and St. Ives draw up at the ranch house and Tom Addis come out to talk with them. They saw Brood Shotwell dismount, say something more to Addis, then speak to

St. Ives over his shoulder. And then they saw the treacherous deputy drag a gun and shoot Brood Shotwell down.

Bud Tharp, who had been carrying his Winchester across the saddle in front of him, reacted with automatic and bewildering speed. Even before the first cough of report had died from St. Ives's gun, Bud had tossed up his rifle and it spat its challenge. St. Ives went down like a pole-axed calf.

"The damned, rotten dog!" Bud cried. "He shot Brood in the back!"

The next second the entire group of riders was spurring down the slope. Buck, his heart cold with dread and fury, rode in the van, with his eyes fixed on Brood Shotwell. He saw the sheriff pull himself up on one elbow, then collapse again. A moment later Buck was out of the saddle and on his knees beside the sheriff.

Shotwell was unconscious now, but not dead. He was wickedly wounded. The bullet from St. Ives's gun, striking him just below and to the back of the right shoulder, had ranged downward.

Johnny Frazier, helping Buck, swore softly and shook his head as he saw the wound. "Looks bad," he opined. "Damned bad. Brood ain't as young as he used to be."

"We got to do all we can," gritted Buck. "That damned, treacherous rat of a Saint Ives, to shoot a man like Brood Shotwell in the back . . . a man who had worked with him, paid him wages, trusted him. Did Bud make a center shot on Saint Ives?"

"Plenty, I'd say," said Frazier. "Bud saved us the chore of swinging him. He's dead."

Bill Morgan pushed Buck aside, dropping on his knees beside the wounded sheriff. "I'll take care of Brood," he rumbled. "You talk to Addis, Buck. He's got something interesting to tell you."

Buck, a little bewildered, found Bud Tharp holding a gun on

Addis, who seemed to be having a fit of ague. A few yards away, three riders who worked for Addis were being faced by the rest of Buck's party.

"We came to the right place, Buck," growled Bud Tharp. "Addis has got that Harper girl locked up in the house. He's trying hard to say something, but he's so shaky it don't make much sense."

Buck caught Addis by the shoulder, shook him. "Get hold of yourself, Addis. What's this about Miss Harper?"

Addis jerked a thumb toward the house. "She's in there," he said in a quavering voice. "Jaeger and Cutts brought her here. Put her in my storeroom. M-made me do it, damn their black souls. They been ironing me down and down and now. . . ." Addis began to shake again and his tight chin grew so loose and wobbly his words became an unintelligible mutter.

"Keep a gun on him, Bud," said Buck. "When he quits shaking, we may learn something."

Buck ran to the house and went in. More than once he had been in the Stirrup Cross ranch house, and he knew where the storeroom was. He stopped before the door of it, noted the heavy hasp and padlock. A cold, white rage went over Buck. Somehow the thought of that slim, black-haired girl held like some criminal behind that padlock reached far down in him and stirred to life a fury and resentment the like of which he had never known before. Jaeger and Cutts had done this.

He knocked on the door and called out. "Miss Harper? Miss Harper? This is Buck Comstock."

He heard her muffled cry of surprise. Then she was beating with her fists on the inner side of the door.

"Buck . . . Buck Comstock!" came that muffled voice. "Thank God! Please, Buck! Please get me out of here."

Buck ran into the kitchen and found a heavy iron poker. Back at the storeroom door, he set to work. He jammed the end of the poker under the hasp and began to pry. The set of that hasp was stout and stubborn, but Buck was full of angry, furious strength. He drove the poker to a better purchase, and strained against it with all his strength. There sounded the slow, squealing pull of staple and bolt. The hasp clanged loose and free. Buck pushed open the door.

Jean Harper stood there for a moment, looking at him, her eyes wide and swimming. She was twisting her slim hands. Her soft lower lip began to tremble. "Buck," she whispered. "Buck, I knew . . . you'd come for me."

Then she ran to him and, somehow, she was in his arms. She clung to him, sobbing convulsively. Buck stood very tall and still, holding her, saying no word, patting her shoulder to comfort her.

As abruptly as she had given away, she quieted. She pulled away from him, dabbing at her eyes. "I-I'm sorry," she whispered. "I did not mean to go to pieces. But the relief . . . to know that a friend, to know that I would be out of there. . . ." She choked up again.

"I savvy," drawled Buck gently. "You're a mighty brave little lady. And you're safe now. Later, when you're feeling better, you can tell me. . . ."

"I can tell you now, Buck Comstock." She spoke swiftly, intensely. She told him how Jaeger and Cutts had overpowered her at the J Bar C ranch house, how they had brought her down here, and locked her up. She told of the several times they had come and bullied and threatened her, of how Cutts had been particularly offensive in his threats. "And all because they were determined to get control of my ranch," she ended. "But I told that beast, Cutts, that, no matter what they did, I'd never sign that property over to them."

"Good girl," commended Buck. "And Addis . . . did he bother you?"

"No. In a way, he was kind enough. He brought my meals to me. He always seemed so frightened, so nervous. But he was kind enough."

"Good," said Buck. "You wait right here. I'll be back for you in a minute. I'm taking you to Bill Morgan's ranch, where you'll be perfectly safe."

Outside, Buck saw that a blanket litter was being swung between two horses, evidently to carry Brood Shotwell. Bud Tharp still held a gun on Old Man Addis.

"The girl all right, Buck?" asked Bud. "On your answer depends whether this damned old coyote goes on living."

"You can put up your gun, Bud. Miss Harper is all right." Buck turned cold eyes on Tom Addis. "How long you been in cahoots with Jaeger and Cutts?"

"I'm not in cahoots with them!" cried Addis. "They made me keep that poor girl prisoner. They made me, I tell you." Addis had steadied a lot by this time.

"That," said Buck sharply, "sounds like so much talk, Addis. How could they make you do a thing of that sort?"

"This ranch. . . ." Addis waved an encircling hand. "It's all I have. The best part of my life went into building up this ranch. Jaeger and Cutts threatened to drive me to the wall, to take it away from me. And they could do it, too. They have the men, the power. What could I do? My partner and me. . . ."

"Your what?" cut in Buck. "Since when did you have a partner?"

"For years. No one knew of it besides Judge Henning and myself. How Jaeger and Cutts found it out, I still don't know. But they did."

"Where does Judge Henning come into the picture?"

"Judge Henning is my partner. All he and I own in the world is tied up in this ranch. We're old men, too old to fight a combine like Jaeger and Cutts. What could we do under the threat of their power?"

"Judge Henning," breathed Buck. "So Judge Henning is your partner. That makes the picture complete. I see it now. I see it all."

One of Bill Morgan's riders came over to them. "The three Stirrup Cross 'punchers want to talk to you, Buck."

Buck nodded and followed the rider over to the three men. Buck knew these boys—Andy Devine, Sig Loftus, and Dave Burke.

Andy Devine spoke. "Buck, I want you to believe us when we say we had no idea that girl was locked up in the old man's storeroom. If we had, we shore as hell would have tore the roof off. We knew somethin' was on the mind of Addis, for he was worried and scared and crotchety. We figgered he'd gotten into some kind of a business deal with Jaeger and Cutts and was gettin' the worst of it. But that was none of our business. We were hired to punch cows, not iron out his business troubles. But we didn't know about the girl. That's gospel, Buck."

Buck nodded gravely. "I believe you, Andy. We're holding nothing against you three. You can go or stay or do as you please."

"Me," growled Dave Burke, "I'm not staying on for any damn' man who'd do what Addis done. I'm drawing my time. When I ride, I want to ride for a man, not a jellyfish. What the hell ever made him do it, anyhow?"

Buck told them, briefly, what Addis had just told him. "In a way, I can see his point, boys. He's an old man. Give him the advantage of the doubt."

"How about that girl?" asked Sig Loftus. "Did Jaeger or Cutts really hurt her in any way? If they did, by God, I'm going scalp-hunting."

"Miss Harper is all right," said Buck. "But that doesn't excuse Jaeger and Cutts . . . none whatever. There are two coyotes whose hides need hanging up, boys. We're going to have to do it, if this range is to be a fit place to live on. If you boys want to help in that chore, we'll be glad to have you."

"We're in, up to our necks!" exclaimed Andy Devine. "We're with you, Buck. Where do we start?"

"Right at this ranch. You stay here. Forget about handling cattle for a few days. Keep Winchesters handy, and don't let Jaeger or Cutts or any of their outfit within rifle shot of this place. Do that, and you'll be helping plenty."

"It'll be done," attested Dave Burke. "Done to a queen's taste. How about the old man?"

"He'll stay here, too. I think this scare has pounded some sense and maybe some backbone into him. I think he'll be willing to fight now."

Buck went over to Bill Morgan and Johnny Frazier, who had lifted Brood Shotwell into the litter. "How's he making it?" Buck asked.

"Pretty fair," said Morgan. "We're taking him to my place. I've sent Gus Howard to town for Doc Pollard. They'll be waiting at the ranch when we get there. The girl all right?"

"All right. I'm bringing her out to your ranch, too, Bill. She's got spunk. She'll help take care of Brood."

XII

Doc Pollard, stocky, cheerful, and ruddy-faced, came out of the sickroom, wiping his hands on a towel. "What're his chances, Doc?" asked Buck Comstock.

"Fifty-fifty. I got the slug. The good Lord must have guided that bullet. An inch right or left, and Shotwell would have been dead immediately. I'll have a better idea twenty-four hours from now. Right now, I'm worried, but not too much. That girl is a dandy. Having her here as Brood's nurse don't hurt his chances any."

Buck went outside and relayed the news to Bill Morgan, Johnny Frazier, Bud Tharp, and the rest. This group had been discussing the mysterious killing of Judge Henning, the news of which had been brought by Doc Pollard.

"Well," said Johnny Frazier, "that much is settled. Where do we go from here?"

Buck put his right hand in his pocket, turned to Bill Morgan, and, with a swift movement, pinned something on Morgan's shirt front. It was a nickel, ball-pointed star—a sheriff's star. "I took that off of Brood when I first went looking for his wound," he told Bill. "Right now, what this country needs is a sheriff . . . law, the kind of law Jaeger and Cutts can't bluff or buy or dodge. Brood Shotwell is down on his back. Saint Ives, the treacherous skunk, is dead. If Brood was able to talk, he'd be more than willing for Bill to wear that star and go about cleaning house. We know that all of this crowd can be trusted. In the light of the things that have happened, that's important. Bill, you're the oldest, the most level-headed of this crowd. Everybody knows you, and you pack a lot of weight. Wear that star, call us your posse, and we'll go get Jaeger and Cutts. We've got absolute proof that they run off with Jean Harper. That's plenty of charges for their arrest. We'll carry this fight right into their faces and jam it down their throats. Let's get going now!"

There was a yell of approbation to this. Bill Morgan nodded slowly. "With you boys behind me, I'd tackle a nest of poison wildcats." He turned to Gus Howard. "See that all of the crew comes along, Gus, except two men to stay here with Bones."

They left Coyote Valley, cut straight across the heart of Timber Valley. Two miles due north they could see the buildings of the J Bar C headquarters. Beyond, swimming in the heat mists, loomed East Butte and West Butte. Well up toward the buttes, and east, a long, low cloud of yellow dust peeled like a ribbon across the world. Buck Comstock, watching that dust, laid a hand on Bill Morgan's arm, and pulled to a halt. He pointed.

"Cattle," he said. "A big herd. They're heading east. Bill, the Wineglass spread is over there. Do you think . . . ?"

"Think nothing," growled Morgan. "That's plain sign. The J Bar C is moving in on the Wineglass. Jaeger and Cutts are forcing their luck too far. We can forget the job we started on. Right now, the thing for us to do is head that herd off. Once they get a foothold in Cotton Valley, they'll be tougher than hell to dig out. Come on. We head for the Wineglass."

They whipped about, set the spurs, and tore away to the east and north. Again they crossed Coyote Valley, angled up into the harsh land beyond, and drove for the upper end of Cotton Valley. The grim troop rode, intently silent, on horses that flattened out like scared wolves. The fury of their pace lifted another banner of dust, which was not missed by the men driving that moving herd. And so it was that when they burst out into the open, where they could see the Wineglass headquarters, they saw also a tight group of riders racing in at another angle toward the buildings.

Bill Morgan gave a wild yell, waving his arm. The men with him knew what he meant. It was to be a race between them and that other group. Spurs dug deep, quirts were used. The straining horses were smeared with foam.

Buck Comstock, squinting his eyes against the whip of the wind, shouted exultantly: "We've got the edge! We're going to beat 'em in!"

Evidently that other group of riders realized this fact, also, for they suddenly whirled to a stop. The sun glittered on gun barrels as rifles were dragged from scabbards and levered into action.

The range was long, a good five hundred yards, yet something crackled through the air and told with a fleshy thud. Gus

Howard's bronco lunged, staggered, missed its stride, and went down, Gus kicking his feet out of the stirrups in the nick of time and rolling free. He came up, roaring mad, jerked his rifle from under the shoulder of the stricken horse, and clambered up behind Buck, who had spun his mount to a stop.

"Damn their rotten hearts!" yelled Gus in Buck's ear. "They killed the best little cutting-out bronco that ever packed a kak. Make this goat of yours ramble, Buck. I want to get a cut at those jaspers."

More long-range lead whispered savagely about. Bill Morgan, wise in the ways of battle, roared a command, and his men spread out, no longer riding in a compact group, thus giving the J Bar C gunmen small individual targets instead of one solid bulk to shoot at. This strategy carried them safely to the Wineglass headquarters without further casualty.

"Find what shelter you can for the horses," ordered Morgan. "We'll need 'em later. Bud, take half the men and hole up here around the buildings. The rest of us will mosey out on foot to meet that crowd. Horses are swell to ride on, but tough to shoot off of, especially with rifles. We can spread out and raise hell with that gang if they try and rush us. Come on!"

Rifles in hand, the doughty little group moved away from the ranch buildings, straight toward the first file of cattle, which could now be seen swinging across the wide curve of the upper valley. The riders, who had failed in their attempt to reach the ranch buildings before Morgan and his crowd, were still out there, evidently holding council.

Buck Comstock measured the distance with his eye. "Between six and seven hundred yards, Bill!" he yelled. "What say we show 'em we mean business?"

"Fair enough," answered Bill. "Try 'em a gun full . . . everybody!"

Rifles lifted, steadied, began their thin, snarling challenge.

For a moment, it seemed to have no effect. Abruptly, however, one of those distant riders threw his hands high and fell backward from his saddle. At the same instant, a horse began bucking wildly, only to collapse a moment later. That distant group immediately split away in retreat, heading back to the herd.

"So far, so good," said Morgan. "We'll wait right here."

Bill Morgan, grizzled and wise, had chosen his strategy perfectly. That herd, to get into the heart of the Wineglass range, had to pass within a short distance of the ranch buildings. To swing it farther north meant that it would leave the head of Cotton Valley and end up at the fringe of Big Sage Desert, in the *malpais* country. The Wineglass headquarters was the key to the whole thing, and Morgan had known it from the first. That Jaeger and Cutts also recognized this fact was immediately apparent. Riders dashed out to the point of the herd, halting its progress, circling it, holding the cattle in a compact mass, ready to move in any direction. Now other riders, over a score of them, moved out in front, broke into little groups, and began riding in a wide, circling movement, with the evident intent of surrounding the Wineglass headquarters.

Bill Morgan met this move by spreading his defenders in a thin line, all around the ranch buildings. "Get down on your bellies," he told them as he placed each man. "Looks like they're going to rush us. They won't have much chance of tagging you if you stay flat. If the pressure gets too heavy, give back to the buildings and take cover. But make 'em pay plenty for every inch they get."

Buck Comstock found himself on the north of the ranch house. Some seventy-five yards to his left was Johnny Frazier. An equal distance to his right was Gus Howard. Crouched low and peering up ahead of him, Buck saw the same oat-topped ridge on which he had been lying when the scream of Jean Harper had brought him to her rescue from Toad Black. A man coming over the top of that ridge on a horse, he mused, would make a perfect target against the sky. He spread a handful of cartridges on the ground beside him, cracked the action of his rifle to be sure it was ready, then settled into tense waiting.

The J Bar C force had cut over the ridge, well back to the north. For some time, there was nothing in sight. Buck lifted his head slightly and glanced over at Johnny Frazier, who caught the look and waved. Johnny, thought Buck, was one swell guy, in a fight or out of one. Long, lean, and coolly drawling, Johnny would do to ride the river with, any old time. Good-natured and slow to anger, but a buzz saw on wheels when he did get his roach set.

Well over on the other side of the buildings a lone rifle snarled. It was as though it had been a signal, for the voice of it was picked up and swelled to a roar. Buck, unconsciously twisting his head, to see what was going on, was brought abruptly to matters out in front of him when a bullet chugged savagely into the ground not a foot from his face, spattering him with stinging bits of earth. He ducked, his slitted eyes searching along the rim above him. Up there a man was kneeling, gun trained, so it seemed to Buck, dead on him. Buck snapped his own rifle up, but before he could get it into line, Johnny Frazier's rifle crashed. That kneeling figure on the ridge seemed to turn a complete backward somersault. From the corner of his eye, Buck saw the peak of a sombrero lifting into sight in that fringe of oats against the skyline. His rifle settled against his shoulder. The sights steadied into line and the gun slammed back in recoil. The sombrero disappeared. Yet the thin, wicked lashing of smokeless powder along the top of the ridge grew in volume.

Buck, his eyes straining to pick up another target, could hear lead hissing past him, most of it well above him as it reached for the ranch buildings behind. But soon bullets began chugging into the earth about him, and he knew that another sharpshooter up on the ridge had spotted him. A muffled, metallic clash sounded. Buck felt a quick, twisting jerk of his left foot and ankle. For a moment he thought he'd been hit, then realized that a speeding slug had split itself on his jutting spur rowel. Buck tried to flatten himself deeper into the hard, sun-baked earth, while he searched the ridge top for sight of the sharpshooter.

For a moment that marksman left Buck alone. Buck looked to his left, just in time to see Johnny Frazier cut loose another shot. He looked to the right, where Gus Howard pulled high on his elbows to work the lever of his rifle. Gus suddenly jerked spasmodically as a slug told with a fleshy clout. Buck saw the tense life in his arms and shoulders flow out of him, saw the half-opened rifle drop from his hands, saw the stricken man's head roll forward and drop. And then Gus Howard looked just like a discarded bundle of clothes. A chill went over Buck Comstock, a chill that turned instantly into hot, blind fury. Gus Howard was dead. Buck knew that. Even a mortally wounded man, while life exists at all within him, has substance. But there is no substance to a dead man—just a flattened, shrunken bundle of clothes. Buck rose to his knees, to his feet, a hoarse, feral cry of fury in his throat. He started up that slope, running. He heard a dim shouting, but it made no impression on him. He did not know that it was Johnny Frazier, aghast at Buck's reckless, lone charge, howling at him to get down. But when Buck did not heed, Johnny reared up and dashed after him.

Back in the ranch buildings, Bud Tharp began to curse brokenly as he saw those wild two, apparently gone loco, dashing up that slope toward the hungry guns atop it. Bud did the only thing he could to help out. He bawled orders to the men about him, pointing to Buck and Johnny. The cowpunchers understood. They began lacing the top of that ridge with a hur-

ricane of lead, laying down a virtual barrage ahead of that lo-
coed pair.

All too soon, Buck and Johnny were so close to the top of the
ridge that the men below had to slacken their fire to keep from
hitting them. Buck, oblivious to all except the wild fury in him,
surged clear on the top of the ridge. A swarthy, savage-eyed
figure, moving at a crouching run, showed along the far side of
the ridge, trying to keep down below the range of lead which
had lashed the ridge top a moment before. He saw Buck at the
same instant that Buck saw him. The fellow jerked his gun up.
Buck fired at him as he would at a running deer, and the man
spun around and dropped. The next second something crashed
against the back of Buck's legs, knocking him sprawling. That
something was Johnny Frazier's body. And Johnny rolled right
on up to the small of Buck's back, and held him down.

"You raving, wild-eyed lunatic!" panted Johnny. "Stay flat
before I larrup you one with a gun. D'you want to get both of
us killed?"

Buck struggled to get free. "They killed Gus Howard," he
gulped hoarsely. "They killed Gus, I tell you! I saw the bullet
hit him."

"Getting yourself killed won't help Gus," growled Johnny.
"You can't lick this whole gang single-handed. Stay down, you
spavin-brained tarantula bug. Promise to stay down, or I'll hold
you here until you grow whiskers."

Buck's brain cleared of that first wild, feral fury. He dropped
his head against his forearm and nodded. "OK, Johnny. You
win."

Johnny slithered out beside Buck. "You watch south, I'll
watch north," he said. "We lather these jaspers on the flank and
they'll hightail it in a hurry."

Buck lifted himself high enough in the wild oats to look south
along the ridge. He could not see anyone, but just for luck he

searched the sun-dried grass with three or four slugs. This brought a startled, wild-eyed waddy into view, who popped from the grass like a jumped coyote. The fellow seemed to understand the situation in a glance, for with no attempt to fight back he angled down the east slope of the ridge at a dead run, tearing for a group of ground-reined horses in the hollow. It would have been simple enough to have knocked him over, but Buck had no stomach for the deed. He contented himself with dusting those flying boot heels with whistling lead, which brought an amazing burst of speed from the fleeing cowpuncher. Into the midst of the snorting horses charged the fellow, to pop immediately into a saddle, and swing out to the east at a dead run.

Farther down the ridge someone was yelling wildly. Then, from various points. four more men appeared, racing for the horses. Buck allowed them to reach their broncos and spur away. Panic is an insidious thing, stampeding even the most valiant at times. Convinced by the sight of their fleeing comrade that something was decidedly wrong, the attackers cleared out in a hurry, swinging beyond rifle range and circling back toward the cattle herd, well to the north.

Things were quiet along the ridge now. But there were still three riderless horses down in that hollow. Buck's brain was working logically again. That kneeling man Johnny Frazier had cut down, that sombrero he himself had driven a bullet through, and then that swarthy ridge-hopper—three men and three riderless horses. The account was pretty well squared for Gus Harper.

Johnny Frazier came over to Buck. "Looks like things have kinda fallen apart on their side," he drawled.

Buck nodded. "They scared easier than I thought they would."

Johnny looped his rifle under one arm and built a cigarette.

"Those jaspers are only fighting for wages," he said. "We're fighting for our range. That makes a difference, Buck."

A survey of the situation on all sides showed that the attack had broken up. Gunfire had died to only a few last sporadic reports, long-range shots that carried an expression of hate, rather than any hope of hitting. Buck and Johnny, from the elevation of the ridge, could see the J Bar C forces circling wide of the Wineglass ranch buildings and drifting back to the herd. There was more than one empty saddle among them.

"The party," drawled Johnny Frazier, "is over. Mister Jaeger and Mister Cutts seem to have burned their fingers. They made a fool play, in the first place, trying to rush this ranch with all the boys holed up and ready for 'em."

Buck agreed. "Let's go down . . . and get Gus."

They carried the body of Gus Howard into the ranch house, where grim, hard-eyed men met them. Bud Tharp came toward them. He asked no question, for he had eyes to see. "A good man," he said softly. "We'll miss him."

"Any more?" asked Johnny.

"Tim Donavan is pretty hard hit. I'm afraid for him. Jigger Lewis has a smashed arm, and Porky Powers got nicked in the shoulder. Bill Morgan has a broken leg."

Bud had a smear of blood along the angle of his jaw. "They didn't miss you more than a mile," said Johnny Frazier.

Bud felt his jaw, looked at his hand, shrugged. "Come on. We got work to do."

While they were checking up and caring for their wounded, Tim Donavan died. The others were not too seriously wounded, though Bill Morgan was cursing harshly over the pain of his wounded leg. Bud Tharp sent out a couple of riders to scout the future moves of the J Bar C contingent.

Buck Comstock went over to Bill Morgan. "This," said Morgan, touching his wounded leg, "makes me of little use with the star. Who'll we put it on next, Buck?"

"That's easy," said Bud Tharp. "Here!"

He took the star, turned, and pinned it on Buck. "What you say goes, Buck. We'll follow you to hell and gone."

"Correct," chimed in Johnny Frazier.

"Fair enough," said Buck soberly. "I'll do my best. The quicker we can settle this, the less good men will have to die. I'm going after Jaeger and Cutts."

XIII

The scouts that Bud Tharp had sent out came back to report that the J Bar C herd had been turned and started back the way it had come.

"Maybe they mean it, maybe it's only a bluff," said Buck. "Either way, we play our cards careful. The wounded will head for the Circle Star. Chances are Doc Pollard is still there, looking after Brood Shotwell. The rest of us will follow that herd and make sure it isn't a bluff. After that . . . Jaeger and Cutts. I'll put 'em behind the bars . . . or in their graves . . . if it's the last thing I ever do."

Bill Morgan, Jigger Lewis, and Porky Powers, rudely bandaged, were lifted into their saddles. "Think you can make it, Bill?" asked Buck anxiously.

"Hell, yes," snorted Morgan. "It'll take more than a smashed leg to put me all the way down. And listen, kid, don't get too reckless. The way things are shaping now, we got a definite edge on that pair of polecats. But play your cards careful. There won't be no satisfaction for us in winning, if you go get yourself killed. Was I you, I'd let those two jaspers stew in their own juice for a time, while I went to work and gathered up a few loose ends and found where they led to."

"What're you driving at?" Buck frowned.

"Who killed Judge Henning, and why?" clarified Morgan.

215

"And why did Saint Ives shoot Brood Shotwell in the back?"

"I think I can answer that last one," said Buck, his eyes narrowing. "Saint Ives was another rat bought by J Bar C money. He knew that Jean Harper was held at the Stirrup Cross, and, when he realized that Brood Shotwell was going to search the place, he shot him in the back. That's the way it looks to me. Well, you get along and have that leg taken care of. I'll try and keep a head on my shoulders, Bill."

"You do that," affirmed Morgan. "Don't go charging up any more ridges with the idea of licking the whole wide world single-handed. You may be a lot of man, but there's limits. Damn this leg!"

The three wounded men rode off for the Circle Star. At the Wineglass there ensued a period of grim-faced labor with pick and shovel. Then Buck took Johnny Frazier and Bud Tharp aside and explained what Bill Morgan had said.

"I think he's right," said Bud Tharp. "If we go pile-driving in on that outfit, there'll be a lot of us where Gus and Tim are now. The sane, sensible play is to work around until we can snap up Jaeger and Cutts without tangling with their crew. Without them, the crew won't fight."

"We'll try it," said Buck. "Johnny and me are cutting out for town. Bud, you take the rest of the boys and kind of hang out behind that herd, to make sure it's driven back where it belongs. Once it is back on J Bar C range, you can cut for town if you feel like it and see how things are shaping up. Fair enough?"

"Fair enough," agreed Bud.

At a little past midday, Buck Comstock and Johnny Frazier rode into Twin Buttes. The town seemed a trifle busier than was usual at this time of day.

"Not all of the J Bar C crowd was with that herd," drawled Johnny softly.

Buck nodded. "We'll look around," he said briefly, reining in

216

and dismounting before Pete Allen's store. They went in and found Pete Allen alone, a stocky, powerfully built man with a square jaw, bristling hair, and direct, shrewd eyes. He stared at Buck in patent amazement.

"Well," he said slowly, "I'll be eternally damned."

Buck smiled. "I reckon it does sort of surprise you, Pete, to see me here, wearing Brood Shotwell's star."

"Surprised," ejaculated Allen, "is hardly the word. I'm plumb flabbergasted."

"There's a story behind it all, Pete," said Buck.

"There must be. There sure must be. Where the hell is Brood? And where is Spike Saint Ives? And what's going on out on the range that's keeping Doc Pollard? There's a lot of damn' funny things going on around here that's got a lot of us fighting our heads. Here somebody put a slug through Judge Henning. Not two hours ago Buss Shugrue got the shock of a lifetime. He went to the livery barn barley bin to do a little feeding. And when he opened the bin, what did he find? I'll tell you what he found. He found Duke Younger in that bin, dead as a mackerel. He'd had his skull knocked in."

Buck looked at Johnny Frazier. "That's news aplenty, Pete, about Younger, I mean," he said. "Who, I wonder, would have killed him?"

"Don't ask me. I tell you I'm plenty spooked the way things are going," complained Allen. "And you still ain't told me how you, a fugitive of justice, is waltzing around free and easy and wearing the star of the man supposed to be out looking for you."

Buck looked Allen straight in the eye. "Pete, you're square . . . and sensible. Here's the story." He told then of the dastardly attempt on Brood Shotwell's life by Spike St. Ives, and of the abrupt finish of St. Ives. He told of the attempt of the J Bar C to take over the Wineglass and throw a herd of J Bar C cattle

217

onto the Wineglass range. He told of finding Jean Harper and her story of abduction by Leek Jaeger and Frank Cutts. He told of the confession of Duke Younger and Toad Black that the jury had been bought. "All of that, Pete, is why I'm here, wearing this star," he said. "Saint Ives is dead and Brood Shotwell badly wounded. Somebody has to represent the law, with hell breaking loose the way it is. Bill Morgan started out to wear this star, but he got a smashed leg in that brawl out at the Wineglass. So he moved the star onto me."

"There'll be some who'll question that authority . . . from you, Buck," said Pete Allen gravely.

"Do you?"

"No. I never was satisfied the way you were treated in that trial. I know several folks who feel the same way. It won't be us you'll have to worry about. But Jaeger and Cutts will buck plenty."

"I expect them to," said Buck. "It won't do 'em any good, though. Pete, back of all the hell on this range stand Jaeger and Cutts. Think over all I've told you and see if you don't get the same picture."

A shadow darkened the store doorway. A man, squinting into the gloom, came a few steps inside. It was Rope Tenny, one of the J Bar C cowpunchers. Of a sudden he froze. He had recognized Buck Comstock. His breath gave out in a startled hiss. He turned quickly toward the door.

"Hold it, Tenny!" Buck commanded. "I've got a gun on you."

"And I'm backing Buck's play all the way, Rope," added Johnny Frazier.

Tenny halted, his hands lifting slightly. "What you want with me?" he asked. "I ain't done a thing."

"No," drawled Buck. "But you would have. Come over here."

Johnny Frazier, at a nod from Buck, took Tenny's gun.

"Who," demanded Buck, "is over in the Yellow Horse?"

Tenny shrugged. "Just a few of the gang."

"Are Jaeger and Cutts there?"

"No."

"Will they be there anytime today?"

"Mebby, mebby not," growled Tenny. "I don't know what their plans are."

"Keep your eye on him, Johnny," said Buck. "I want to take a look-see."

He moved up at an angle to the door and peered out. Over across the street, grouped about the door of the Yellow Horse, were nearly a dozen riders. The eyes of all of them were on the store. In the forefront of the crowd stood a wiry, compact man, carrying two guns slung low and tied down. Even at the distance a livid, ugly scar across the man's face was visible.

Buck turned back into the store, shot out a long arm, and caught Rope Tenny by the slack of his shirt. "They sent you over here . . . to find out what?"

"Nobody sent me," blurted Tenny. "I came over here to get some smoking."

"That's a lie. You can buy Durham in the Yellow Horse. There's a dozen men over there, with Whistler Hahn in front of them, watching this store. Untangle that crooked tongue of yours or. . . .'"

Tenny licked his lips. "I was to find out who was with Frazier," he admitted. "Nobody saw you two jaspers ride in, but one of the boys spotted that claybank of Frazier's. They didn't recognize the other bronco, and they wondered who was with him. That . . . that's all I know."

Buck pushed him away, went back to the door. Whistler Hahn was haranguing the group in front of the Yellow Horse. Abruptly the group split up, some going up the street, some down. Hahn, with three others, started toward the store.

"We're in for it, Johnny," said Buck over his shoulder. "Tie

Tenny up. Pete, your store may get some holes shot in it."

"Fair enough," said Pete Allen calmly. "Close the door if you want to, Buck."

"Not yet. Maybe in a minute or two. How's your back door?"

"I'm going to lock it right now."

"Watch that Hahn jasper close, Buck," warned Johnny Frazier. "He didn't get his reputation because he was slow on the draw. Quiet down there, Tenny, or I'll bend a gun over your head."

Buck drew both belt guns and poised himself just off the flare of daylight that came in the open door. A moment later his voice rang out, cold and crisp: "Far enough, Hahn! What's eating you?"

Outside, Whistler Hahn stopped, as did the three men behind him. His hand dropped to his gun. "We're looking for Rope Tenny," he said, his words carrying that sibilant, whistling note that had given rise to his nickname. "He in there?"

"He's in here," answered Buck. "And he's staying here. Anything else?"

"I know that voice," cried one of the men with Hahn. "It's Buck Comstock!"

Buck knew the gag was up. He leaped to the heavy, sliding door, threw his weight against it. The door slid shut with a bang. Pete Allen, appearing from nowhere, threw the heavy, locking hasp into place.

Outside, sounded a volley of shrill, whistling curses, then a thudding roll of gunfire. Lead cracked through the door, peeling back big, white splinters. The two front windows, one on either side of the door, small and high up, dropped shattered glass as lead cut through them. Long, pealing yells echoed over the town.

Johnny Frazier, finished with the task of tying up Rope Tenny, came over beside Buck. "This," he drawled, "looks interesting."

Buck nodded. "It's tough on Pete, though. I was a damned fool to come here."

"Don't worry about me or the store," said Pete Allen quietly. "I ain't altogether blind. I've seen a showdown coming up for a long time between the J Bar C and the rest of the Twin Buttes range. All the time, I knew there was only one side for me. That's the side I'm on now. I'll see your crowd through, Buck."

"That's white of you, Pete. When this is over, our side won't forget."

At that moment there sounded several heavy blows at the back of the store. "They're working on the back door!" exclaimed Pete. "I'll discourage that *pronto.*"

He grabbed a six-shooter from under his counter and ran to the rear of the place, back where the shadows were deep and thick amid piles of merchandise that filled the gloom. The next moment the confines of the store shuddered under the rolling snarl of several shots. Outside, rose a howl of pain, then a string of bawling curses.

"I gave 'em a gun full!" yelled Pete Allen. "They won't get so close again."

Answering lead crashed through the back door. And Allen, with Johnny Frazier's help, quickly threw up a barricade of sacked flour.

"Let 'em shoot and be damned now," Allen panted. "They won't get far."

Out in front, things quieted somewhat. Then came the challenge of Whistler Hahn's voice: "Listen to gospel, Allen. Turn Frazier and Comstock out here or it'll be the worse for you. If you want your store left in one piece, turn 'em out."

"I stick to my friends, Hahn," Allen answered him. "And you're not one of them."

Again came that burst of furious cursing and another volley of lead into the heavy front door.

"I reckon," said Johnny Frazier, drawing a gun and moving over to one of the front windows, "we might as well start shooting for keeps. If we could get that wolf of a Hahn down, it might take a lot out of that crowd. I'm gonna try."

"Take it easy," warned Buck. "They'll be watching those windows."

Johnny flattened against the wall, tipped his gun over the sill, and started to rise up for a quick snap shot. The next moment a livid stream of sparks bloomed and Johnny's gun was smashed from his grip and to the floor. Johnny whirled away from the window, gripping his right hand and swearing savagely.

"You hit, boy?" cried Buck anxiously.

"No," rasped Johnny. "But they shot my gun out of my hand."

In the dim light, Buck examined Johnny's hand. There was new blood on it, but Buck saw with relief that the blood came from shallow surface cuts where the lead of the speeding slug had spattered. Also, there was a slight cut on Johnny's jaw. Now another slug came through that same window and slogged into a barrel of dried apricots, not far from the door.

"Thought so!" exclaimed Pete Allen. "Somebody is up high, shooting down through that window. The slug that hit your gun, Johnny, came from a rifle. I could tell by the report."

Buck glanced from the apricot barrel to the window, judging the angle. "Break me out a new rifle, Pete," he ordered. "Wipe the grease out of it and bring it here with some cartridges."

Over the roar of battle outside, sounded the tattoo of speeding hoofs. Buck sought the safer window and took a quick look.

"Jaeger and Cutts!" he exclaimed. "With six or eight more men. Now we do catch hell, boys."

"Here's your rifle," said Pete Allen, thrusting the weapon into Buck's hand. "And it's loaded."

Buck nodded, moving to the left-hand window and back a trifle from it. He could see the enemy rifleman now. The fellow was standing on a support behind the false front of the Yellow Horse, with head and shoulders visible, a rifle cuddled to his face. Even as Buck looked that rifle leaped in recoil and another whistling bullet came through the right-hand window, slamming into the floor.

Buck did not hesitate. His own rifle spat flame, with a ringing report. It was as though a hurricane's gust had struck that man on the false front across the street. He was whipped back from his perch, and Buck distinctly heard the crash of his fall as he struck the roof of the Yellow Horse. A moment later his body came into view again, rolling down the slant of the roof and plummeting to the ground. "They want hell," growled Buck savagely. "They can have it."

The killing of the J Bar C sharpshooter brought a reaction of curses and angry yells, and then a hail of lead, ripping through both windows and both doors.

"I'm sorry, Pete," said Buck. "They're going to make a mess out of this store."

"Sorry, be damned," snorted Pete. "I'm not sorry. I'm mad . . . plenty. Just because they want to get hold of you, is no excuse for that gang to shoot my store all to hell and gone. It's high time Jaeger and Cutts and their crowd got their ears knocked down. And I'm aiming to sit into this thing until that comes to pass. Don't you worry none about my store. I'll take the pay for all damage out of their cussed hides."

Buck and Johnny made no attempt to answer the shooting. They crouched, out of line, and let the slugs drive past. If the hostile force did nothing more than shoot through door and window, they never would get any results.

As though realization of this came to the attackers, the fire dwindled and died. Pete Allen came sliding over beside Buck. He had a double-barreled shotgun in his hands. "I ain't got a load of buckshot in the joint," he lamented disgustedly. "I got some ordered, but they ain't showed up yet. I got plenty of quail loads, though. And at close range they'll discourage some of those bimbos."

Outside, came a shout. It was Leek Jaeger, and he addressed his remarks to Pete Allen. "We want Comstock!" he bawled. "We're going to get him, one way or another. Better listen to reason, Allen. If you want any store left, run Comstock out of there. You won't get another chance."

"If he's in the open," promised Pete, "I'll answer him."

The doughty storekeeper slipped over to a window, stood on his tiptoes, and looked out. Instantly his shotgun leaped to his shoulder and roared. From the far side of the street sounded a shriek of pain and surprise. Pete Allen came back to Buck and Johnny, laughing softly. "It was Jaeger," he chuckled. "He had turned to talk to somebody in the Yellow Horse and I sure lathered his britches with birdshot. I sure woke him up, and he hit for shelter lickety-larrup."

There came another flurry of shots, then another period of silence. This stillness lasted so long it became ominous.

Buck prowled to a window, took a quick survey. "Nobody in sight," he announced. "But they're figuring up some devilry. I can feel it."

As if in answer to this observation, the whole store building shook under the impact of a terrific crash. Wood splintered and metal hinges squealed in protest. It was as though an earthquake was shaking the store.

"The back door!" yelled Buck. "They've rammed it in!"

At the same moment another hail of lead smashed into the front of the store.

It was Pete Allen, with his scatter-gun who turned the tide. He leaped to one side, so that he could see back the length of the store. There the splintered, unhinged door, transfixed on the end of a heavy timber that had served the attackers as a battering ram lay crookedly across the barricade of sacked flour Pete had thrown up. A group of men fought to crowd their way through the aperture. Once that group got inside the store, the answer would be quick. Pete Allen swung up his scatter-gun and drove two loads of birdshot into their midst.

That hail of fine shot was not fatal, but it was painful and blinding and disconcerting. The charge broke and the men scattered, cursing frenziedly.

But the respite was of short duration. Through that shattered door now came a veritable sleet of lead, fanning right and left, the length of the store. Johnny Frazier gasped, reeled, and went down. Instantly Buck Comstock was on his knees beside him. "Johnny! Johnny! God, man, where did they get you?"

But Johnny did not answer. His head, as Buck tried to lift it, lolled limply from side to side. Down one cheek, staining Buck's lifting fingers, was a thickening fan of blood. Buck went cold all over. His eyes seemed to sink into his head and the muscles of his face tautened until his profile was bony and rigid. He rose to his feet, caught up his rifle, started for that back door.

"Watch the front, Pete!" he said.

The shooting through the rear door had stopped. Then there sounded a rush of booted feet, and again the opening was jammed with charging men. Into the very center of that mass, Buck levered his rifle empty. He grabbed it by the barrel then, and hurled it after the lead it had thrown. He whipped out both belt guns and began rolling them. Before that fusillade dead men slumped limply down. Wounded men fell on top of them. Others, who by some miracle had escaped that merciless lead, fought their way free of the shambles and rushed away, terror-stricken.

Mechanically Buck Comstock punched the empty shells from his guns, thumbed fresh loads into the cylinders, then started for that open door. He was through skulking in cover, through with situations that had brought death to his friends—first Gus Howard, then Tim Donavan, now Johnny Frazier. And there were Jigger Lewis and Bill Morgan and Porky Powers wounded—while he, who was really the crux of the whole set-up, was still untouched. Yes, he was done with skulking. He was going out after Leek Jaeger and Frank Cutts. He was going to punch their tickets—with hot lead.

Behind Buck, Pete Allen was yelling at him, begging him to wait, begging him not to go out. Buck never heard him. He stalked to that rear door, climbed over the tangle of dead and dying men, and swung outside. He went up the alley, a tall, lean, figure, bending slightly forward, as though he was following the trail of some stampeded quarry. His eyes, set far back in his tight-locked countenance, burned like feverish coals. And then, when he was less than a dozen steps from the end of the alley, two men turned into it from the street. Recognition was instantaneous. Those two were Leek Jaeger and Whistler Hahn.

The advantage of surprise lay with Buck. He was strung to a state of cold, rigid, mechanical purpose. He was beyond a condition where anything might surprise or upset him. On the other hand, Buck Comstock was the last person in the world Jaeger and Hahn would expect to find marching up the alley toward them. Buck threw his first shot at Whistler Hahn, almost as though his subconscious self had analyzed the situation and warned him that Hahn was the more dangerous of the two. The lead went home, for Hahn spun around, staggered, and leaned against the outer wall of the store for support. But he did not go down. He whipped out one gun and began to shoot.

Buck minded that shooting not one whit. His blazing eyes were on Leek Jaeger's stumpy figure now, and he was throwing lead at that man. He was throwing bullets much as he would have thrown his fists, with an unconscious hunching of his shoulder at each shot, and a low panting, as though he was driving that lead home with physical as well as mechanical force. Jaeger had started for his guns, but got neither of them out of the leather. Buck's first slug took him deep in the body. Jaeger reeled backward, his hands thrown up before his face as though he would ward off some dread specter. Then he began to sag. Suddenly he halted in his backward stagger, rocked forward on his toes, and pitched out on his face.

At that moment something struck Buck a terrific blow in the chest. It sent him reeling the entire width of the alley. His knees started to sag under him, but somehow he kept himself erect, his burning eyes whipping over to Whistler Hahn. The gunman had slid down until he was half lying, half sitting on the ground. Hahn's rodent teeth were bared in a set snarl and his eyes were a weasel red. He was trying to set his gun on a line with Buck's heart.

Buck shot twice, mechanically. Hahn's head jerked back and he flattened out in a twisted, awkward heap. Buck staggered and went down on one knee. For a moment, he stayed there. There was a livid fire burning in his chest now, and a deathly weakness gripped at his vitals. A haze was gathering before his eyes. He shook his head savagely in an effort to clear his vision.

Slowly he got back to his feet. The job wasn't over with yet. Frank Cutts still remained. He had to wipe out the last of that rat nest. He had to get Cutts. He took one step. He took another. He went up the alley to the street in staggering lurches, like a man in the last stages of drunkenness. This alley, which always before had seemed reasonably level, had suddenly become filled with dips and ridges and hollows, countless hazards to stumble over. And that agony in his chest was spreading now, and his legs were growing numb.

Suddenly the alley was gone and he was in the street. There was a roaring in his ears, a rapidly growing thunder. Up the street came a madly riding bunch of men. Was that damned haze before his eyes tricking him or was it really Bud Tharp riding at the head of that charging group of riders? Damn that haze. He hadn't realized it was so late. The sun must have gone down. It sure as hell was getting dark.

Over across the street, in the doorway of the Yellow Horse, a single shot blared. Another terrific force struck Buck Comstock, this time high in the right shoulder. The impact spun him around. His knees gave way entirely this time. He vaguely felt the impact of the ground striking him, and then blackness carried him away. And so it was that Buck did not see Bud Tharp, shooting from the saddle at a wild riding speed, cut down on Frank Cutts as the latter stood in the doorway of the Yellow Horse, just in the act of levering another cartridge into the rifle he held. Bud Tharp never made a better shot. His .45 slug took Cutts just above the left eye. Cutts crumpled where he stood.

XIV

Buck Comstock had the feeling that he had been away on a long, long journey, before coming back to the world of men. He climbed up and up from immeasurable depths, through a pit full of grisly horrors. He reached the top of the pit and floated away on soft, white, restful clouds. Then, even in this haven of clouds, were the devils from the pit. They stuck their damned fingers into his chest and shoulder, torturing him with a million prying pitchforks. He tried to curse them, but somehow it was too much trouble. Maybe if he pretended not to notice, they'd leave him alone. Then he went back to sleep.

There came a day when a bright, living warmth lay on his face and made him open his eyes. He blinked painfully. Why, it was the sun, the good old sun that made that brightness and warmth. Buck sighed, grinned, and fell asleep once more. His strength came back quickly after that.

One fine morning he awoke to discover that it wasn't white

clouds he was resting on, but clean white sheets. He was in bed. He looked around him, turned his head to one side. There, on another bed not far away, was Johnny Frazier. Johnny had a big, white bandage about his head and was sitting up, propped against some pillows, reading a lop-eared magazine.

"Hi," whispered Buck weakly. "Hi, you old leather-pounder. How's things?"

Johnny's bandaged head jerked around, and a look of keen pleasure came over his face. He grinned. "Hi, yourself, old thunder bug! How you feeling?"

"Hungry," Buck whispered. "Hungry as hell. Don't they ever feed a man around this spread?"

Before Johnny could answer, a door creaked slightly as it opened. Through the door came Doc Pollard—and Jean Harper, prettier than any girl had a right to be, in starched, spotless gingham. Johnny nodded toward Buck.

"He's awake at last, Doc. And he's hungry."

"Fine," effused the doctor. "He's got his feet back on the trail."

Doc Pollard and Jean Harper came over and stood beside Buck's bed. "So you're hungry, eh?" The doctor grinned. "About time you perked up. You've given us some mighty tough moments, Buck. Four different times I gave you up. But Jean here . . . say, this girl don't know what it is to cry quits. She insisted you'd live. And by golly, you're going to. Jean, you can get him a cup of thin broth."

The girl nodded and went out, while Doc Pollard peeled back the covers and prodded around Buck's chest and shoulder. "So you're the old devil that kept sticking his fingers into me all the time," Buck accused weakly. "I used to cuss that devil."

Doc Pollard laughed. "I had to dig deep, Buck, to get out the lead you were packing. But I got it."

He covered Buck as Jean Harper came in with the broth. She

pulled up a chair beside Buck's bed, to feed him, while Doc Pollard turned to examine Johnny Frazier's head.

"Hate to be a baby," Buck muttered. "Be able to feed myself one of these days."

She laid a cool, fragrant palm on his lips. "Hush. No more talking. Go to sleep now."

She smiled gravely at him and Buck obediently closed his eyes and drifted off, remembering how soft her hand had been on his lips.

Two weeks later Buck Comstock was sitting up in bed. Doc Pollard had sent old Tony Chavez, the town barber, up, and Buck was shaved and shorn for the first time in a month. He was eating solid food now, and the pinched tightness of his face was gone. He was feeling like a real human again.

The door opened and Bud Tharp came in. Behind him, stumping along on a clumsily handled pair of crutches, came Bill Morgan.

"About time," said Buck. "You two jiggers would leave a guy in this danged hotel to rot before you'd come around and say howdy."

"We'd have come sooner, only Doc wouldn't let us," explained Bud. "I suppose you're honing to hear the story?"

"Yeah," Buck said. "I've got things figured out up to the time that last slug hit me. Who threw that one, anyhow?"

"Cutts. I dropped him cold the next second. There ain't no J Bar C any more, Buck. You did for Jaeger and Whistler Hahn, and I got Cutts. Things are healthy once more on Twin Buttes range."

"Did you find out who killed Judge Henning and Duke Younger?"

"No. Maybe we never will. Brood Shotwell . . . he's coming along fine now . . . well, he figures that maybe Spike Saint Ives might have killed Judge Henning . . . either him or Toad Black. And he figures that maybe Toad Black killed Duke Younger. Brood said it was Younger who first caved and admitted that jury was bought. Maybe Black killed him because he squealed."

Buck nodded. "That whelp, Toad Black . . . I'm sorry he got away. He tried one trick . . . the dirtiest of all. I'd feel better. . . ."

"Calm yourself," insisted Bill Morgan. "Don't get excited, kid. Toad Black is all done. He made the mistake of trying to get even with Bones Baker. The day after the big brawl here in town, Bones went out to get a armful of stove wood. Black was hid out up west of the ranch house and cut loose at Bones. Bones came right back at him. He let go a slug that removed Toad Black from this earth . . . plumb complete."

Buck grinned. "Good of Bones." He sobered again. "Money can be all right," he murmured. "But when it's dirty money and buys up the honor and souls of men, it's the lowest thing on earth. Call the roll and see what J Bar C money did. But all that is history. Might as well forget it now. It seems good to be square with the world once more . . . and to know you've got friends."

"Come on, Bill," scoffed Bud Tharp. "We stick around here any longer and that big walloper will be weeping on our shirts. Besides, we got work to do. You"—he leveled a forefinger at Buck—"had better be up and doing, young feller. You got a ranch to handle. Besides, your neighbor at the Wineglass, being what you might call a lady tenderfoot, she'll probably need some advice on how to run a cow outfit from an up-and-coming young gent about your size and complexion."

"You can go plumb to hell," said Buck, grinning.

Bud Tharp and Bill Morgan were both laughing as they went out.

Their departure left Buck restless. When Doc Pollard dropped in for a couple of minutes later in the day, Buck broached the subject of getting up and forking leather again.

The doctor shrugged. "Take it easy, cowboy. No sense in rushing things. Ask me the same question a week or ten days from now, and I might consider it. You've got to learn to walk again before you can ride."

This, Buck found, was mighty true, and it was nearer three weeks than ten days before, one warm, drowsy morning, he led a pony from the livery barn, swung stiffly into the saddle, and reined away from town.

It sure was good to be in the leather once more, watching a pony's ears bobbing in front of you. And the old range country, though it was plenty familiar, looked different, somehow. Take East Butte and West Butte, for instance. Funny that he'd never noticed how rich their coloring was, with that pale violet sun haze misted about them. The range itself was all tawny and gold, with the larks whistling and the bees digging out a winter store of sage honey. You had, Buck mused, to go away down into the cold depths and watch death leering at you and grabbing at you, before you could really appreciate the sun and the world. Yes, you had to go through all that really to know the pleasure of living.

Buck crossed Timber Valley, where the former J Bar C headquarters stood forlorn and deserted. He crossed Coyote Valley, stopping only once to look at a white-face cow fondly licking a knobby-kneed, shaky-legged little white-face bummer. When the cow bellowed deep in her throat and eyed Buck suspiciously, he laughed aloud.

"Take that kink outta your tail, old girl," he told the cow. "I ain't going to hurt your pop-eyed darling. The little devil ain't much to look at now, but he'll make a real beef one of these days."

In the end he came into the north end of Cotton Valley, and looked out ahead of him, where the Wineglass ranch buildings stood. There were two cowpunchers working around the corrals when Buck drew up there, Dave Wilkins and Hobey Sayre, both former Circle Star riders. They hailed him with broad grins.

"Time you was up and around, you damned old sissy." Dave Wilkins chuckled. "How's it feel to be forking leather once more?"

"Swell! How come you boys are working here?"

"Bill Morgan sent us up sort of to keep things moving for Miss Jean until she could get a crew together. Now it looks like Bill has lost two danged good cow nurses. Miss Jean does the cooking around this spread. And man, do we eat!"

Buck built a cigarette. "Where is your new boss, anyhow? Maybe I'll hit her up for a riding job myself."

"Oh, yeah?" snorted Hobey Sayre skeptically. "You ain't fooling me and Dave . . . not one little bit. But if you must know, she's up at the house, probably brewing a couple more pies for supper."

"Pie!" exclaimed Buck. "Say, I'm a drunkard where pie is concerned. I'm going up and see if I can't beg a couple of wedges from her."

He left his pony at the corrals and stalked up the low slope to the ranch house. He was thinner than he had been, but his step was sure and buoyant. His eyes were clear and bright and filled with a quick eagerness.

The prophecy by Hobey Sayre was a good one. Buck found Jean in the kitchen, her cheeks flushed with the heat of the stove, her hands and bared forearms dusted with flour. She greeted him with a grave, still sweetness.

"I'm glad to see you up and around again, Buck," she told him quietly.

"I couldn't hang around that hotel room any longer," he said. "You wouldn't come and see me any more, so I had to come out here to you. Why have you stayed away so long, Jean? Soon as Doc was certain I'd get well, you pulled out, and I haven't seen you from that day to this."

She met his eyes for just a second, then looked away and became busy over her kitchen table again. "I had a ranch," she murmured. "I had to get out and look after it. Besides"—here her voice became very low—"I knew you knew the trail out here."

Buck moved over and stood beside her. The top of her dark, little head came just to his chin. "There's been a lot of water under the bridge, Jean, since I first saw you. There's a lot of things been done I wish could be undone. But life sort of throws things at a person, and you got to step around 'em and keep on going. There is one thing I'm wondering if you can ever forget."

Her hands rested flat on the table top. She was very still. "You're speaking of Ben Sloan?" she said.

"Yes. Ben Sloan."

"I think we can both forget that, Buck. The first day I ever talked to you . . . that day when Toad Black . . . well, that day I believed your story. I still do. There was a time when what happened between you and Ben Sloan would have filled me with horror. But this country has done something to me. It has made me see a lot of things more clearly. I only know that you can forget what happened between you and Ben Sloan. I have forgotten it."

"Then," said Buck, "you. . . ."

She looked straight at him now, and her eyes were clear and deep and glowing. "Yes, Buck," she told him.

His arms went around her and she came to him without the slightest hesitation. After a bit, when her lips were free once more, she sighed.

"Buck, I thought you never would get well enough to ride . . . the trail . . . to me."

ABOUT THE AUTHOR

L. P. Holmes was the author of a number of outstanding Western novels. Born in a snowed-in log cabin in the heart of the Rockies near Breckenridge, Colorado, Holmes moved with his family when very young to northern California and it was there that his father and older brothers built the ranch house where Holmes grew up and where, in later life, he would live again. He published his first story—"The Passing of the Ghost"—in *Action Stories* (9/25). He was paid 1/2¢ a word and received a check for $40. "Yeah . . . forty bucks," he said later. "Don't laugh. In those far-off days . . . a pair of young parents with a three-year-old son could buy a lot of groceries on forty bucks." He went on to contribute nearly six hundred stories of varying lengths to the magazine market as well as to write numerous Western novels. For many years of his life, Holmes would write in the mornings and spend his afternoons calling on a group of friends in town, among them the blind Western author, Charles H. Snow, who Lew Holmes always called Judge Snow (because he was Napa's Justice of the Peace in 1920-1924) and who frequently makes an appearance in later novels as a local justice in Holmes's imaginary Western communities. Holmes produced such notable novels as *Somewhere They Die* (1955) for which he received the Spur Award from the Western Writers of America. His Five Star Westerns mark his more recent appearances. In these novels one finds those themes so basic to his Western fiction: the loyalty that unites one man to another, the pride one must take in his work and a job well done, the innate generosity of most of the people who live in Holmes's ambient Western communities, and the vital relationship between a man and a woman in making a better life together. His next Five Star Western will be *Sunset Trail*.